Acclaim for **ALBERT MURRAY**

and THE BLUE DEVILS

OF NADA

"Renaissance man and raconteur extraordinaire, Murray is too eclectic and wide-ranging in his interests, too cosmopolitan and wily, to be easily pigeonholed.... The essays in *The Blue Devils of Nada* cover a wide terrain."
—*The Boston Sunday Globe*

"Albert Murray is possessed of the poet's language, the novelist's sensibility, the essayist's clarity, the jazzman's imagination, the gospel singer's depth of feeling."
—*The New Yorker*

"This is Albert Murray's century; we just live in it."
—Henry Louis Gates, Jr.

ALBERT MURRAY
THE BLUE DEVILS
OF NADA

Albert Murray was born in Nokomis, Alabama. He was educated at Tuskegee Institute, where he later taught literature and directed the college theater. A retired major in the United States Air Force, Murray has been O'Connor Professor of Literature at Colgate University, visiting professor of literature at the University of Massachusetts, writer-in-residence at Emory University, and Paul Anthony Brick Lecturer at the University of Missouri. He is the author of many works of fiction, including *Train Whistle Guitar*, *The Spyglass Tree*, and *The Seven League Boots*, and nonfiction, including *The Hero and the Blues*, *South to a Very Old Place*, *Stomping the Blues*, and *Good Morning Blues: The Autobiography of Count Basie* (as told to Albert Murray). Murray was awarded the 1996 Ivan Sandrof Award by the National Book Critics Circle for his contribution to American arts and letters. He lives in New York City.

INTERNATIONAL

THE
BLUE
DEVILS
OF
NADA

ALBERT MURRAY

THE
BLUE
DEVILS
OF
NADA

*A Contemporary American Approach
to Aesthetic Statement*

VINTAGE INTERNATIONAL

VINTAGE BOOKS

A DIVISION OF RANDOM HOUSE, INC.   NEW YORK

Grateful acknowledgment is made to the following for permission to
reprint previously published material: *Little, Brown and Company*:
Excerpt from *Louis. The Louis Armstrong Story* by Max Jones, copyright
© 1971 by Max Jones and John Chilton. Reprinted by permission of
Little, Brown and Company. • *University of Washington Press*: Excerpt
from "Louis Armstrong and the Development & Diffusion of Jazz" by
Dan Morgenstern from *Louis Armstrong—A Cultural Legacy*, edited by
Marc H. Miller (Queens Museum of Art, 1994). Reprinted by permission of the University of Washington Press. • *The Village Voice*: Excerpt
from "Duke Ellington Vamps Till Ready" by Albert Murray (*The
Village Voice*, June 28, 1976). Reprinted by permission of the author
and *The Village Voice*.

The Library of Congress has cataloged
the Pantheon edition as follows:
Murray, Albert.
The blue devils of Nada / Albert Murray.
p.   cm.
Includes index.
ISBN 0-679-44213-8
1. Afro-American arts. 2. Afro-American artists—Psychology
3. Blues (Music)—Influence. I. Title.
NX512.3.A35M87   1996
700'.89'96073—dc20
Vintage ISBN: 0-679-75859-3

Book design by M. Kristen Bearse

Random House Web address: http://www.randomhouse.com/

Printed in the United States of America

BVG 01

FOR
MOZELLE
AND
MICHELE

CONTENTS

PROLOGUE

Q

Black fiction stems from a largely realistic tradition. Your novel, Train Whistle Guitar, and recent nonfiction books are written in a lyrical, indeed musical style. Do you consider this a departure from the realist tradition?

A

I am searching for an adequate metaphor or "objective correlative" for my conception of contemporary actuality. Realism, regardless of academic definitions, is essentially only a literary device among other literary or narrative devices—no less than naturalism, fantasy, surrealism, and so on. Yes, in a sense I suppose you can say that many writers from my ethnic background have relied on "realistic" devices. But it seems to me that they have mostly been preoccupied with the literal document as agitprop journalism, so much so that for all the realistic details to make the reader feel that all this really happens, their stories seldom rise above the level of one-dimensional patently partisan social case histories. The Afro-U.S. tradition of idiomatic storytelling on the other hand (not unlike others elsewhere) is largely concerned with the exploits of epic heroes who are involved with the complexities of human motives and with the contradictions of human nature and with the ultimate inscrutability of nature as such.

Q

In line with that, I wonder if there are any other novelists today doing the same kind of innovative fiction—and nonfiction—that you are doing, imbuing jazz rhythms into fiction and prose?

A

There is Ellison of course, and there are others that I like for one reason or another, but as of now, aside from the outstanding exception of Leon Forrest, I'm unaware of any others who share either Ellison's or my involvement with the blues as a literary device. Over the years there has been a tendency to confuse the blues with folk expression, but where the hell did all those writers get the idea that folk, which is to say peasant or provincial, art (or artlessness), is adequate to the complexities of black experience in contemporary America? Louis Armstrong knew better than that and so did Jelly Roll Morton, King Oliver, and Duke Ellington—as did Charlie Parker, Dizzy Gillespie, Miles Davis, and Thelonious Monk, all of whom extended, elaborated and refined that folk stuff as far as talent and craft enabled them.

Q

I've long felt that the English epic poem, which grew into the novel, was in many ways an extension of the ballad. In America there doesn't seem to be much of a musical underpinning to our literature—I guess because our literature was borrowed, historically speaking, from England. Do you think many critics today are receptive to, or aware of, the changes going on in black fiction.

A

I'm not so sure that the English novel is as directly derived from the epic and the ballad as you suggest. Perhaps some influence of poetry was inevitable, but a much more obvious source seems to have been the old practices of diary and journal keeping and letter writing. Nor do I think American literature was borrowed from English literature. It is rather an extension of English language and literature. Also, I don't know how far you can take that musical underpinnings business. What about Melville and Mark Twain? It seems to me that the oral tradition out of which they worked had musical underpinnings. Man, those old New England preachers were not only musical as hell but they were also a major source of the down-home pulpit style and manner. There are Afro elements in most down-home things to be sure; but what they represent is an Afro dimension or Afro accent, which sometimes adds up to an idiom—but an idiom within an existing tradition or convention. (As with basketball, if you get what I mean. The game is from the Northeast, but idiomatically it is more and more an extension of down-home and uptown choreography.) But back to your point, James Joyce's work was obviously influenced by Irish poetry and music, but Gertrude Stein was not less preoccupied with the music inherent in language as such.

Critics? Man, most critics feel that unless brownskin U.S. writers are pissing and moaning about injustice they have nothing to say. In any case it seems that they find it much easier to praise such writers for being angry (which requires no talent, not to mention genius) than for being innovative or insightful.

Q

I am fascinated with the influence of Hemingway on your work. In one article you say that his heroes are blues heroes, which makes a lot of sense.

But your style and his are quite different. In what stylistic sense, if any, has he influenced you?

A

Hemingway writes a prose that strikes you as being realistic, and it is indeed more accurate than most reportage, but it is at the same time the very essence of ritual. His cadence is that of process and of ritual re-enactment as well. As casual as it seems, his style achieves its realistic effect through what amounts to incantation.

Q

Lastly, and I hope you won't horse-laugh when I say this, but would you consider yourself a romantic?

A

I most certainly do not regard myself as being romantic in any under-graduate academic sense that suggests Byron, Shelley, Keats, and Wordsworth. On the other hand, take a look at The Hero and the Blues. *Look at the very last paragraph. In view of what we now think we know about the physical nature of the universe, anybody who thinks of human life as a story is romantic. The thing to avoid is sentimentality. To struggle against the odds, to continue in the face of adversity is romantic, which is to say heroic. To protest the existence of dragons (or even hooded or unhooded Grand Dragons for that matter) is not only sentimental but naïve, it seems to me.*

· · ·

After all, on the one hand there is always the threat of entropy (the tendency of all phenomena to become random), but on the other there is also human consciousness, to which modality is ineluctable, for even chaos is "perceived" as particles and/or waves! In any case, art is a species of deliberate modality derived from reenactment through ritual and play. Thus, the creative act is an effort to give enduring shape or pattern and meaning to perpetual-seeming flux of ongoing experience.

Interview with Jason Berry
in Southern Booklore *magazine, 1977*

Addendum 1995:
The objective of the following observations on the nature of the creative process is to suggest (as does The Hero and the Blues*) that the affirmative disposition toward the harsh actualities of human existence that is characteristic of the fully orchestrated blues statement can be used as a basis upon which (and/or a frame of reference within which) a contemporary storybook heroism may be defined.*

PART ONE

THE INTENT OF THE ARTIST

REGIONAL PARTICULARS

AND UNIVERSAL IMPLICATIONS

A s a very ambitious writer who would like to create fiction that will be of major interest not only as American literature but also as a part of contemporary writing in the world at large, I must say I am not primarily concerned with recording what it is like or what it means to be a Southerner or even a down-home grandson of slaves. My concerns are more fundamentally existential, which is perhaps to say epical, if by epic we mean to suggest an account of a hero involved with elemental problems of survival rather than with social issues as such. In any case, my stories are really about what it means to be human. They are concerned with what Suzanne K. Langer calls the life of human feeling.

Which is most certainly not to say that I am not at all or even only a little concerned with being a Southerner, for it is precisely by processing the raw materials of my southern experience into universal aesthetic statement that I am most likely to come to terms with my humanity as such. The condition of man is always a matter of the specific texture of existence in a given place, time, and circumstance.

But the point is that the regional particulars—the idiomatic details, the down-home conventions, the provincial customs and folkways—must be *processed* into artistic statement, *stylized* into significance.

Art, as André Malraux points out in *The Voices of Silence*, is the means by which form is rendered into style. And art is also, as Kenneth Burke has said, fundamental living equipment for our existence as human beings. What these two notions suggest to me is a concern with the quality of human consciousness. Which might also be said to be the basic concern not only of education, whether formal or informal, but also of religion and of all ceremonial occasions including holidays, red-letter days, and pastimes as well.

Applied to literature, this becomes, for me at any rate, a concern with the adequate image, by which I mean the image of the hero or effective protagonist, that personification of human endeavor, if you will, which most accurately reflects the complexities and possibilities of contemporary circumstances or indeed any predicament, and also suggests its richest possibilities. Perhaps one could say that an indispensable function of such an image is either to inform or remind us of these possibilities.

As for a working definition of adequacy, why not measure it in terms of its statistical validity, reliability, and comprehensiveness? It must yield a solid deduction. It must work time and again, and it must have broad applicability. It must work in the world at large; otherwise it has to be rejected as too exclusive, too narrow, or, to get back to the theme, too provincial. Too southern. Of some down-home significance, perhaps; if you like that sort of thing. But not of very much immediate use elsewhere.

So, yes, it is precisely the regional particulars that the storyteller as full-fledged artist processes or stylizes. But it is the universal statement he should be striving for. Beneath the idiomatic surface of your old down-home stomping ground, with all of the ever-so-evocative local color you work so hard to get just right, is the common ground of mankind in general.

The storyteller either says or implies as follows: *Once upon a time in a place far away or nearby or right on this very spot or wherever, where people did things this way or that or however, there was whoever who was in whichever situation (to wit, et cetera) and who did whatsoever.*

Once upon a time. But perhaps also time after time after time and so on up
to this time and this very day. So take note.

In other words as a serious writer and also as an engaging and
entertaining storyteller, you are always concerned with what
Kenneth Burke calls the *representative anecdote,* which I take to be
that little tale or tidbit of gossip, that little incident that is in effect definitive in that it reflects, suggests, or embodies a basic attitude toward experience.

Ever mindful of the guidelines suggested by Malcolm Cowley in *The Literary Situation,* you approach your anecdotal tidbit
not as a symbolic action per se, but rather by treating a basic
southern occasion as a basic American occasion, which is in turn
a basic contemporary occasion, and thus a basic human occasion.
According to Cowley: *"If it isn't real, it isn't a symbol. If it isn't a*
story, it isn't a myth. If a character doesn't live, he can't be an arche-
type...."

Another definition. Art is the ultimate extension, elaboration,
and refinement of the rituals that reenact the primary survival
techniques (and hence reinforce the basic orientation toward experience) of a given people in a given time, place, and circumstance much the same as holiday commemorations are meant
to do.

It is the process of extension, elaboration, and refinement
that creates the work of art. It is the *playful* process of extension,
elaboration, and refinement that gives rise to the options out of
which comes the elegance that is the essence of artistic statement.
Such playfulness can give an aesthetic dimension to the most
pragmatic of actions.

It is indeed precisely play and playfulness that are indispensable to the creative process. Play in the sense of competition. Play
in the sense of chance-taking. Play in the sense of make-
believe and play also in the sense of vertigo or getting high. Play
also in the direction of simple amusement as in children's games,
and play in the direction of gratuitous difficulty as in increasing

the number of jacks you can catch or the higher distance you can jump, and as in the wordplay in *Finnegans Wake* or soundplay in a Bach fugue.

Incidentally, implicit in the matter of playful option-taking extension, elaboration, and refinement is the matter of the function of criticism in the arts. For wherever there is extension, elaboration, and refinement, there is the possibility of overextension, overelaboration, and overrefinement, and as likely as not, attenuation.

Perhaps the very first function of criticism is to mediate between the work of art and the uninitiated reader, viewer, or listener. As mediator, the critic decodes and explains the elements of the game of stylization and makes the aesthetic statement more accessible. Then, having indicated what is being stylized and how it is being stylized, the critic may also give a "professional observer's" opinion as to how effectively it has been stylized and perhaps to what personal and social end. In doing all of this, criticism proceeds in terms of taste, which is to say a highly or specially developed sense of the optimum proportion of the basic elements involved and of the relative suitability of the processing. But all of that is a very special story in itself.

To get back to the matter of the representative anecdote. My primary vernacular, regional, or indigenous, or yes, down-home source is the fully orchestrated blues statement, which I regard and have attempted to define and promote as a highly pragmatic and indeed a fundamental device for confrontation, improvisation, and existential affirmation: a strategy for acknowledging the fact that life is a lowdown dirty shame and for improvising or riffing on the exigencies of the predicament. What is that all about if not continuity in the face of adversity? Which brings us all to the matter of heroic action and the writer to the matter of the heroic image.

I don't know of a more valid, reliable, comprehensive, or sophisticated frame of reference for defining and recounting heroic action than is provided by the blues idiom, which I submit enables the narrator to deal with tragedy, comedy, melodrama, and farce simultaneously. Obviously I do not hear the blues as a simple lamentation by one who has not loved very wisely and not at all well; and certainly not as any species of political torch song. I hear the music counterstating whatever tale of woe (or worse) the lyrics might present for confrontation as part and parcel of the human condition.

The ancient Greek playwrights, remember, addressed themselves to tragic happenings in one form, dealt with comic confusions and resolutions in another (*even on other days*), and for satiric and farcical matters they used still other forms. I associate melodrama with medieval romance. The great Elizabethan tragedies, to be sure, did come to include comic relief sequences as a matter of course.

But the fully orchestrated blues statement is something else again. Even as the lyrics wail and quaver a tale of woe, the music may indicate the negative mood suggested by the dreadful, or in any case regrettable, details, but even so there will also be tantalizing sensuality in the woodwinds, mockery and insouciance among the trumpets, bawdiness from the trombones, a totally captivating, even if sometimes somewhat ambivalent elegance in the ensembles and in the interplay of the solos and ensembles, plus a beat that is likely to be as affirmative as the ongoing human pulse itself.

There is much to be said about the literary implications of this aspect of my down-home heritage, and I have written not only in direct terms of it in *South to a Very Old Place, The Spyglass Tree, and Train Whistle Guitar,* but also in no uncertain terms about it in *The Hero and the Blues* and in *Stomping the Blues,* both of which may be read as being among other things books about literary terminology and as attempts at a functional definition of improvisation as heroic action, as a way of responding to traumatic situations creatively.

So I will reiterate only in passing that (1) blues lyrics should not be confused with torch songs, which wail the heart-on-sleeve frustrations and yearnings of those rejected or discarded ones who still love not wisely and not at all well; and (2) that the improvisation that is the ancestral imperative of blues procedure is completely consistent with and appropriate to those of the frontiersman, the fugitive slave, and the picaresque hero, the survival of each of whom depended largely on an ability to operate on dynamics equivalent to those of the vamp, the riff, and most certainly the break, which jazz musicians regard as the Moment of Truth, or that disjuncture that should bring out your personal best.

The point of all this is that your representative anecdote also provides your representative man, your *hombre de época*, your all-purpose protagonist, whose personal best is exemplary. Incidentally, speaking of the South as such as a locus of motives, as a context for heroic action, I read fellow Southerner William Faulkner's great novel *The Sound and the Fury* as a story about the absence of truly heroic action. Neither poor Benjy, sad Quentin, nor mean Jason can riff or solo on the break, or set a personal pace for a truly swinging ensemble. They are all stuck with stock tunes that only add up to sound and fury, signifying a big mess.

But for all the restrictions that you inherited as a Southerner during the days of my coming of age as an apprentice in literature, being a Southerner did not automatically mean that my mind, my interests, and my aspirations were limited to things southern; moreover, it is not at all unsouthern to read a lot. In any event, it was in a down-home library that I discovered the Joseph in Thomas Mann's *Joseph and His Brothers, Young Joseph, Joseph in Egypt,* and *Joseph the Provider,* who as I have suggested in *The Hero and the Blues* is a hero whose playful creativity is his stock in trade, and also the salvation of his people.

My attempt to suggest an image of the hero as improviser is Scooter, the first-person narrator of *Train Whistle Guitar, The Spy-*

glass Tree, and *The Seven League Boots,* in which I try to make the literary equivalent of an Ellington orchestration of a little blue steel and patent leather down-home saying that goes: *my name is Jack the Rabbit and my home is in the briar patch,* which for me is only an upbeat way of saying: *"woke up this morning [with the] blues all around my bed"*. . . . which means that Scooter could also say: *I live in a land menaced by dragons and even Grand Dragons, and that's why I have to be as nimble in brain as in body—or else!—and must either find or forge my own magic sword and be heroic or nobody.*

All of this is nothing if not down-home stuff. Which brings us to our out chorus: it is precisely such southern "roots" that will dispose and also condition my protagonist to function in terms of the rootlessness that is the basic predicament of all humankind in the contemporary world at large.

PART TWO

TWO ALL-AMERICAN ARTISTS
FIRST PERSON SINGULAR

DUKE ELLINGTON VAMPING TILL READY

The personal recollections and reflections that Duke Ellington has left in *Music Is My Mistress* were programmed or routined into acts rather than orchestrated into a literary equivalent of, say, *Reminiscin' in Tempo*. So the overall effect is somewhat like that of an all-star variety show, including special guest appearances. But formal structure aside, time and again the actual narration as such becomes so suggestive of Ellington's unique speaking voice and conversational mannerism that you find yourself all but literally backstage looking on and listening in as he recalls people, places, times, circumstances, and events somewhat as if nudged into nostalgia by old friends or some very lucky interviewer.

Not that backstage is ever altogether offstage. But then Duke Ellington himself was never very far from the footlights for very long either. Nor did he ever show or express any overwhelming need to be. What he always needed was listeners, even at rehearsals. And audiences were as essential to his recording sessions as was the accustomed excellence of the studio equipment. After all from him, in whom the instrumentalist, composer, and conductor were so totally and inextricably interrelated, performing music was absolutely indispensable to writing it. Not only was there almost always a keyboard instrument of some kind in his dressing room whenever space permitted, such was also the case with his hotel suites and even his hospital rooms. And he was forever noodling and doodling and jotting and dotting no matter who else was there or what else was going on.

In any case, among the anecdotes, vignettes, plugs, takeoffs, put-ons, whatnots, and what-if-nots in *Music Is My Mistress* there are also some that even seem not so much written as jive-riffed into the microphone *onstage between numbers*. Nor are they thereby any less representative than the rest. Ellington was mostly himself no matter where he was. Indeed, the man behind the legend, as the interviews published several years ago by Stanley Dance in *The World of Duke Ellington* bear out, was if anything even more of a legendary figure to his closest associates than to his millions of worshipful admirers all over the world.

As for his mike spiel, what with the orchestra there in the background, he was (for most intents and purposes) quite possibly as much at home on the job as he was ever likely to be lounging in an armchair by a fireside on a rainy night.

Which is not to say that he was ever given to making public such private (but by no means secret) personal involvements as his schedule permitted. References in *Music Is My Mistress* to his adult family life, for instance, are oblique at best: "I took him [arranger Billy Strayhorn] to 381 Edgecombe Avenue and said, 'This is my home, and this is your home. I'm leaving for Europe in a few days, but you stay here with my son Mercer and my sister Ruth. They will take good care of you.'" So much for that. Mention of previous and subsequent adult addresses is less than oblique. And while there indeed was, as he says he discovered very early, always a pretty girl standing down at the bass clef end of the piano, the only "love interest" discussed concerns music. No kissing and telling for him, or perhaps there was too much kissing for telling. But then the title of his book may have been intended as a statement of precisely the delimitation he wanted.

But even so, *Music Is My Mistress* is an authentic autobiographical document that is strong at precisely those points where so many other books by and about so-called black Americans are so often so exasperatingly weak.

Seldom are such books concerned with making anything more than a political statement of some kind or other, mostly polemical. Rarely do they reflect very much personal involvement with the textures of everyday actuality as such. On the contrary, most often they are likely to leave the impression that every dimension of black experience is directly restricted if not inevitably crippled, by all-pervading (and always sinister) political forces.

More often than not it is as if all of the downright conspicuous orientation to style in general and stylish clothes in particular, all of the manifest love of good cooking and festive music and dancing and communal good times (both secular and sacred), all of the notorious linguistic exuberance, humor, and outrageous nonsense, not to mention all of the preoccupation with love and lovemaking (that blues lyrics are so full of)—it is as if none of these things, otherwise considered to be so characteristic of the so-black American's lifestyle, is of any basic significance whatever once a so-called black American becomes the subject of biographical contemplation.

Actually, most biographies and autobiographies of so-called U.S. black folks tend to read like case histories or monographs written to illustrate some very special (and often very narrow) political theory, or ideology of blackness, or to promote some special political program. Such writing serves a very useful purpose, to be sure. But the approach does tend to oversimplify character, situation, and motive in the interest of social and political issues as such, and in the process human beings at best become sociopolitical abstractions. At worst they are reduced to clichés.

The *Narrative of the Life of Frederick Douglass, an American Slave, Written by Himself,* is as much a classic of nineteenth-century American prose as are the works of Emerson, Long fellow, Hawthorne, Thoreau, Lowell, Holmes, and the rest. Moreover, the story it outlines is nothing less than an unsurpassed representative anecdote (or epic or basic metaphor) of the American ideal of self-realization through the resistance to tyranny. But still it is more of an autobiographical *political* essay than a full-scale comprehensive autobiography. And so were Douglass's *My Bondage and My Freedom* and the *Life and Times of Frederick Douglass*.

Booker T. Washington's *Up from Slavery* is another case in point. It is an autobiographical essay on post-Reconstruction education that is far more concerned with promoting the Hampton-Tuskegee emphasis on normal, agricultural, and trades courses as a basic means of black uplift than with the story of Booker T. Washington himself. And the same is true of Washington's *The Story of My Life and Work* and *My Larger Education*.

In the "Apology" for *Dusk of Dawn*, which he called an essay toward an autobiography of a race [*sic!*] concept, W. E. B. Du Bois flatly states that because midway through the writing he realized he was approaching his seventieth birthday "It threatened . . . to become mere biography. But in my own experience, autobiographies have had little lure; repeatedly they assume too much or too little; too much in dreaming that one's own life has greatly influenced the world; too little in the reticences, repressions, and distortions which come because men do not dare to be absolutely frank." And then curiously, he adds, "My life had its significance and its only deep significance because it was part of a problem. . . ."As if people involved with problems have not always been as great a preoccupation of biography as of fiction and dreams. Still, in *Dusk of Dawn* and in his *Autobiography* there is much richly textured autobiographical writing.

But all told, perhaps the most noteworthy exception to the general run of one-dimensional biographical writing by so-called black Americans is James Weldon Johnson's *Along This Way*. Johnson, who not only wrote the lyrics to "Lift Every Voice and

Sing" (The Negro National Anthem) but was also the first executive secretary of the NAACP, was actively involved with problems of civil rights as few have been. But *Along This Way* is not
political propaganda. It is a full-scale personal record of a marvelous American who was, among other things, also a professional
music hall entertainer, poet, lawyer, diplomat, editor of antholo-
gies of poetry and spirituals, and novelist. Indeed, for historical
perspective, comprehensive grasp of circumstance, and sensitivity to the texture of life as such, it may well be the very best autobiographical treatment to date of the experience of a descendant
of U.S. slaves.

   None of which is to imply that *Music Is My Mistress* is comparable in overall literary merit to *Along This Way*. The two, however, do share basic virtues so often absent from so many
autobiographical monographs geared primarily to political statement. To begin with, Ellington, like Johnson, always regarded
himself not as a political theory but as a flesh-and-blood human
being, a person of capability with many possibilities. Like Johnson he remembers his parents, for instance, not as if they were
mostly social problems in urgent need of white liberal compassion, but rather as good-looking, affectionate, prideful, and au-
thoritative adults who expected one to grow up and amount to
something. Nor did his black elders treat him as if he were born
under a curse. He was always somebody special. "Edward, you are
blessed," his mother, who certainly knew the facts of life, told
him. That he didn't have anything to worry about. And he believed her, and storybook Duke-designate that he already was, he
went out and forged a magnificent sword and conquered the
world.

   In other words, as is entirely consistent for one whose all-
pervading commitment is to an art form, the frame of reference of
Ellington's most basic functional conceptions and definitions of
himself and his purposes is not political but metaphorical. For all
its concrete details including such specifics as employment and

budgets, his is the fairy-tale world of heroic encounters and endeavors, where obstacles are regarded not as occasions for welfare-oriented protests, but as a challenge to one's creativity. Thus, the eight "acts" of *Music Is My Mistress* consists mostly of a recounting of the initiation rituals of the apprentice, the trials and contests of the journeyman, and the offerings of the full-fledged craftsman-practitioner. Then comes some modest (and some tongue-in-cheek) words of wisdom and advice from the long since venerable Old Pro, followed by a listing of ceremonial honors and awards and finally a catalog of his good works and exploits.

Such day-to-day actualities were no less the symbolic terms and underlying rituals of Ellington's existence. And to be sure, all of the key *felidae* (as he calls them) in his cast of characters were blue steel fables in the flesh. Which is also why, the dynamics of aesthetic feedback being what they are, references no matter how offhand to James P. Johnson, Willie "the Lion" Smith, Will Marion Cook, Will Vodery, Sidney Bechet, Louis Armstrong, and Fletcher Henderson, among others, are absolutely indispensable sources of insight. Even the sketches of the personalities of the musicians in his orchestra over the years—plus what he includes about Irving Mills, the agent who promoted him into the big time—provide more understanding of the structure as well as the content of Ellington's music than is ever likely to be derived from any examination of deep-seated anxieties resulting from political oppression, or ever likely to be revealed by even the most exhaustive confession of long-hidden personal hangups.

Moreover, although far too many students of history seem far too oversubscribed to the methodology of psychiatric case surveys to realize it these days, in making references to people who struck him as being literally *fabulous,* Ellington is also addressing himself to precisely those basic rituals and myths that all truly serious scholars must discover in order to come to comprehensive terms with the definitive forces that motivate the effort and achievement (or lead to the failures) and shape the lifestyle of the person who is the subject of any biographical study. After all, what the comprehensive, valid, and reliable biography or history must always add up to for all its entirely proper preoccupation with specific fact, is fiction. The subject's vital statistics are such and such and his doings and accomplishments are already a matter of public record and widespread acclaim. *But what is his story?* What, in other words, is his functional mythology, his personal frame of reference?

That Duke Ellington had no intention whatsoever of writing a conventional autobiography on the scale of James Weldon Johnson's *Along This Way*, or even on the lesser scale of W. C. Handy's useful but somewhat stilted *Father of the Blues*, need hardly be argued. Nevertheless, in *Music Is My Mistress*, along with all of the firsthand information and expert but seldom pontifical observations, he has left future biographers and historians the literary equivalent of some of the indispensable piano vamps he used to sit noodling, doodling, and riffing until the ensembles and soloists were ready for the downbeat. He has, that is to say, improvised a prelude, an overture, an introduction that establishes the key, the tempo, mood, direction, and overall treatment for those who wish to deal with his life in his own personal terms, for those who wish to come to terms with what he was really about rather than what they think he should have been about.

As for the biographical or autobiographical social science monograph, its shortcomings are inherent not so much in its methodology as such (aside, of course, from the fact that it cannot be *scientific* enough) but rather in the all too obvious assumption that generalizations, findings, and conclusions drawn from measurable fact are *not fiction*. But aren't all formulations necessarily fabrications? In all events, what finally matters most about both formula and metaphor is the extent of their functional immediacy or comprehensive applicability. As for those historical research specialists who set out to replace the legendary, the fabulous, or the mythical with scientific fact, what they end up with are all too often only stereotypes derived from social science assumptions—which, of course, is to say social science fiction.

COMPING FOR COUNT BASIE

I

In autobiography as in fiction, nothing has more to do with what the story is really about than the voice of the narrator. So the main thing was to get his voice on the page. Everything else came after that. Incidents mean only as much as the way they are told makes them mean. If you couldn't help him sound like himself in print, you'd probably be better off working on a book *about* Count Basie rather than one *by* Count Basie about himself.

Obviously it is the voice of the narrator that establishes not only the physical point of view including the relative sharpness or vagueness of focus and the limits of the field of vision, but also the listening post, which determines the reader's distance from the alarums and excursions if any, and also whether what is being said is heard verbatim or second remove—and how much is to be heard in either case.

It is also the storyteller's voice that creates the overall atmosphere as well as the specific mood for each situation and sequence of action. The on-the-page equivalent of vocal cadence, tone, and timbre, together with vocabulary, syntax, and imagery determines just *how* whatever is being recollected and recounted is to be taken. Whether the narrator is deadpan or scowling or smiling or laughing or has his tongue in his cheek makes all the difference in the world. The tone of voice may not only represent a sense of life that is not otherwise stated, it may also of its very nature counterstate or cancel out any direct assertion or avowal.

Unlike the narrator of stories in the third person who can either maintain one position and one voice or shift position and voice source at will, the autobiographer speaks in his own voice at all times. Even when the conversation with and between others is quoted as if with total recall, it is still only an approximation. It is, in fact, the narrator mimicking others with his own voice barely disguised, and indeed what really counts is the impression he wishes to convey. Sometimes he may go so far as to put words and phrases that are obviously his own into the mouths of others to create a desired effect. But after all, this is only a storytelling device that has been employed since the days of talking animals during the age of fables and that also permits the ever-so-earthy peasant language of the aristocrats in most folk tales.

Third-person dialogue, on the other hand, can almost always be taken as literal transcription. Moreover, such is also the convention of third-person narration that the degree of intimacy and omniscience the storyteller chooses enables him to represent and indeed give voice to as many memory banks and individual streams of consciousness and to reveal as many private thoughts, anxieties, fears, wishes, confusions, and even motives as suit his purpose.

Even when fiction is narrated in the first person there are many more options than the autobiographer has. You may be an outsider with only a spectator's view of things. Or you may be personally involved in the action to some small or large degree. Or you may exist at the very center of all the action with everything happening around you and to you.

As autobiographer, you have only one position and that is at the center of everything that matters. Even though you may represent yourself as being only a passive witness to the times, you still occupy what Henry James called the "commanding center." Yours is the central informing intelligence, the comprehensive or overall sensibility that determines the operative frame of refer- ence. And so it is that the autobiographer's voice is the vector of the basic sense of life, attitude toward experience, and hence the value system that everything in the story represents.

And so it is also that the limitations of the autobiographer's awareness are ultimately also an important part of what his story is about. Inferences may also be drawn from deliberate omissions. After all, since what is at stake is not a matter of *guilt* but of *attitude*, there is no literary Fifth Amendment. Language, as Kenneth Burke once said, is symbolic action, the dancing of an attitude. So, under certain conditions, is silence. In the context of a discourse, ellipses, omission, and silence are also *verbal actions* and as such also represent the dancing of an attitude.

But the point is that it is always the storyteller's story because it is his voice that is the vector, even when he is anonymous, as when he is working in terms of the third person and seems totally concerned with depicting *somebody else* as the compositional center if not the protagonist. It is still his voice that provides the emotional as well as the physical context in terms of which everything else is defined.

II

And yet as literary craftsman, the cowriter of an as-told-to autobiography is also present on every page. Never as a partner in a duet, to be sure, but he is there nonetheless! Actually, his role is very much the same as that of the piano accompanist who comes on stage with the solo vocalist or instrumentalist. Once the performance gets under way, it is as if the very best accompanists are neither seen nor heard.

Even as the accompanist vamps till the soloist is ready, what he plays is like so many bars of preparatory silence. And the same is almost as true of his obbligatos and fills. Everything he plays is specifically designed to enhance the presence and the unique traits of the featured soloist, not to divert attention from him in any degree whatsoever. Nor does such background support compromise the integrity and authenticity of the solo as solo statement. Few soloists perform a cappella. Many singers accompany themselves on the piano, and perhaps even more do so on guitar.

Sometimes the accompanist, for all his unobtrusiveness, actually leads and prompts the soloist. Sometimes he only follows, perhaps most often as if he were whispering yes, yes, yes; and then, and then, and then; go on, go on, go on; amen, so be it. Even when he engages in call-and-response exchanges, it is always as if the soloist is carrying on a dialogue with someone who is either absent or totally imaginary. But always the accompanist is there to keep the melodic line and its frame of reference intact and the soloist in key, in tune, and in time.

For all that, however, it is only at the *end* of the performance when the bows, if any, are being taken that the accompanist shares a brief moment with the soloist in the spotlight. And yet two of the most prominent and influential contemporary American musicians, both of whom were easily identifiable by their piano styles, were also two of the very best comp artists who ever did it. One was Duke Ellington, and the other was Count Basie himself.

III

Count Basie's conception of the role of the literary craftsman (and research assistant) as cowriter of an as-told-to autobiography was just about everything you could want it to be. All-time exemplary bandleader and performing artist as improviser that he always was to his very fingertips, he was completely aware and appreciative of the fact that what he was involved in was an act of composition. He knew very well that getting his voice down on the page was not simply a matter of making a literal transcription of his recollections and then tidying them up for the printer.

As for dictating sequences and anecdotes into a tape recorder, very few people seem able to do that in their most natural or characteristic cadence, syntax, and tone of voice. More often than not, they become so self-conscious and spend so much time choosing words, revising their phrases, and measuring their statements that they not only interrupt the normal flow of discourse, but even lose the train of thought from time to time and have to begin again, and again, only to end up sounding stilted at best. Not that there are not those who do manage to maintain a steady on-mike flow. But more often than not, they sound more like overstylized media types than like the individuals they project otherwise. Indeed, in such instances their words are only likely to become on-the-page equivalents of masks and costumes. In any case, Basie knew that the microphone patter that he used on stage and in interviews with entertainment page reporters would not do for the kind of book he had in mind.

In point of fact, a small Sony tape recorder with a tiny clip-on microphone was used at every working session over a period of six years, and transcriptions were made from most of them. But the trick was to get him to respond to questions, not by speaking into the microphone, but to you in a casual person-to-person conversational tone and tempo. And that meant getting him in the frame of mind that made him try to take you back into his past with him, much the same as he was soon to do when he took you to Kansas City and later on to Red Bank, New Jersey. Then instead of addressing himself to abstract issues as such, he would simply become anecdotal and evoke people and details about places and days and nights and ongoing actions and relationships. Once he got an anecdote going, the I said, he said, she said particulars tended to fall into place with no effort at all.

The whole procedure worked as smoothly as it did because it was not really a new approach to composition for Basie. After all, he had been collaborating with staff arrangers and freelancers as well for almost fifty years. Also entirely in line with his definitive orientation to improvisation, he had his own functional conception of dictation. For him it was mostly a matter of feeding suggestions and instructions directly from the keyboard to band members during rehearsals, or perhaps as often as not during an actual performance. In either circumstance, it was only sometimes that his statements were repeated literally. And other times they were to be complemented—perhaps as often as not through counterstatement.

So he was already all set to utilize the services of a cowriter as the literary equivalent of the piano accompanist or comp artist who would supply him with chordal structures and progressions in the form of documentary notes, press clippings, photographs, recordings, and data from various colleagues over the years. But at the same time you were also to be his staff arranger and copyist who would prepare tentative score sheets that the two of you would rework and polish together, as if rehearsing the band.

Which made you Count Basie's literary Count Basie and also Count Basie's literary extension of such legendary arrangers as Eddie Durham, Buck Clayton, Buster Harding, Jimmy Mundy, Andy Gibson, Ernie Wilkins, Frank Foster, Frank Wess, and Thad Jones all rolled into one. No mean task or honor for you, but everyday stuff for him. And when he realized that you, for your part, already conceived your own writing in terms of vamps, choruses, riffs, call-and-response patterns, breaks, chases, and so on to outchoruses and tags, all he could do was point his finger at you as if at a sideman and say, "You got it." Which became "You got it, Mister Bateman" after you began addressing him by his nickname in the Gonzelle White troupe, only to have him turn it back on you. "Where the hell are we, Mister Bateman? How did I get off on this, Mister Bateman? Get me out of here, Mister Bateman. Stop pointing and just get us out of here, Mister Bateman. Hell, you the one with the dates, Mister Bateman, you tell me when I was supposed to do whatever it was, and I'll tell you what I remember about it."

Not only did he appreciate the fact that getting the voice on the page, with all of its distinctively personal inflections, was the *sine qua non* of an autobiography, he also understood that once there, it also had to function as a series of paragraphs and chapters in a book. And what he wanted was the kind of book that made you see and hear as you read. Indeed, he really wanted a book that would unfold like a movie script, with long and medium camera shots and closeups, with montage and flashback sequences, and all the rest, including panning, zooming, cutting to, crosscutting, fading in, and fading out, among others.

IV

Very much in line with the many recapitulations and revisions required by an as-told-to autobiography was the fact that being a performing artist, Basie was as used to regular rehearsals as he was to improvisation. So you could count on taking him back over some details time after time until the replay turned out to be a statement that he was willing to release to the public. As should surprise no one, he was no more inclined to release raw material as a writer than he was given to doing so as a musician.

He did not think that unguarded or loose expression represented one's true, honest, and material self. It represented one as careless, unorganized, and confused. As far as he was concerned, you should always get yourself together before you made any kind of presentation to others. Nor was this unusual for a bandleader. Very rarely do any musicians worthy of the name ever presume to play, or even rehearse, anything without first tuning up their instruments and getting in key, if only to get deliberately out of key. In any case, as fresh and impromptu as the best Basie bands always sounded, they were always well drilled. Even the widely celebrated unwritten, informal, or head arrangements were worked up during rehearsal and also reworked during subsequent rehearsals. Although many riff patterns and ensemble figures also came into being during actual performances, those that became a part of the repertory were reworked and refined in rehearsal after rehearsal. Such arrangements were called "heads" mainly because the band had memorized them long before they were copied out on the score sheets.

As relaxed and as basically geared to improvisation as Basie's bands always were, his musicians always looked and sounded well rehearsed and together. Nor was there ever any ring-around-the-collar sloppiness about their appearance. Their uniforms were sharp, and their deportment on the bandstand was beyond reproach. There was always room to hang loose and swing, but careful preparation was as characteristic of the Basie approach to performance as were the unexpected accents, on-the-spot obbligatos and extended vamps, solos, and outchoruses. One more time, indeed.

V

Even when it is offered as an entirely unprepossessing personal record of one's own life, undertaken with great reluctance, an autobiography is still of its very nature an exercise in exemplification, concerned with the narrator's sense of endeavor, fulfillment, and failure. As such it is really a species of *fiction*. It is a story with an explicit or implicit moral.

Sometimes it may be structured in terms of a dramatic plot (one thing *leading* to another) that enfolds on the dynamics of tragedy, comedy, melodrama, or farce. Or, as is perhaps just as often the case, its story line may be only a simple matter of one thing *following* another as in the genre of the picaresque novel, that literary extension of the logbook, diary, and journal (and perhaps also the rogue's deposition!). In either case, it is a story and as such it takes people and events from the context of vital statistics and the facts of everyday life into the realm of legend, myth, fairy tale, and fable (which, by the way, also has the effect of transforming the profane into the sacred).

It is the stuff of legend, myth, fairy tale, and fable, not the concrete facts per se, that accounts for the widespread interest in such classics of autobiographical writing as the *Confessions of Jean-Jacques Rousseau, The Autobiography of Benjamin Franklin, Narrative of the Life of Frederick Douglass, an American Slave, Written by Himself,* and *The Education of Henry Adams* (written in the third person!) that persist from generation to generation. Not that factual precision is unimportant, but rather that such books are read not nearly so much for the information per se as for the story.

But the autobiography is also a form of history even so. Being a personal record of one's own life, it is of its very nature an exercise in chronological documentation, which, however skimpy the details, is obviously intended to convey historical data. Thus it is in itself a historical document that may be the object of scholarly investigation, and its usefulness as such depends on its accuracy and its scope, both of which may be limited in some degree (but not necessarily compromised) by the author's inevitable subjectivity.

Whatever its limitations, however, the autobiography is still an indispensable form of historical documentation. So, along with all considerations based on the assumption that style functions as statement in autobiography, much the same as it does in fiction, there is also the matter of content as such: what is included and to what purpose and what is omitted either by design or through oversight. After all, whatever the story line of an autobiography is, the book itself is made up of factual details about real people involved in actual events.

VI

What Basie had in mind was a book giving his own account of some of the highlights of some of the things he had been involved in during the course of his career as a musician and bandleader over the years, including a few incidents thrown in for laughs. As far as he was concerned, there were no axes to grind, no special ideological points to make, and no old scores to settle. He did not even express any overall urge to set the record straight. He simply dealt with longstanding misrepresentations and misinterpretations as they came up in the normal sequence of putting the book together.

That was the way he put it for the cowriter at the very outset of the collaboration, and not only was it justification enough for undertaking an autobiography at any time, it was also precisely what was most urgently needed. Not a gossip or sensation-oriented show biz confession, which, as far as he was concerned, was out of the question anyway.

What was needed was the first book-length treatment of the Count Basie story by anybody at all. Because although he had never suffered for lack of publicity and promotion, but had been one of the most famous men of his time for nearly five decades, with a musical signature that is to this day still perhaps almost as instantly identifiable in international circles as the national anthem, there had at that time been only one book about him. It was titled *Count Basie and His Orchestra* and was written by an Englishman named Raymond Horricks, but it was mostly about the personnel of this orchestra over the years, with only a thirty-four-page sketch of Basie himself. *The World of Count Basie* by Stanley Dance didn't come out until Basie's own project was under way, and it, too, was mostly about members of the band.

Moreover, the personality sketches that had appeared as features in various journalistic publications were, for the most part, either based on very brief entertainment reporter interviews usually given on the go or backstage, and almost always off the cuff, or they were derived from secondary source materials, including other articles and unverified eyewitness and hearsay accounts.

Anyway, what he wanted the cowriter to help him put together was a book giving his own version of what struck him as the key elements and turning points of his life. And he was very aware of the fact that once released it would become the prime source (as likely to be double-checked as taken at face value) and point of departure for more detailed monographic studies and attempts at full-scale biographical undertakings as well.

The most obvious model for what he had in mind was the souvenir booklet that record companies sometimes include in deluxe boxed sets. It would contain more information about his childhood in Red Bank and Asbury Park, his apprenticeship in Harlem, and on the entertainment circuits, and also more about his years as a Kansas City journeyman than had ever been published anywhere before. In addition, it would also provide the most comprehensive running account of the band's extensive travels over the years, because he wanted future readers to realize that the band did not spend most of its time in theaters and dance halls in places like Harlem or the Chicago South Side, but was not only a national but also an international institution.

Also, instead of a formal discography as an appendix, he decided to treat the performance and reworking of key items in the band's repertory as the integral part of the main action of the narrative that it indeed was. When he thought of the book as a bound volume, he visualized it as standing on the record shelf at one end of the Basie collection with a complete discography by experts like Jorgen Jepsen or Chris Sheridan at the other.

VII

Most of the outstanding omissions from *Good Morning Blues* were intentional. Naturally there were also some that are due to faulty memory, but there were some lapses that were also deliberate. As Freddy Green pointed out to the cowriter early on, Basie was a much more reliable source of historical particulars than most of the self-styled experts. But he was also the type of person who would pretend not to know something, just to find out what somebody else knew. He was never one for showing that he knew more about anything than somebody else. But when he said, "Is that where that happened? Boy, my memory is gone! I thought that was out in Washington," anytime he said something like that, you'd better recheck your sources!

Sometimes he would say, "Let's skip that because I might not have it right, and I don't want anybody saying, 'See there, he don't know what he's talking about.' " But in writing about Kansas City, for instance, he just simply had no intention of going on record with everything he had seen or heard about the workings of the Pendergast machine, the business interests and invisible associates of Ellis Burton and Piney Brown, or the political connections of Benny Moten. About the Reno Club, for instance, he said, "Goddammit, somebody is always asking me to paint them a detailed picture of everything that went down in there, and name names. But why the hell should I get into that? My business in there was music, and that didn't have a damn thing to do with naming names and meddling around in somebody else's gig. Hell, ask them about it, not me. If they make a movie and show some other stuff, that's okay as long as it's true. But I don't want it in my book. Don't care how true it is. You don't have to go around talking about other folks' business just because what you're saying is true."

On the matter of the tells-all confession memoir, Count Basie was no less insightful than Somerset Maugham, for instance, who in *The Summing Up* said: "I have no desire to lay bare my heart, and I put limits to the intimacy I wish the reader to enter upon with me. There are matters on which I am content to maintain my privacy. No one can tell the whole truth about himself. It is not only vanity that has prevented those who have tried to reveal themselves to the world from telling the truth; it is direction of interest. . . ."

There was also Basie's unimpeachable sense of propriety. Never a blabbermouth, once he became a public figure he was not only extremely concerned with not becoming embroiled in controversy of any kind, he was also always very much alert to the untold damage a mean or even a careless word from him could do to other people's reputations and careers. Nor did he recognize any statute of limitations on promises made in the course of tipping on the q.t.

If the story he has chosen to tell is thereby made short on scandalous self-exposé, it is also short on outrageous self-inflation. If it is short on explanation, it is also short on false claims and pretentiousness. It is obviously a success story. But he does not presume to have a formula. And if it is short on advice, it is also short on condescension and pontification. If it also is short on the usual protest and polemics that are so predictable in the personal accounts of so many other so-called black Americans, it is also short on gratuitous (and politically naïve) self-degradation and the rhetoric of sackcloth and ashes or phony despair.

Behind all of that super cool, laid-back understatement, Old Base was mostly having himself a ball, and in his daily contacts with white people over the past forty-five years, he was much less concerned with keeping from being done in by hostile ones than with keeping from being bored to utter exhaustion by worshipful ones *(saying Bill this and Bill that in no time at all, curiously oblivious to the fact that true intimates were calling him Base).* He did not presume to speak for other so-called black Americans; instead, he set them an impeccable example of how to carry yourself in a way that always commands respect, as well as admiration, and even awe.

VIII

In the case of *Good Morning Blues*, some key answers to very basic and entirely appropriate questions about the influence of the cowriter, whether insidious, thinly disguised, or obvious, on both form and content, are already a matter of public record. There was *Stomping the Blues*. There was the essay titled "Duke Ellington Vamping Till Ready." There was *The Omni-Americans*, and there was also *The Hero and the Blues*.

The invitation to collaborate with Count Basie on his memoirs was a signal honor indeed, but it was also a great responsibility, which was accepted not only because the subject matter as such was so interesting, but also because it fell so neatly into the context of section nine of *Stomping the Blues*. So much so that it was like working on an elaborate representative anecdote as an extension of "Kansas City Four/Four and the Velocity of Celebration" to be called "For Instance Count Basie and His Orchestra."

There were also the notions about the special shortcomings of so much so-called black American biographical documentation as expressed in "Duke Ellington Vamping Till Ready." (See page 21.)

None of which should come as any surprise to anybody already familiar with *The Omni-Americans*. For one of the most obvious concerns of that book is that any image of "black" experience that is geared to the standard materialist assumptions about human fulfillment underlying most of the so-called findings of American social science technicians is very likely to fall into the trap of reinforcing the folklore of white supremacy and the fakelore of black pathology.

The Hero and the Blues, a book about the nature and function of the heroic image in fiction, is based on the assumption that endeavor, whether in quest, in conquest, or defense, is what storytelling is really about. Accordingly, it rejects protest and elects to view the eternal necessity to struggle not only as the natural condition of mankind but also as a form of antagonistic cooperation without which there is no achievement and fulfillment, no heroic action, no romance.

There were also specific assumptions about the Basie project. One was that in addition to providing useful documentation of Count Basie's successful career as a bandleader it would of its very nature also be in effect a natural history of the very distinctive Basie style. As little interest as he himself ever had in analyzing and explaining *how* and *why* he played the way he did, as a casual account of what he was doing from time to time in place after place, his book would also be a story of his musical evolution. For example, when he went west on the vaudeville circuit, he used the striding left hand of an eastern ragtime piano player, but when he came back home from the stomp-oriented West, the *stride* hand had somehow been all but replaced by the *walking* bass of Walter Page.

Another of the cowriter's very personal assumptions was derived from a discussion about the refinement of aesthetic statement in "The Style of the Mythical Age," by Hermann Broch, published as the Introduction to Rachel Bespaloff's *On the Iliad.* In a passage about expressing the essential and nothing but the essential as in childhood before entering the cluttered world of subjective problems, and in old age after leaving the cluttered behind, Broch goes on to discuss the style of old age, which he described as being not so much the product of maturity as "the reaching of a new level of expression, such as old Titian's discovery of the all-penetrating light which dissolves the human flesh and the human soul to a higher quality, or such as the finding by Rembrandt and Goya, both at the height of their manhood, of the metaphysical surface which underlies the visible in man and thing and which nevertheless can be painted; or such as *The Art of the Fugue* which Bach in his old age dictated without having a concrete instrument in mind"—and so on. There he defines it as "a kind of *abstractism in which expression relies less and less on the vocabulary, which finally becomes reduced to a few prime symbols, and instead relies more and more on the syntax . . ."*[1]

Count Basie himself had no particular concern with such observations, but to the cowriter they were as directly applicable to the evolution of the quintessential style of understatement that Basie, not unlike Ernest Hemingway in literature, not only achieved and received universal recognition for, but did so at a relatively early stage of his career. Indeed, so far as the public at large was concerned, it was as if both had expressed themselves that way all along.

Another pet notion of the cowriter was that the distillation and refinement achieved by the all-powerful yet laid-back and understated Basie style were analogous not only to the seemingly purely pragmatic but nothing if not poetic and indeed ritualistic prose of Ernest Hemingway, but also to the visual simplifications of Henri Matisse, especially but not exclusively during the late years when Matisse settled on the cutouts as if to echo Hokusai, the great Japanese master who, at ninety and at the peak of his mastery, said, according to Broch, "Now at last I begin to learn how one draws a line."

There was (or so the cowriter liked to think) also a noteworthy resemblance between the music of Count Basie and the paintings of Matisse during the years of their apprenticeship. There were the tinkling, sparkling, and cascading notes and the fancy runs and finger-busting figures of young Basie during his Harlem stride or eastern ragtime phase, culminating in the *Prince of Wails,* recorded with Benny Moten's orchestra in 1932. Just as there was, or rather had already been, the mosaic density sometimes of brush strokes and sometimes of detail, that characterized many of the early Van Gogh and Pointillist-influenced Matisse paintings, such as *Luxe, Calme, et Volupté* (1904–5), *The Open Window, The Moorish Screen,* and the various odalisques in which, as John Russell has said, he aimed "to fill the entire surface of the canvas with a unified decorative pattern and to achieve ever more exciting interactions of color." Also: Behind Basie there was the all-pervading influence of Louis Armstrong, much the same as there was old Cézanne for Matisse.

Naturally, the analogy does not apply to all particulars. Analogies seldom, if ever, do. Nevertheless, two more: Both men foreshadowed their mature reliance on syntax in much of their earlier work, but neither seems to have realized at the time that the subsequent development and refinement of their craft would take them back in the direction of their early efforts, not away from them. Young Matisse seems to have regarded his simplifications not as distillations, but as preliminary sketches and studies—and as such they were really throwaways. Basie regarded his purely functional vamps, riffs, and obbligatos as the stock in trade of the comp artist, which made them throwaways in the theatrical sense of the throwaway line!

But the point here is not that either old master was ever dead set on eliminating all density from all of the later work on the basis of some rigid principle. It is rather that such density as is so obviously there is even more obviously less a matter of vocabulary and detail than of syntax. In Matisse's *Tabac Royal* (1942), *The Egyptian Curtain* (1948), *The Parakeet and the Siren* (1952), and *Ivy in Flower* (1953), the density is based on fewer colors, less color nuance, and less detailing than in *The Moorish Screen* (1921), *Decorative Figure on an Ornamental Background* (1927), or *Odalisque in Red Pantaloons* (1922).

As a performing maestro, Basie, who thought in terms of

perennials as well as new productions, always included items from every period of his repertory with no noticeable preference for the less complex ones. However, when earlier recordings of such vintage items as *Jumping at the Woodside* (1937) and *9:20 Special* (1941), for example, are compared with later ones, even when the sidemen are obviously geared to a rococolike density, strongly influenced, no doubt, by Charlie Parker, the overall statement is still more a matter of basic blues idiom syntax than of lush additions to the vocabulary. Indeed, against the unison and ensemble backgrounds so typical of the later-day Basie arrangements, the effect of the high-speed note solos is not unlike that of Matisse's use of decorative figures against the flat backgrounds in such final cutouts as *The Sorrow of the King* (1952) and *Large Decoration with Masks* (1953).

Anybody who has hung out with him knows very well that Count Basie had no concern whatsoever with such juxtapositions and speculations. He regarded them as being academic at best and a bit too highfalutin in any case. The suggestion that Matisse's reproductions be used as Basie album covers struck him as being very nice and appropriately contemporary. But so far as the rest: "Okay. I see what you mean, but that's you saying that now, not me."

Matisse, on the other hand, was highly conscious of musical parallels in his painting. He was theorizing in terms of "harmonies and dissonances of color" as long ago as 1908, and in 1946 he spoke of black as "taking a more and more important part in color orchestration, comparable to that of the double-bass as a solo instrument." And, of course, over the years there were *Harmony in Blue*, which became *Harmony in Red, Music, Dance, Joy of Life, Piano Lesson, Music Lover*, and so on. Then in fruitful old age there was the book of twenty prints (from cutouts) that represented "crystallizations of memories of the circus, of popular tales, or of travel," which he called *Jazz* because they were composed on unspecified principles of improvisation, but which resemble no other jazz in existence more than that of Count Basie's band in general and Count Basie's piano in particular.

One of the best possible models for keeping all of these and other personal assumptions and opinions under control was Count Basie himself. As universally popular as his uniquely individualistic piano style made him, few soloists, vocal or instrumental, ever sounded more like they had all of their own special attributes and nuances under more effective control than when they had him in there doing what he did in his own special way in the background, usually unattended by most of the audience.

But even so there is finally no getting around the fact that regardless of how self-effacing certain accompanists might seem to be, what they do has a crucial and even definitive influence on the manner as well as the substance of the performance of any soloist. Thus no matter how distinctively individual your personal identity remains, when, say, Duke Ellington supplies the accompaniment, you are very apt to sound even more rather than less like yourself than ever, to be sure, but at the same time your voice becomes Ellington music. And when you perform with Count Basie the chances are that you are going to sound very much like yourself on a Basie beat.

The implications of this aspect of the as-told-to autobiography for oral history projects in general should be obvious enough. After all, such projects are hardly ever initiated by the subjects, who as a matter of fact are seldom if ever in a position to exercise any basic control over context, theme, direction, emphasis, or nuance. Indeed, far from having any definitive editorial prerogatives, many do not actually know what use will be made of the data their interviews produce.

Such was certainly not the case with Count Basie and *Good Morning Blues*. In the first place, he himself initiated the project in his own good time. Then he chose an accompanist who met criteria that he himself had established. Moreover, in doing so he enjoyed the same position of unassailable authority that gave such headliners as Billy Eckstine, Sarah Vaughan, Ella Fitzgerald, Tony Bennett, and Frank Sinatra the option of having themselves showcased by Ellington, Basie, Nelson Riddle, some pickup combo, or an anonymous studio aggregation.

In any case, it was not for nothing that for all of his widely celebrated gracious deportment toward the press corps throughout his long career Basie was nevertheless one of the most reluctant and reticent of interviewees. He was admittedly extremely sensitive to and wary of the crucial influence that the reporter's frame of reference and editorial slant could have on what was to be printed as an objective rendering of verbatim quotations, and he dreaded the misrepresentation and destructive distortions that were so often the result.

Then there was also his longstanding suspicion that reporters were mostly concerned about getting credit for some sensational revelation, regardless of who was embarrassed or hurt in the process. In addition, there was also the matter of sharing idiomatic experiences with an insider rather than having to explain routine details to someone who, however curious and genuinely sympathetic, is nevertheless an outsider. Obviously this is not a matter of "for your ears only," but rather of "for your ears first," with everybody else getting the benefit of the more relaxed, natural, and revealing discourse. That storytellers do better with some audiences than with others should surprise no one.

When Basie asked prospective as-told-to collaborators what kind of book they thought his story would make, he already knew that he himself wanted a literary equivalent to the "class act" that his no less refined than down-to-earth orchestras always were. He also knew that he did not want to become involved with anybody who was going to try to maneuver him into reducing the chronicle of his career as one of the most successful of American musicians to a polemic about racism. He wasn't one to brag about his achievements, which were considerable; but he didn't stand for any putdowns either. The condescending rhetoric of do-gooders turned him off.

He was all for including anecdotes for laughs and for humor in general and especially for jokes on himself. But as for publicizing delicate indiscretions of no fundamental significance to his development as a musician, he felt that any man well into his seventies who did that was only putting tarnish on his own trophies and graffiti on his own monument.

PART THREE

THE ARMSTRONG CONTINUUM

THE TWENTIETH-CENTURY
AMERICAN HERALD

L ouis Armstrong claimed that he was born on the Fourth of July in 1900. True or not, such a birth date was not only appropriate to the status he achieved as a twentieth-century American legend, but it is entirely consistent with the crucial role he came to play as the quintessential embodiment of the spirit of his native land as it is expressed in contemporary music.

Moreover, if as some researchers now report, the date given by Armstrong was a personal choice rather than a documented fact, the symbolism of the choice may well suggest that Armstrong was not unaware of the fact that he was in effect a culture hero (not unlike, say, Prometheus), the bringer of indispensable existential equipment for the survival of humanity.

In any case, what the elegant innovations of his trumpet and vocal improvisations added up to was the American musical equivalent of "*emblems for a pioneer people who require resilience as a prime trait.*"

Nor, given the transitional nature of life in the twentieth-century world at large, is such resiliency or ability to maintain equilibrium through swinging and improvising any less an imperative for experiment-oriented people in the contemporary world elsewhere.

· · ·

Whether he was born on July 4, 1900, or on August 4, 1901, as recorded in military conscription records of 1918, Louis Armstrong was destined to make music that is if anything even more representative of American affirmation and promise in the face of adversity than the festive reiterations of the most elaborate display of any Fourth of July fireworks. And it is received as such around the globe. Indeed, during the years following World War II, the sound of Ambassador Satchmo came to have more worldwide appeal than the image of Yankee Doodle dandy ever did, not to mention the poster image of Uncle Sam, who by then had become synonymous with Uncle Sugar.

Generally acknowledged or not, much goes to show that it was through Louis Armstrong's definitive influence on jazz that the United States has registered its strongest impact on contemporary aesthetic procedure.

Yes, it was an American named Louis Armstrong, not such justly celebrated avant-garde Europeans as Igor Stravinsky, Béla Bartók, Georges Auric, Darius Milhaud, Louis Durey, Paul Hindemith, Arthur Honegger, Francis Poulenc, Germaine Tailleferre, or any of the heirs of the theories of Rimsky-Korsakov, Erik Satie, and Nadia Boulanger, whose music matched the innovations of such twentieth-century sensibilities as are represented in the visual art of Picasso, Braque, and Matisse, for instance, or in literature by Joyce, Proust, Mann, Malraux, Hemingway, Eliot, and Faulkner, or in architecture by the skyscraper, the Bauhaus, Frank Lloyd Wright, Le Corbusier, and Mies van der Rohe.

Louis Armstrong, yes, Louis Armstrong from back o' town New Orleans, Louisiana, whose American apprenticeship during the first two decades of the twentieth century made him the intimate beneficiary of ragtime and stride, the shift from the popularity of the 3/4 waltz beat of the operetta to the 4/4 of the fox trot, the one-step, the two-step, the drag, the stomp, the Afro-U.S. emphasis on percussion and on syncopation, the break, stop time, and so on.

On the other hand, by the way, in spite of all the unmistakable clues so readily available to them on ballroom floors and vaudeville stages across the nation, none of the most publicized twentieth-century American choreographers has yet risen to the challenge of Armstrong's trumpet affirmations. Nor do their productions share his universal appeal and acclaim, as might be the case if they did. Why choreographers of all people did not rise to the challenge is perhaps a very special American story in itself.

"All this life I have now," the mature and long since world-famous Armstrong told Richard Meryman in an interview, most of which was printed as a memoir in *Life* magazine of April 15, 1966, "I didn't suggest it. I would say it was all wished on me. Over the years, you find you can't stay no longer where you are, you must go on a little higher now, and that's the way it all came about. I couldn't get away from what's happened to me."

"But man," he went on to say, "I sure had a ball there growin' up in New Orleans as a kid. We were poor and everything like that, but music was all around you. Music kept you rolling."

He also told Meryman that he had spent about a year and a half in the Colored Waifs Home (that has become such a famous part of accounts of his childhood) and that he never did go back to school. "I was about the fifth grade—and I regret that to a hell of an extent. But I had to take care of Mama and I was the only one to put somethin' in the pot. And at that time I didn't need school . . . I had the Horn."

In all events, what he also told the editors of *True* magazine when they published his memoir of Storyville in November of 1947, makes it clear enough that, whatever social science technicians might think, his hometown was not a God-awful place in which he grew up wishing to get out of: "*Every time I close my eyes blowing my trumpet, I look right into the heart of good old New Orleans.*"

About all of which he went on to say in the opening paragraph of the Meryman interview, "*I'm always wondering if it would have been best in my life if I'd stayed like I was in New Orleans, having a ball. I was very much contented just to be around and play with the old-timers. And the money I made—I lived off of it. I wonder if I would have enjoyed that better than all this big mucky-muck traveling all over the world...."*

What Armstrong told Meryman and the editors of *True* magazine was not social welfare or civil rights propaganda to ring the condescending hearts and shallow pockets of self-styled do-gooders and patron saints of socioeconomic uplift, but the very stuff not only of legendary adventure and romance, but also of the world of epic achievement in terms of which national character is described.

As for those who are either critical of or defensive about the close interrelationship of jazz and the goings-on in Storyville in the New Orleans of Armstrong's childhood, let them remember not only what a disreputable place the Globe Theatre and environs was during the heyday of Shakespeare, Marlowe, and Jonson, but also that the great classic dramas of Aeschylus, Sophocles, and Euripides were not written for the approval of college professors but for the entertainment of revelers during the festival of Dionysus, the god of wine, whose celebration was as noted for sexual indulgence and food as for drunkenness.

"When I got to the station in Chicago I couldn't see Joe Oliver anywhere. I saw a million people, but not Mr. Joe, and I didn't give a damn who else was there. I'd never seen a city that big. All those tall buildings. I thought they were universities. I said, no, this is the wrong city. I was just fixin' to take the next train back home—standin' there in my box-back suit, padded shoulders, double-breasted, wide-legged pants...."

So said the long since legendary Louis Armstrong in the Meryman interview. But even so, he never was the young man from the provinces come to seek his fortune in the big city by hook, crook, or whatever, such as was depicted by Balzac in *Le Père Goriot* and *Lost Illusions,* for instance. *He had come to Chicago because he had been asked to join his New Orleans mentor, then playing at one of the choice spots in town.*

As impressed as he undoubtedly was by the size of Chicago, then the second largest city in the United States, he was no hayseed from the sticks; he was a very promising young journeyman from New Orleans, a city of revelry, widely celebrated for the international flavor of its sophistication; and long before he had enough free time on his hands to wander around and be overwhelmed by Chicago, he himself was not only well on his way to becoming one of its most dazzling elements, but was also being invited to join the even more famous Fletcher Henderson Orchestra, then playing at the Roseland Ballroom at Fifty-second Street and Broadway, a choice midtown venue in the even greater city of New York.

Not that Chicago was not a world-class metropolis to be sure. It was not only the railroad center of the nation, but also the major U.S. port city on the Great Lakes outlet to transoceanic trade. And along with its exclusive position as the capital of the meatpacking and distribution industries, it was also the major regional focal point of the vast midwestern agricultural, manufacturing, and mail order enterprises.

Also, when you thought of the great city that Chicago had become at the time Armstrong arrived, you realized that by then it had not only surpassed Boston and Philadelphia, for instance, in its cosmopolitan outlook, but was also well on its way as a possible contender for New York's position as the nation's cultural capital. Certainly its architects had become pacesetters. Its newspapers were more powerful than most elsewhere, and its output of phonograph records and radio broadcasts was second only to New York's.

Nor as busy as he was kept could Armstrong not have known about and have been impressed by the fact that in addition to the sensationally popular jazz spots on the South Side, there was also the *Chicago Defender*, one of the two top black weekly newspapers (the other being the *Pittsburgh Courier*), with the largest nationwide circulation.

When Armstrong arrived in New York to join the Fletcher Henderson Orchestra, he felt some twinges of the old momentary uncertainty of his first night in Chicago. But not for long. Indeed, before the end of his very first rehearsal, his cornet was already inspiring other sidemen and the arranger as well to expand their approaches to music. And among many other New York-based musicians who heard him, either in person or on record, his impact seems to have been no less instantaneous and even more widespread.

In addition to the several dozen records on which he played with the Henderson Orchestra (most of which are generally thought to owe such lasting interest as they have mainly to his contributions, although he's featured on none), he also made a noteworthy impression as a member of recording studio groups backing the great blues singer Bessie Smith, among others.

But as Max Jones and John Chilton point out in *Louis: The Louis Armstrong Story, 1900–1971*, there were also his studio dates with another group: "Of more consequence to students of music—and probably to Armstrong himself, since they reverted to the spontaneous type of jazz-making he loved and excelled at—were the quintet sides he cut with Clarence Williams's Blue Five and similarly constituted group known as The Red Onion Jazz Babies, after a New Orleans dive named the Red Onion. In spite of the acoustic recording which muffled the tone of Armstrong's cornet, these tracks give a clear enough presentation of his authority and expressiveness as both solo and lead player."

It is also in *Louis*, the best Armstrong biography to date, that Jones and Chilton make the following summary and assessment of Armstrong's initial New York experience: *In his first New York stay Armstrong scored a success only with musicians and those dancers and music fans who bothered to note who was playing what. He commented once that five years after his visit Broadway finally accepted him. The experience, however, had been vastly worthwhile for him professionally. In the year with Henderson he gained confidence, improved his knowledge of reading and interpreting a score, learned many new tricks of showmanship, and picked up ideas from dozens of musicians he heard and in some cases recorded with.*

Of Armstrong's second stay in Chicago, Jones and Chilton go on to write: *"New York was the last of Louis's universities. There were still finer points of the music game to be mastered, and he was as eager as ever to learn them, but he returned to Chicago a marvelous and mature all-around musician. Once back he launched himself on a variety of enterprises which established him as the jazz sensation of the city. A long series of recordings by his Hot Five and Hot Seven, the first made under his own name, carried his reputation beyond the United States to wherever Jazz records were sold. They were soon to be rated by connoisseurs in many parts of the world as the most advanced of all performances in the rough-and-ready or gutbucket style. To this day they are recognized as absolute classics of their field. In the opinion of thousands of collectors they have never been bettered."*

Dan Morgenstern, in an essay entitled "Louis Armstrong and the Development and Diffusion of Jazz" in *Louis Armstrong: A Cultural Legacy*, writes: *"The more room Armstrong gave himself on these records the better were the results, and with such masterpieces as 'Big Butter and Egg Man,' 'Wild Man Blues,' 'Potato Head Blues,' and 'Hotter Than That,' the revolutionary young Armstrong is clearly displayed. With solos such as these, he created a vocabulary of phrases that would echo in the music for decades, even unto this day—in the work not only of such older players as Ruby Braff (b. 1927) but also Wynton Marsalis (b. 1961) and other young neo-traditionalists (or post-modernists). Armstrong now proceeds with utter fearlessness and freedom, crossing bar lines, extending the working range of the horn, mastering breaks and stop time and other rhythmic devices, and creating lovely melodies and phrases that linger in the mind and stir the emotions. Hundreds upon hundreds of musicians, not only in America but wherever jazz records were sold, studied these solos, learning them note for note—to sing if not to play, for the technical demands, not to mention the rhythmic and harmonic ones, were well beyond the capacity of most. In 1927 the Chicago music publisher Melrose put out a book of Armstrong solos and breaks.*

"Armstrong's phraseology now began to enter the mainstream of jazz; it would remain a cornerstone at least until the advent of bebop—and a close analysis of Charlie Parker's vocabulary will show that he, too, was steeped in Armstrong, willy-nilly."

In a reminiscence written especially for Chilton and Jones, Armstrong himself accounts for a significant transition in his development during his return to Chicago: "I changed from the cornet to trumpet while I was with Erskine Tate at the Vendôme; Jimmy Tate (Erskine's brother) played trumpet, and they figured that it would be better if I did, too. We played some difficult shows with that orchestra, good for reading, you'd suddenly get the call to turn back five pages in the overture or something like that. I never tried to be a virtuoso or the greatest; I just wanted to be good. I learned a lot playing under the direction of Erskine Tate, we played all kinds of music. I really did sharpen up on my reading there. We played the scores for the silent movies and a big overture when the curtain would rise at the end of the film. I got a solo on stage, and my big thing was *Cavalleria Rusticana*. That always stayed with me, sometimes I used to warm up with snatches from it."

The memoir edited by Meryman also sketches other moves (many suggested by his wife, Lil, King Oliver's piano player, whom he had married before going to New York) that led to his spectacular success in Chicago, including making the Hot Five and Hot Seven records. And then he also says: *"Toward the end in*

Chicago it was tough, as Lil and I went along through the years, she didn't dig me—and I picked up a gal named Alpha. . . . eventually I married her. My last job in Chicago was at the Savoy Ballroom with Carroll Dickerson's band, and every time payday come around, oh, oh, another hard-luck story. I figured it was time to go to New York."

There was a quick trip to New York for a two-day guest shot with Luis Russell's band in March of 1929. But Armstrong's second stand there began in the third week of May, when he was invited to rejoin Fletcher Henderson to rehearse for a spot in Vincent Youmans' ill-fated musical *Great Day*, and on his own he took Dickerson and his orchestra along with him and picked up a two-night engagement at the Savoy Ballroom, followed by a four-month stand at Connie's Inn beginning in June. It was during this time that in addition to fronting Dickerson's orchestra he began doubling in the musical *Hot Chocolates*, backed by an orchestra led by one Leroy Smith in which he was featured on Fats Waller's and Andy Razaf's *Ain't Misbehavin'*.

Armstrong went out to the Pacific Coast for the first time in July 1930 because he had been offered a spot as soloist with a band, soon to be led by Les Hite, playing at Frank Sebastian's Cotton Club in Culver City, a favorite hangout of Hollywood personalities. It was a very successful engagement, but he returned to Chicago in March 1931. Meanwhile, however, his recordings of new popular tunes had already begun to make him a major stylistic influence on singers of mainstream popular song. Indeed, as Rudy Vallee, one of the most celebrated conventional dance band leaders of the decade, was to say in 1936: *"That Armstrong's delightful, delicious sense of distortion of lyrics and melody had made its influence felt upon popular singers of our own day cannot be denied. Mr. Bing Crosby, the late Russ Colombo, Mildred Bailey, and many others have adopted, probably unconsciously, the style of Louis Armstrong. Compare a record by Crosby, in which he departs from the 'straight' form of the melody and lyric and then listen to an Armstrong record and discover whence must have come some of his ideas of 'swinging.' Armstrong antedated them all and I think most artists who attempt something other than the straight melody and lyric as written, who in other words attempt to 'swing' would admit, if they were honest with themselves and with their public, that they have been definitely influenced by the style of this master of swing improvisation."*

Moreover, the fact that Armstrong began including pop tunes in his repertory not only led other jazz groups to do so because it was in vogue, but also to use either the most sophisticated show tunes as if they were only other folk ditties to be extended, elaborated, and refined into jazz.

It was not until he came back to Chicago from California in 1931 that Armstrong, with the aid of second trumpet man Zilner Randolph, organized his first full band. This was a group he took on tours through Illinois, Kentucky, Ohio, and West Virginia, to the Greystone Ballroom in Detroit, and then down to New Orleans for his first homecoming after seven years, and for a three-month residency in the swank Suburban Gardens. Then between September 1931 and March 1932 his tours with the band included Dallas, Oklahoma City, Houston, Memphis, St. Louis, Columbus, Cincinnati, Cleveland, Philadelphia, and Baltimore before he disbanded.

He returned to California for a second stand as featured soloist in Sebastian's Cotton Club in April 1932, but stayed only until early in July and sailed for England.

By one of Armstrong's own accounts, he made his first trip to England and France in the summer of 1932 not because he had bookings to fill there but as a vacation and as a chance to do some sightseeing. Others have said that he also did so in order to escape from personal problems and business complications for the time being. Along with him went Alpha Smith, his third wife-to-be and his manager. But he took no musicians and left none on alert in case any engagements turned up.

Whatever his reason for making it, the trip actually turned out to be mostly a series of concerts in response to the astonishingly great enthusiasm his recordings had stimulated abroad. So, for a two-week stint at the London Palladium, a group of jazz musicians were brought over from Paris, and for tours that included the Glasgow Empire, the Nottingham Palais, York, Liverpool, and Buckingham he used a group of British jazzmen.

It so happened that he did not get around to his vacation until he crossed over from England to Paris for a short stay that fall before returning to New York on November 2, the day, incidentally, that Franklin D. Roosevelt was elected president.

Meanwhile, however, Armstrong had not only achieved a deeper appreciation of the significance of the beachhead that he had only just discovered that his records had established but had also become personally aware of the fact that his music and musicianship were taken to be a much more serious matter by intellectuals abroad than by their counterparts in the United States, where it was regarded as entertainment rather than so-called serious (i.e., classical) music. Indeed, in the United States more than sixty years later, the regular music critics leave jazz to entertainment page reporters who are regarded as specialists in pop music.

Not that Armstrong was ever to concern himself about the general cultural significance of his efforts, which were generally directed toward being as good a musician as he could become. But in the process, he took jazz from the level of popular entertainment and into the realm of a fine art that requires a level of consummate professional musicianship unexcelled anywhere in the world.

The crucial factor involved in distinguishing between fine art and folk art and between fine art and pop art, it should be remembered, is not the raw material or subject matter as such. It is rather the quality of the extension, elaboration, and refinement involved in the creative process, the process, to reiterate yet again, that transforms or stylizes raw, direct experience into aesthetic statement. In other words, it was Armstrong's phenomenal technical mastery of his instrument coupled with the unique emotional range of his sensibility and the elegance of his imagination that gave his renditions the range, subtlety, and profundity that placed his best performances in the category of fine art.

On his second trip to Europe, which began in midsummer 1933, Armstrong played in the Halborn Empire in London in August and then toured Denmark, Sweden, Norway, and Holland and came back to England that December. Then he was booked for engagements in England until April, following which he moved to Paris for a vacation before playing two concerts at Salle Pleyel and setting out for a tour that included Belgium, Holland, Italy, and Switzerland as well as other cities in France. In *Swing That Music*, he (and/or his ghostwriter) wrote: *"Just as I was about getting homesick again and ready to take my boat, a European impresario named N. J. Canneti asked me if I could tour the Continent and I decided I might as well since he had most everything arranged. . . . At Torino, we played before the Crown Princess of Italy. I remember we spent New Year's Eve 1935 in Lausanne. We went over the Alps into Switzerland by bus and that was a very thrilling thing to me. . . .*

"When that trip ended up in Paris, I packed up and took my boat back to America. It seemed I had been gone ten years when we landed in New York, and I was glad to be back home."

European response to Armstrong and his music included some embarrassingly provincial emphases on black exotica to be sure, but after all there was that downright worshipful fascination with the Josephine Baker phenomenon (which, much goes to suggest, was far more a matter of their own concoction than of her show biz self-promotion ingenuity).

But for all that, there were European musicians, reporters, and insightful students of the implications of twentieth-century aesthetic theories and innovations, who made Armstrong aware, as he never seems to have been before, of the fact that the music that his absolutely astonishing musicianship was now playing such an indispensable role in developing and disseminating was to be taken as something with profound implications far beyond its delightfully hypnotic and kinetic appeal as popular entertainment.

With the publication of *Made in America* (republished in paperback as *The Arts in Modern American Civilization*), John A. Kouwenhoven was to make much of the aesthetic and pragmatic significance of products resulting from the interaction and synthesis of the "learned" conventions, traditions, and implements imported mainly from Europe with improvised or homespun solutions and devises evolved from or inspired by frontier situations indigenous to the United States.

Some thirty-odd years earlier, Armstrong's impact on jazz musicianship had already placed in the international domain exemplary evidence of a magnificent achievement of the crucial and definitive learned/vernacular interaction that Kouwenhoven was to write about in *Made in America* and again in *Beer Can by the Highway*.

Before Kouwenhoven, the all too prevalent attitude among those regarded as the most sophisticated American students of and commentators on twentieth-century morals and manners led them to regard jazz as an exciting and amusing novelty, an obviously transitory popular art, and the term Jazz Age was widely used as a synonym for the post-Eighteenth Amendment or Prohibition decade also known as the Roaring Twenties, the lifestyle of which was characterized by the behavior of the so-called flaming youths whose symbolic setting was the speakeasy and whose personification of post-Victorian and postwar "liberated" morality was the cigarette-smoking, cocktail-sipping, bobbed-hair-sporting flapper, who zipped about town and out to fun country in the new widely available fancy automobiles of the postwar manufacturing boom.

To the popular culture theorists the new musical phenomenon called jazz was only a postwar boom time fad, and perhaps most continued to regard as unworthy of the serious attention and assessment they were giving post-Cubist collage painting and even Art Deco. And for the most part such continued to be their attitude even as jazz continued to develop and to increase its international prestige during the very unfrivolous Depression and war years of the 1930s and the 1940s.

Nor did the intelligentsia of the so-called Harlem Renaissance of the teens and twenties seem to have had any special insight into or appreciation of the profound universal, existential implications of Armstrong's pied piper influence, which was tantamount to a major aesthetic continuum. Not that they didn't think that jazz was wonderful. On the contrary, to them it was (or so it seems) mostly just a lot of fun (some of which many feared was also questionable). So it was thus more a part of the world of entertainment and sometimes dangerous amusement than something they regarded as being serious enough to be a part of the rarefied world of the fine arts.

In any case, as serious students of the role of their people in contemporary culture (or cultivated society), the music they seemed to have identified most closely with consisted mainly of folk songs, work chants, field hollers, spirituals, jubilee songs, and the conservatory-oriented compositions and arrangements of "certified" composers and arrangers such as Harry T. Burleigh, R. Nathaniel Dett, J. Rosamond Johnson, and William Grant Still, among others. They celebrated the concert hall triumphs of singers such as Roland Hayes and Paul Robeson but not the far greater impact of the singing of Ma Rainey, Bessie Smith, and the likes of Louis Armstrong.

Back in Chicago after his second European tour and a stopover in New York, Armstrong began what was to become a lifelong relationship with a local entertainment business insider named Joe Glazer by engaging him as his manager.

Then after a debut in Indianapolis with another orchestra organized and supervised for him by Zilner Randolph, Armstrong hit the road on a tour that took him through the Midwest back down into the South and New Orleans once more and also included dates in Pittsburgh, Detroit, Washington, and New York, where he broke the attendance record at the Apollo Theatre in Harlem before disbanding in September.

In late October of 1935, fronting Louis Russell's band again, Armstrong opened at Connie's Inn in Harlem once more and stayed until February 1936. Then there were ballroom club and theater bookings (plus a film part in Hollywood) that kept him crisscrossing the country until he returned to Chicago for Christmas.

After being hospitalized in Chicago at the beginning of the following year, he hit the road again, and in April he began a series of radio broadcasts (as suggested by Rudy Vallee) for the top-rated Fleischmann's Yeast program. Later on, after dates in major cities in the East and Midwest, he made another tour through the South and by October was back out on the Pacific Coast for more film work as well as band bookings.

By this time such was the pervasive influences of devices derived from Armstrong's instrumental and vocal innovations, not only on other jazz musicians but also on the popular music of standard songwriters, that the decade of the 1930s was already being called the Swing Era. In fact, the impact was so strong that the general public still seems to be unable to distinguish between Swing Era bands who played music that qualifies as fine art, and excellent jazz-influenced conventional ballroom bands, a confusion not made less difficult by the fact that in following Armstrong's lead, so many jazz bands came to include so much pop fare in their repertory. But of course, in all matters of fine art the distinguishing factors are range, precision, profundity, and the idiomatic subtlety of the rendition.

Armstrong continued to lead full ballroom-size dance orchestras throughout the thirties and went on doing so until mid-1947, after which he initiated the Louis Armstrong All-Stars, a sextet consisting of trumpet, clarinet, trombone, piano, bass, and drums, the type of combo he was to lead for the rest of his career.

Meanwhile, in 1942 he divorced his third wife and married Lucille Wilson, a dancer with whom he was to spend the rest of his life. Also during the war years, in addition to his boom-time schedule of ballroom tours and posh nightclubs and first-run theater stands, he also played an endless number of U.S. Savings Bonds rallies, troop morale concerts, and dances, and made numerous V-disk transcriptions for broadcast in worldwide overseas combat zones.

Also between 1936 and 1969 he appeared in at least thirty-two soundies, cartoons, and movies.

Many conventional jazz journalists give the impression that by the late 1940s the so-called Swing Era had been succeeded by a post–World War II jazz stylistic emphasis known as be-bop, and modern jazz [sic!]. But in point of fact for all the promotion of it as the postwar new thing, and in spite of its undeniably chic appeal to and influence on a great number of young musicians, bop never achieved the widespread appeal and universal impact that swing as such enjoyed. Dizzy Gillespie became the most influential trumpet player since the arrival of Armstrong, and the influence of Charlie Parker's alto on all instruments was also comparable to Armstrong's. Ironically, however, the so-called bop years were also a period characterized by a very enthusiastic revival of interest in the New Orleans of Armstrong's earlier years.

But even as bop boosters like Leonard Feather, for instance, tried to write such revival enthusiasm off as the reactionary hostility of those they referred to as "moldy figs.," jazz musicians of all persuasions were beginning to express their longstanding reverence for Armstrong by referring to him as Pops (as in "old father, old artificer, stand me now and ever in good stead"). To this day jazz musicians prefer Pops to Satchmo.

In any case, Armstrong's popular appeal was far from being diminished by bop competition. On the contrary, while the typical venue of bop groups was to remain the small club in a number of the larger cities, Armstrong's audiences filled the largest theaters, concert halls, and stadiums around the globe.

The worldwide acclaim for Armstrong's genius and the unsurpassed sense of earthy well-being that his music generated everywhere he went seems to have meant very little if anything to spokespersons in the ever so dicty circles of the neo-Victorian watchdogs of proper black decorum. To them, apparently, there was no such thing as a genius who sometimes doubled as a court jester. In their view Louis Armstrong was only a very popular "entertainer" anyway. But even so, he owed it to "his people" to project an image of progressive if not militant uplift.

Ironically, offstage Armstrong in his heyday was not only a preeminent influence in sartorial matters but also a major source of the fashionable speech of the most elegant and sophisticated "men about town" from border to border and coast to coast. Nor at any time after he became a public figure was his offstage presence any less awe-inspiring than that of the sparkling tongue-in-cheek regal bearing of Duke Ellington or the laid-back banker-calm Count Basie. People from the bossman down to the hired help became downright reverential when they approached him in person. No matter how informal the situation was, this sometime court jester was always given the deference of royalty.

And he was such a genuinely nice and unpetty person, always generous with cash handouts, supportive of worthy causes, and thoughtful of old friends. *But don't make him mad. And don't try to boss him around or try to pull any one-upmanship on him. He preferred merrymaking to conflict but could be devastating when crossed. He publicly rebuked one president of the United States over civil rights and angrily refused an invitation from another to be honored at the White House.*

As for his response to caricatures of himself in the media (mostly early on) and misguided attacks by the ever sensitive brotherhood of proper black behavior in front of white folks, what must not be forgotten is the fact that along with his incredible orientation to elegance and soaring magnificence, Louis Armstrong was also endowed with an irrepressible sense of humor and merriment, not to mention an acute awareness and profound appreciation of the ridiculous, the absurd, and the downright outrageous. After all, he did get away with addressing the king of England as Rex as he dedicated "I'll Be Glad When You're Dead, You Rascal, You" to him; and he caused no offense when he referred to devoted music fans among the British aristocracy as Lord (or Lady) Dishrag!

In all events, as his long career of continuous creativity goes to show, Armstrong, like most other truly great achievers, was one who took most things in stride—as if his music would counterstate and counteract caricatures, stereotypes, and stupid misperceptions and misinterpretations as well, much the same as it had the derisive nickname of Dippermouth, Dipper, and Dip early on, and Satchelmouth and Satchmo forever afterward.

On the other hand, as for himself, Armstrong never seems to have been given to causing embarrassment to others. And perhaps best of all there was nothing at all pretentious about him.

When he made mistakes, he made corrections, not excuses. No wonder vicious satire and hostile caricatures didn't ever really work against him. There was nothing pompous to deflate. Indeed, did anybody set out to ridicule him without ending up having a ball imitating him?

After all, what Louis Armstrong did was mug *back* at the blues, saying Yeeeeah as in Oh, yeah??? or in Oh, Yeah!!! And then go on and riff all of that flashy-fingered elegance out into the atmosphere as if there were no such thing as the blues!

Armstrong's music made him a globetrotting goodwill ambassador for the irrepressible idealism of his native land because it was such an irresistible expression of what so many people elsewhere think of as being the American outlook on human possibility.

But long before he became Ambassador Satchmo to the world at large, there was the absolutely fundamental existential response that such music stimulated among people within the continental limits of the United States. All of the ever-resilient and elegantly improvised ballroom choreography was nothing if not the dancing of a definitively American attitude. It was an idiomatic representation of an American outlook on possibility and thus also was an indigenous American reenactment of affirmation in the face of the ever-impending instability inherent in the nature of things.

When Armstrong used to say, "They all know I'm there in the cause of happiness," nobody seems ever to have been inclined to insist otherwise. Because nothing was ever more obvious than the fact that he had come to town not to complain about the presence of the blues but to blow them away and hold them at bay—always with more subtlety and elegance than power, as overwhelmingly powerful as all of those astonishing high C's always were.

Nor, conditioned as he so profoundly had been by the ambivalence of those New Orleans funeral corteges he grew up marching in, was happiness ever a simple matter of thoughtless frivolity. To him, it was a hardearned and extremely fragile thing indeed. After all, the blues were only at bay; they can never be blown entirely away once and for all. But (it should be remembered) such is the nature and function of art that it can foil them time and again. Hence standards, masterworks, and the classics that add up to the canon.

When Louis Armstrong, whatever the exact date of his birth, used to say that he and jazz music grew up together, not only could he have gone on to point out that he and jazz music had helped each other grow up, but he could also have added that being born in the first decade of the twentieth century, he and the automobile and the airplane and the movies and phonograph records and radio and television, not to mention the theory of relativity, subatomic physics, space technology, automation, and so on.

In fact, Armstrong's trumpet, symbolizing as it does the very spirit of the exploration and readjustment that are so indispensable for survival in such unstable times, qualifies him as the herald of the age that may not end with 1999.

PART FOUR

THE ELLINGTON SYNTHESIS

THE VERNACULAR IMPERATIVE

A pantheon, as you probably already know even if you don't remember your elementary Latin because you never studied any to begin with, is a sacred place dedicated to all of the gods, whether of a tribal community, a city-state, or an empire of one sort or another.

The original of such consecrated places was a domed circular temple created in honor of all of the gods of ancient Rome by the Emperor Hadrian, and the idea has long since been adopted and adapted and institutionalized for secular purposes. Indeed, much goes to show that pantheons are now used for the express purpose of giving a sacred dimension to the secular.

Thus public buildings commemorating and dedicated to the great citizens of a nation are now also regarded as pantheons. Such buildings may or may not contain tombs, statues, busts, and various other memorabilia. In all events there is also a world-famous public edifice in Paris that honors the most outstanding rulers and citizens of France that is also known as the Pantheon: Panthéon Français.

Sometimes, as common usage makes clear enough, a pantheon is not an actual temple of any sort but rather a metaphorical place. In this sense it refers to all of the gods, heroes, and outstanding champions and achievers of a particular people or nation (or even an organization or line of endeavor) taken collectively as if existing somewhere in an imaginary place, say not unlike Olympus, if you will, which was not so much a mountain as it was a metaphor. But then as for the gods themselves of pre-Roman-Greek antiquity, certainly it was not their physical presence but their spiritual presence (always in the disguise of a human being) that counted.

In one sense the National Museum of American History and also the Smithsonian Institution as a whole is a temple. In effect, it enshrines and deifies and even idolizes human beings. At the same time, however, it is nothing if not a secular place, obviously concerned to a very great extent with the nuts and bolts of works and days in factories, fields, and offices, with weather vanes and windmills and so to airfoils and beyond. To many Americans, the very word *Smithsonian* is synonymous with the natural history of U.S. science, technology, and industry.

And yet, as a repository of indigenous and vernacular artifacts and memorabilia, the Smithsonian also serves, intentionally or not, the very express purpose of providing compelling documentary evidence that a very functional and, in fact, indispensable metaphorical American pantheon really does exist (even as the constellation of Roman gods [some adapted from the Greeks, some not] was already in existence, and Hadrian already regarded himself as their beneficiary long before he caused a temple to be consecrated to them).

And why not? Certainly much goes to show that such metaphorical or godlike national forces or influences and also inspirations have as much to do with the quality of American works and days and pastimes and notions of self-fulfillment as any other environmental factors, so to speak. In any case, to be in the national pantheon is to have a place of definitive influence among the aggregate forces that determine the fate of a people, for even as such forces shape rituals, customs, and traditions, which is to say, the way things are done, they modify expectations, define values, and, in effect, set the direction of endeavors.

So much for the nature and function of pantheons. But still, an extremely important thing always to keep clearly in mind about a position in the metaphorical pantheon with all of its god-like influence is that even in the most democratic of republics, it is not a matter of election campaigns. You must earn your own way in as gods and heroes have always had to do, through the intrinsic merit of what you do and how you do it, and as a result of the undeniability, the depth and scope, and the durability of its impact.

And, of course, that is exactly what Duke Ellington had done. He, whose name has for so many years been a proper noun, became a very uncommon common noun and in consequence a transitive and intransitive active voice verb as well, has been brought into these hallowing halls and archives precisely because he already existed and was already exercising so much, yes, Olympian influence *out there*, as if already *up* there where he has been awe-inspiring, emulated, and as yet never quite successfully ripped off.

Yes, you earn your own way into the national pantheon by fulfilling in an exemplary manner the basic national imperatives as they apply to your particular line of endeavor. That is the *sine qua non* and in the arts this becomes the *vernacular imperative to process (which is to say to stylize) the raw native materials, experiences, and the idiomatic particulars of everyday life into aesthetic (which is to say elegant) statements of universal relevance and appeal.*

Nor should such a requirement be confused with nationalism as the term is generally used in art history and criticism, for it has nothing to do with flag-waving, chauvinism, and Fourth of July jingoism. What makes it ancestral is a longtime underlying assumption that there are traits that are basic to and definitive of American character and thus a uniquely American outlook or attitude toward experiences that makes for a native value system and lifestyle.

· · ·

To Constance Rourke, the author of *American Humor,* a study of the national character, and The Roots of American Culture, what characterizes American sensibility and conduct and distinguishes it from that of people elsewhere may be portrayed as a composite image consisting of the legendary Yankee peddler with his shrewdness and ingenuity, the equally legendary backwoodsmen, the Indian-modified gamecock of the wilderness with his ever eager disposition to adventure and exploration, his skill at improvisation and innovation and thus his adaptability, and the no less legendary and by no means invisible, even if not readily acknowledged Negro, with his blues-stomping Afro-percussive banjos and fiddles and his tambos and bones and fifes and triangles plus his sense of humor and "his improvised melodies and verses to match all the occasions of the day," who, says Constance Rourke, "became a dominant figure in spite of his condition [of servitude]."

In *Made in America* (the arts in contemporary American civilization), John A. Kouwenhoven, also the author of *The Beer Can by the Highway: What's American About America,* documents what amounts to still another very closely entwined ancestral source for an indigenous American aesthetic. He relates numerous examples of how vernacular procedures evolved from the modification of established technologies and conventional ideas and customs and learned traditions from Europe and elsewhere as a result of frontier situations and also as a result of the rugged American orientation toward freedom of enterprise in the general as well as the economic sense of the word.

No other music has ever been more directly or more obviously derivative of or compatible with or more comprehensively representative of all of this than is the body of fully orchestrated blues idiom statements that make up the collected works of Duke Ellington. Moreover, no American artist working in any medium whatsoever in any generation has ever fulfilled the vernacular imperatives more completely and consistently. Not even Walt Whitman, Mark Twain, among the most illustrious of his literary ancestors.

Among his contemporaries, Ellington's place in music is equivalent to that of Hemingway and Faulkner in literature and Frank Lloyd Wright in architecture whose buildings were already swinging (or, in any case, appropriately resilient!) long before the one that survived the earthquake in Tokyo. Oh, yes, and there is Alexander Calder, whose stabiles no less that his mobiles were constructed as if on the Ellingtonian principle of it don't mean a thing if it ain't got that swing.

As for contemporary musicians, Ellington is the quintessential American composer not only because he was always mostly concerned with the actualities of life in an American landscape, but also because he was able to process it into such fine art and to such international effect. When Aaron Copland was asked a few years ago why he abandoned the style of his *Variations*, the *Short Symphony*, and *Statements* to do things like *El Salón México*, he replied in part that he became aware "that not only I but most composers I was familiar with were writing music that lacked appeal to a wide audience. It occurred to me that we could write music that would be true to ourselves and yet have a wider potential audience." The easiest way to do that would be to combine your music with ballet action on stage, or perhaps write it as background to a film, or *any other form than just pure concert music*.

All-purpose, ever-pragmatic, workaday bandleader and performer as well as arranger and composer that he always was, Ellington knew all along that such indigenous workaday requirements as were very specific to phonograph recording sessions, radio broadcasts, and moving picture soundtracks were key factors that were of far more crucial importance to the form as well as the content of his music than were any of the essentially academic pieties about the conventions of European music of whatever merit.

Such also were the American musical actualities or stateside facts of a native-born musician's everyday life that he operated in terms of that when Ellington, playing in Paris in 1933, was asked about Rimsky-Korsakov's *Treatise on Harmony* by one of his numerous and very enthusiastic admirers, among whom were the likes of Auric, Durey, Honegger, Milhaud, Poulenc, and Tailleferre, and he replied that he hadn't read it and didn't intend to, he could have added the obvious. The output of Fletcher Henderson, Don Redman, Fats Waller, Jimmy Mundy, and others soon to be joined by Edgar Sampson, Sy Oliver, and Eddie Durham and Count Basie, was what he had to contend with, not any European theories per se.

In any case, what an Ellington arrangement or composition represents is not even a free or even a deliberately iconoclastic appropriation of any European convention, but rather the extension, elaboration, and refinement of the basic twelve-bar (and less frequently the eight-, four-, and sixteen-bar) blues idiom statement of the old strolling and streetcorner folk musician with his train whistle guitar and harmonica and also of his sometimes less folksy honky-tonk keyboard colleague.

No wonder his music always sounds so unmistakably American, for the blues idiom statement (with its dead metaphors from locomotive onomatopoeia, among other things) is not only primarily concerned with indigenous raw material, it is even more preoccupied with its own vocabulary, grammar, and syntax.

Unlike other excellent American composers, whose music is no less involved with the everyday stuff of American life but who work it up mainly by using devices that so often make it sound like the work of irreverent Europeans, or perhaps the admirers and imitators of irreverent Europeans, or maybe just as children of Nadia Boulanger, Ellington proceeded not in terms of the convention of exposition, development, and recapitulation, but almost always in terms of vamps (when not coming on like gangbusters), riffs, breaks, choruses of various kinds, such as ensemble, solo, call, and response, through chases and bar tradings to outchoruses and tags. Then there was all of that idiomatic timbre, harmony, those un-ofay minors and various dimensions of locomotive onomatopoeia. Not to mention all of that inimitable rhythm, tempo, and syncopation, all in the spirit of unrepressible improvisation to achieve, if not grace, at least a tentative equilibrium under the pressure of all tempos and unforeseeable but not unanticipated disjunctures.

But in the end, to say that Duke Ellington's achievements have earned him a place in the national pantheon should imply much more than that he has gained a place of honor for himself as an artist and as a person and has thereby set an example that will be an inspiration to other musicians and also to all people who have high horizons of aspiration, especially those from his own social background.

That is all well and good. The late great expert in international relations Ralph Bunche said more than once that Ellington had always been one of his most important role models, and there are others in many other walks of life who have been saying the same thing for generations.

But as important as the effect of Ellington's achievement has been in the area of career development, even more importance must be given to the legacy that the music itself embodies. It was created for the express purpose of becoming an integral—nay, indispensable—element of the nation's most basic equipment for everyday existence. Call it conditioning equipment, for it provides the very best of all contemporary soundtracks for the nation's workaday activities and its fun and games as well.

And in doing so, it also provides all Americans with a comprehensive score to which the tragedy, comedy, melodrama, and farce of the ongoing, even if mostly picaresque, episodes of their individual stories can be choreographed. Indeed, it is also here for the carefully deliberated purpose of inspiring each individual to choreograph his or her own solos and every couple its duets.

Nor should the implications of Ellington's ensemble writing as an all-American approach to harmony be overlooked.

STORIELLA AMERICANA AS SHE IS SWYUNG; OR, THE BLUES AS REPRESENTATIVE ANECDOTE

I t is a coincidence both appropriate and profoundly symbolic that the quintessential American composer was born, grew to young manhood, came to his vocation, and began his apprenticeship in the capital city of the nation. Such achievement as his is hardly predictable, to be sure. But in this instance it is easy enough to account for, because it is so consistent with uniquely local environmental factors that conditioned the outlook, direction, and scope of his ambition and development.

As little as has been made of it, there is in point of historical fact, much to suggest that circumstances in Washington during the first two decades of the century made it just the place to dispose a bright-eyed and ambitious young brownskin musician to become the composer who has indeed achieved the most comprehensive and sophisticated as well as the most widely infectious synthesis of the nation's richly diverse musical resources, both indigenous and imported.

Duke Ellington (*né* Edward Kennedy Ellington, a.k.a. Ellington and Duke), whose collected works represent far and away the most definitive musical stylization of life in the United States, was born in the house of his maternal grandparents on Twentieth Street on the twenty-ninth of April 1899, and shortly thereafter was taken by his parents, James Edward and Daisy Kennedy Ellington, to their own residence in Wards Place off New Hampshire Avenue, about midway between Dupont Circle on Massachusetts Avenue and Washington Circle on Pennsylvania Avenue.

This was less than ten blocks from the White House of William McKinley, who was assassinated when Ellington was two years old. From then, until Ellington was ten it was the White House of Theodore Roosevelt, who was followed by four status quo ante years of William Howard Taft. From the time Ellington was fourteen until he was twenty-two, it was not only the White House but also very much the sharply segregated Washington of Woodrow Wilson.

The Washington of McKinley is said to have provided much more government employment for black citizens than any previous administration. But even so, post-Reconstruction disfranchisement continued apace, for McKinley's commitment was not to the implementation of the Thirteenth, Fourteenth, and Fifteenth Amendments, but to conciliation of the erstwhile Confederate states. Moreover, his capital city was also the seat of an American expansionism that was all too consistent with the underlying assumptions of the folklore of white supremacy and fakelore of black pathology.

Then there was the Washington of Theodore Roosevelt, whose admiration for the down-home Horatio Algerism of Booker T. Washington, the founder of Tuskegee and author of the best-selling autobiography *Up from Slavery*, was widely publicized, as was his defense of his appointment of William D. Crum as collector of the Port of Charleston. In point of fact Roosevelt's attitude toward black American aspirations was not only inconsistent and undependable, it was at times indistinguishable from that of those who were frankly opposed to anything except a subservient status for Negroes. The obvious immediate effect of his wrongheaded and high-handed overreaction in meting out dishonorable discharges to black soldiers allegedly involved in the so-called Brownsville Raid of 1906, was to embolden whites who advocated terrorism as a means of keeping black people from full citizenship, something against which Roosevelt spoke neither loudly nor softly and against which he seems to have carried no stick of any size.

During the administration of Taft, Washington was the city of a president who in his inaugural address announced that he would not appoint Negroes to any position where they were not wanted by white people. On one of his better days Roosevelt had once written that he would not close the door of hope to any American citizen. But to aspiring black Americans and white reactionaries alike Taft's statement seemed like official capitulation to the forces of white supremacy, not all of them in the South.

During Ellington's adolescence and young manhood his hometown was the Washington of the downright evil forces of Woodrow Wilson, whose campaign promises to black voters were forgotten as soon as he was inaugurated. Once in office, it was as if he had never expressed his "warmest wish to see justice done to the colored people in every matter, and not mere grudging justice, but justice executed with liberality and cordial good feeling.... I want to assure them that should I become president of the United States they may count on me for absolute fair dealing, for everything by which I could assist in advancing the interest of their race in the United States."

But whereas his predecessors had been, on balance, perhaps more indifferent to black aspirations than intolerant of gradual improvement, Wilson's two administrations turned out to be downright hostile. In less than three months he signed an executive order segregating dining and toilet facilities in federal service buildings whose black employees were already being rapidly reduced in number and significance. And this was only the beginning. During the next eight years every effort was made to turn the nation's capital into a typical peckerwood town with a climate of white supremacy. "I have recently spent several days in Washington," Booker Washington wrote to Oswald Garrison Villard in a letter (10 August 1913) that he knew was going to be passed on to

Wilson, "and I have never seen the colored people so discouraged and bitter as they were at that time."

As inevitable as a direct effect of all this was on his daily life, Ellington did not grow up thinking of himself as downtrodden. On the contrary, as far back as he could remember he was treated as though he were a special child, and he never seems to have doubted his mother when she told him as she did time and again that he didn't have anything to worry about because he was blessed.

His father, who was a butler, then a caterer, and then a blue-print technician at the navy yard, was not only a good provider, but a man who saw to it that his family lived in good houses, in good neighborhoods (no slum dweller, he), and Ellington said that he "kept our house loaded with the best food obtainable and because he was a caterer we had the primest steaks and the finest terrapin." Ellington added, "He spent money and lived like a man who had money and he raised his family as though he were a millionaire. The best had to be carefully examined to make sure it was good enough for my mother."

No, James Ellington's outlook was neither negative nor provincial. Nor was young Edward's. Indeed, such were his horizons of aspiration even as a child that when at the age of about eight a slightly older playmate nicknamed him Duke, he accepted it as if it were his natural due, and so did his family and everybody else in Washington who knew him, and in time so did the world at large, including the royal family of England and the ever so proletarian bureaucrats and workers of the Soviet Union.

(Apropos of the personal vanity that this readiness to define himself in aristocratic terms may suggest to some pseudo-egalitarians, let it be said that Ellington was always more charming than vain and not at all arrogant. The fact of the matter is that you would be hard put to find anybody who was ever more discerning and appreciative of other people's assets and as eager to develop and showcase them. His ability to utilize and feature specific nuances was one of the trademarks of his genius as a composer. And no other bandleader ever put up with so many exasperating personal faults in his sidemen just to have them on hand to supply shadings that perhaps most of his audiences would never have missed. What other bandleader always had so many *homegrown* superstars on hand at the same time?)

But to continue the chronology. What Ellington himself always emphasized when recounting the advantages of his coming of age in Washington was that he was born and raised among people to whom quality mattered and who required your personal best no less as a general principle than as a natural reaction to the folklore of white supremacy. In neither case would they accept excuses for failure. You either had what it took or you didn't, as somebody from less promising circumstances than yours would prove only too soon.

Not that Ellington would ever deny or ameliorate any of the atrocities perpetuated by the Wilson crowd between 1913 and 1921. He took them for granted much the same as the fairy tale princes and dukes of derring-do take the existence of the dragon (grand or not) for granted. Also like the fairy tale hero that he was by way of becoming, he seems to have been far too preoccupied with getting help to forge his magic sword (or magic means) to spend much time complaining about the injustice of the existence of the dragon. *Dispatching the dragon, after all, as devastating as dragons are, has always been only incidental to gaining the ultimate boon to which the dragon denies you access.*

According to Ellington himself, the hometown he grew up in was an exciting and challenging place of apprenticeship, in which there were many people of his kind to admire, learn from, and measure up to. As early on as the eighth grade there was Miss Boston. "She taught us that proper speech and good manners were our first obligations because as representative of the Negro race we were to command respect for our people. This being an all-colored school, Negro History was crammed into the curriculum so that we would know our people all the way back."

The mainstem hangout for the young man about town was Frank Holliday's poolroom next to the Howard Theatre on T Street between Sixth and Seventh. "Guys from all walks of life seemed to converge there: schoolkids over and under sixteen; college students and graduates, some starting out in law and medicine and science; and lots of Pullman porters and dining car waiters. These last had much to say about the places they'd been. The names of the cities would be very impressive. You would hear them say, 'I just left Chicago, or last night I was in Cleveland.' " You could do a lot of listening in the poolroom, where the talk "always sounded as if the prime authorities on every subject had been assembled there. Baseball, football, basketball, boxing, wrestling, racing, medicine, law, politics, everything was discussed with authority."

Then when he really began to focus his ambitions on the piano and music, there was a whole galaxy of virtuosi and theorists not only at Holliday's but all over town, and they were always willing to repeat and explain things. Among them were Lester Dishman with his great left hand, Clarence Bowser, a top ear man; Phil Wird from the Howard Theatre; Louis Thomas, Sticky Mack, Blind Johnny, Gertie Wells, Carolynne Thornton, and the Man with a Thousand Fingers.

But most especially there was Louis Brown, who played chromatic thirds faster than most of the greats could play chromatic singles, and his left hand could reach an eleventh in any key. There was also Doc Perry, to whose house the young apprentice used to go as often as possible and "sit in a glow of enchantment until he'd pause and explain some passage. He never charged me a dime and he served food and drink during the whole thing."

There was also Henry Grant, a conservatory-trained teacher who directed the Dunbar High School Orchestra. He volunteered to give the promising young Ellington (a student at Armstrong High School, not Dunbar) private lessons in harmony, and was much impressed with his talent for melody and unusual harmonic nuances *and also with his indefatigable devotion to the mastery of fundamentals.* Hence the incomparable precision that was characteristic of all Ellington bands over the years!

As no true storyteller whether of fiction or the most precisely documented fact should ever forget—such as the indispensable function of the dynamics of antagonistic cooperation (or antithesis and synthesis, or competition or contention) in perhaps all achievement—there is neither irony nor mystery in the fact that Washington during the vicious years of Wilson and his diehard Confederates was also the base of operations for Kelly Miller, dean of the College of Arts and Science at Howard (1907–19) and author of numerous essays on race relations, advocate of courses on the American Negro and on Africa, militant spokesman and pamphleteer, most notably of *As to the Leopard's Spots: An Open Letter to Thomas Dixon* (1905) and the widely distributed *The Disgrace of Democracy: An Open Letter to President Woodrow Wilson.*

It was likewise the Washington of Carter G. Woodson, with his B.A. and M.A. from Chicago and his Ph.D. from Harvard and his background of work and study in the Philippines, Asia, North Africa, and Europe, who taught French, Spanish, English, and history at the M Street School and at Dunbar and was later principal of Armstrong High School, and who was also cofounder of the Association for the Study of Negro Life and History from its beginning until his death in 1950.

And along with Miller and Woodson there was also Alain Locke from Philadelphia by way of Harvard and the Oxford of

Rhodes scholars, who as a professor of arts and philosophy was especially concerned with making Howard a culture center for the development of black intellectuals and artists.

The national fallout of all of this (add to it *the work* of W. E. B. Du Bois) was such that by 1925 Locke could edit an anthology of poems, stories, plays, and essays by black contributors and call it *The New Negro* and introduce it by saying, "In the last decade something beyond the watch and guard of statistics has happened in the life of the American Negro, and the three *norns* that have traditionally presided over the Negro problem have a changeling in their laps. The sociologist, the philanthropist, the Race-leader are not unaware of the New Negro, but they are at a loss to account for him...."

It was during this ten-year period, which included World War I, that Ellington came of age and left Washington for New York.

But a word about usage. The emphasis that Miller, Woodson, and Locke place on race consciousness and even race pride should not be confused with the shrill, chauvinistic, pseudoseparatism of the so-called Garvey Movement. As Arthur Schomburg, who knew very well how easy it was for such matters to degenerate into "puerile controversy and petty braggadocio," was to write in "The Negro Digs Up His Past" for Locke's anthology, race studies "legitimately compatible with scientific method and aim were being undertaken not only to correct certain omissions and not merely that we may not wrongfully be deprived on the spiritual nourishment of our cultural past, *but also that the full story of human collaboration and interdependence may be told and realized.*" And Locke himself wrote, "If after absorbing the new content of American life and experience, and after assimilating new patterns of art, the original (Afro-American) artistic endowment can be sufficiently augmented to express itself with equal power in more complex pattern and substance, then the Negro may well become what some have predicted, *the artist of American life.*" If not Ellington and Armstrong in music, who else?

Ellington's all-American outlook was a direct result not of Howard University but of the Howard Theatre and Frank Holliday's poolroom cosmopolitans, but the fallout from Professors Miller and Locke and from Woodson was there all the same. After all, his impact was not only citywide but also, like that of Du Bois, nationwide.

In all events, when the group of ambitious young musicians with whom Ellington went to New York in 1923 proudly advertised themselves as the Washingtonians they were not presenting themselves as a provincial novelty but rather as a band of sophisticated young men who were ready to get on with it, because they had grown up in the capital city checking out the best in the nation at the Howard Theatre, which, it should be remembered, was on the same T.O.B.A. circuit as the Lincoln and the Lafayette in Harlem. (There was no Savoy yet, no Cotton Club, no Apollo.) New York was a bigger league, to be sure, but the Washingtonians seem to have had no doubts that they were ready to make the most of the breaks. And they were right. In less than four years Ellington composed and recorded *East Saint Louis Toodle-oo, Birmingham Breakdown, Washington Wobble, Harlem River Quiver, New Orleans Low-Down, Chicago Stomp Down* (note the regional diversity), and also *Black and Tan Fantasie* and *Creole Love Call.*

Nor was he to encounter any musical authority in cosmopolitan New York that was more crucial to his development as a composer than that of Will Marion Cook, another Washingtonian. Cook, who was born in 1869, had been sent out to Oberlin to study violin at the age of thirteen and on to Berlin (with the encouragement and aid of the venerable Frederick Douglass) to be a pupil of Joseph Joachim, the greatest music master of the day, and had also studied composition in New York under Dvořák, who had been brought over from Bohemia in 1893 to head up an

American conservatory and to encourage Americans to create a national music based on indigenous sources.

Cook, who had given up the violin to concentrate on composition and conducting, had become passionately committed to exploring and developing the possibilities of the Afro-American vernacular and had written the score for Paul Lawrence Dunbar's *Clorindy, or the Origin of the Cakewalk* in 1898, such musical comedies as *Bandanna Land, In Abyssinia,* and *In Dahomey* for the famous vaudeville team of Williams and Walker. He had also organized, directed, and toured with various jazz bands, most notably the Southern Syncopated Orchestra of some forty-one pieces, which he took to Europe in 1919. When he returned to New York, he became a pioneer arranger and conductor of radio music, leading a hundred-piece Clef Club Orchestra in some of the earliest live broadcasts.

Not only was Ellington, who had named his son Mercer after Cook's son Will Mercer, very much impressed and personally influenced by all of this, but he was especially taken by the fact that Cook, with all of his formal training and all his strictness about technical precision, also insisted, as James Weldon Johnson wrote, that the Negro in music and on the stage ought to be a Negro, a genuine Negro; he declared that the Negro should eschew "white" patterns, and not employ his efforts in doing what the white artist could always do as well, generally better." According to Ellington, Cook's advice was "first you find the logical way, and when you find it, avoid it, and let your inner self break through and guide you. Don't try to be anybody else but yourself."

Not the least of what Cook's advice may have done for young Ellington was to free him to compose in terms of what he liked about such stride or eastern ragtime masters as James P. Johnson, Willie "the Lion" Smith, and Lucky Roberts, such New Orleans pacesetters as Louis Armstrong, Sidney Bechet, King Oliver, and Jelly Roll Morton, and such special in-house talents as Charlie Irvis and Bubber Miley among others, including Johnny Hodges,

Harry Carney, Jimmy Blanton, Ben Webster, and Ray Nance, who became stars even as they became Ellington "dimensions."

What Ellington went on beyond Will Marion Cook and everybody else to achieve was a steady flow of incomparable twentieth-century American music that is mostly the result of the extension, elaboration, and refinement of the traditional twelve-bar blues chorus and the standard thirty-two-bar pop song form. *And in doing so he has also fulfilled the ancestral aesthetic imperative to process folk melodies, and the music of popular entertainment as well as that of church ceremonies into a truly indigenous fine art of not only nationwide but universal significance, by using devices of stylization that are as vernacular as the idiomatic particulars of the subject matter itself.* It is not a matter of working folk and pop materials into established or classic European forms but of extending, elaborating, and refining (which is to say ragging, jazzing, and riffing and even jamming) the idiomatic into fine art. *Skyscrapers, not Gothic cathedrals. And as historians need not be reminded, barbarians eventually produce their own principles of stylization and standards of criticism.*

Moreover, what Ellington's fully conjugated blues statement adds up to is a definitive American Storiella as she is *swyung*, which is to say, a musical equivalent to what Kenneth Burke calls the representative anecdote, the effect of which is to summarize a basic attitude toward experience; or a given outlook on life.

For many U.S. citizens, the representative anecdote would be any tale, tall or otherwise, or indeed any narrative tidbit or joke or even folk or popular saying or cliché that has to do with a self-made and free-spirited individual, or any variation on the Horatio Alger rags to riches, steerage to boardroom, log cabin to White House motif. Among the so-called Founding Fathers, Benjamin Franklin's career qualifies him as a veritable prototype of the picaresque Alger hero and two other classic examples are the *Narrative of the Life of Frederick Douglass, an American Slave, written by Himself,* and Booker T. Washington's *Up from Slavery.*

Everybody knows that even now there are people all over the

world dreaming of the United States in the ever-so-materialistic image and patterns of Horatio Alger. Others, however, see definitive American characteristics in terms that are no less pragmatic but are more comprehensively existential. In their view, the anecdotes most fundamentally representative are those that symbolize (1) affirmation in the face of adversity, and (2) improvisation in situations of disruption and discontinuity.

To this end, nobody other than Ellington as yet has made more deliberate or effective use of basic devices of blues idiom statement, beginning with the very beat of the ongoing, upbeat locomotive onomatopoeia (the chugging and driving pistons, the sometimes signifying, sometimes shouting steam whistles, the always somewhat ambivalent arrival and departure bells) that may be as downright programmatic as in the old guitar and harmonica folk blues but that also function as the dead metaphoric basis of the denotative language of common everyday discourse. The obviously programmatic but always playfully syncopated pistons, bells, and whistles of "Daybreak Express," "Happy Go Lucky Local," and "The Old Circus Train Turn Around Blues" become as dead metaphors in "Harlem Airshaft" and "Mainstem." Incidentally, Ellington's use of locomotive onomatopoeia is resonant not only of metaphorical underground railroad but also the metaphysical gospel train.

As for the idiomatic devices that are basic to the structure of most Ellington compositions, there are the blues (mostly of twelve bars) and/or the popular song choruses (mostly of thirty-two bars), a series or sequence of which add up to a vernacular sonata form known as *the instrumental*, which is also made up of such special features as the *vamp* or improvised introduction or lead-in, the *riff* or repetition phrase, and the *break* or temporary interruption of the established cadence and which usually requires a *fill*.

An excellent instance of the break as both structural device and statement is "C-Jam Blues," which is also a perfect example of how Ellington used the jam session, which consists of an informal sequence of improvised choruses as the overall frame for a precisely controlled but still flexible instrumental composition. In an elementary sense it is as playful as a children's ring game or dance, and yet it is also a basic way of ordering a discourse, not unlike, say, that jam session of a social contract known as the Constitution with its neat piano vamp of a preamble followed by a sequence of articles and amendments. The point here, of course, is not one of direct derivation but of cultural consistency and perhaps a case could be made for occupational psychosis.

Nor is the break just another mechanical structural device. It is of its very nature, as dancers never forget, what the basic message comes down to: *grace under pressure, creativity in an emergency, continuity in the face of disjuncture.* It is on the break that you are required to improvise, to do your thing, to establish your identity, to write your signature on the epidermis of actuality which is to say entropy. The break is the musical equivalent to the storybook hero's moment of truth. It is jeopardy as challenge and opportunity, and what it requires is the elegant insouciance that Hemingway admired in bullfighters. Representative anecdote indeed. Talking about the American frontier Storiella as she is riffed!

As for any question of extended forms, so dear to the reactionary hearts of so many old-line academics, the number of choruses in a jazz composition is determined by the occasion, as is the number of floors in a given skyscraper, depends on the anticipated use and/or the budget! Once there was the three-minute phonograph record, then came the radio sound bite for voice-over, and suitelike sequence of bites that make a movie soundtrack, and now there is the hour-plus LP. Ellington took them all in stride.

The quintessential composer should be so called because he is the one who provides that fifth essence, beyond earth, air, water, and fire, that substance of the heavenly bodies that is latent in all things, that spirit, nay that soul which is the magic means that somehow makes life in a given time and place meaningful and thus purposeful.

Indeed, the fifth essence may well be nothing less than the ultimate boon that the storybook quest is usually, if not always, about. If so, then the golden fleece of the composer's quest is the musical equivalent to the representative or definitive anecdote. *The assumption here is that art is indispensable to human existence.*

Duke Ellington is the quintessential American composer because it is his body of work more than any other that adds up to the most specific, comprehensive, universally appealing musical complement to what Constance Rourke, author of *American Humor: A Study of the National Character,* had in mind when she referred to "emblems for a pioneer people who require resilience as a prime trait." Nor can it be said too often that at its best an Ellington performance sounds as if it knows the truth about all the other music in the world and is looking for something better. Not even the Constitution represents a more intrinsically American statement and achievement than that.

ARMSTRONG AND ELLINGTON

STOMPING THE BLUES IN PARIS

I

In the middle of that October now already almost long enough ago to be remembered as once upon a time, Louis Armstrong and Duke Ellington, two of the most widely celebrated American musicians who ever lived, went to Paris to work on a moving picture for United Artists of Hollywood.

The title of the moving picture, which was to costar Paul Newman, Sidney Poitier, Diahann Carroll, and Joanne Woodward, was *Paris Blues*. The producer was Sam Shaw, also a very well known still photographer, and his director was Martin Ritt. The script, which was an adaptation of a novel by one Harold Flender, was written by Flender, Ted Allen, and others. The executive producer was Ian Woodner.

Armstrong had agreed to perform several instrumental selections on camera in the role of a world-famous trumpet player, obviously based on the living legend that he himself had long since become for great numbers of people in all walks and stations of life at every point of the compass. Appropriately enough, Armstrong, who even then was barnstorming the major European capitals on a concert tour with his all-star sextet, came to Paris not only for the filming of his sequences in the movie, but also to fulfill an already sold-out engagement at the Palais de Chaillot. None of the musicians in the sextet, which included Barney Bigard and Trummy Young, was used in the film, however. Nor was any footage of the concert acquired for use on the soundtrack.

No stranger to movie sets, Armstrong, like Ellington, had been involved with Hollywood for almost thirty years. In addition to having made numerous musical short features over a period dating back to the beginning of sound stages, he had played often brief but always memorable parts in such full-length productions as *Pennies from Heaven, Going Places, A Midsummer Night's Dream, Cabin in the Sky, New Orleans, Glory Alley, High Society,* and *The Beat Generation.*

Ellington, who within the past year or so had not only written the signature music for *Asphalt Jungle,* a very popular weekly television series, but also created the outstanding background music for Otto Preminger's production of *Anatomy of a Murder,* starring James Stewart, Lee Remick, and Ben Gazzara, had been commissioned to compose and conduct an original score. He was also to provide new arrangements for his *Mood Indigo* and *Sophisticated Lady* and for Billy Strayhorn's *Take the A Train.*

The script did not call for him to perform on camera either as a piano player or orchestra leader. The agreement, however, did stipulate that he would record some parts of the score for the soundtrack with his orchestra. Other segments were to be played by locally recruited groups made up of French musicians and American musicians then living and working in Paris. Two especially selected American instrumentalists were used to supply the sound for the trombone and saxophone performances represented on camera by Paul Newman and Sidney Poitier, respectively. *Anatomy of a Murder* was Ellington's first assignment as the composer of a full-length score, but he had made his screen debut as a composer and also a leader and performer in a musical short titled *Black and Tan* more than three decades earlier. He also played one of his own compositions called *Ring Dem Bells* in *Check and Double Check,* a full-length Amos and Andy feature made in Hollywood the following year; and the year after that he was back in Hollywood to appear in *Murder at the Vanities* and Mae West's

Belle of the Nineties. There were spots in *Day at the Races, Cabin in the Sky,* and *Belle of the Beverly.* Other short musical features following *Black and Tan* had included *Bundle of Blues, Black Jamboree, Dancers in the Dark,* and *Symphony in Swing.*

II

Paris Blues was not a major production. It was, alas, only a routinely slick Hollywood adaptation of a story line about two American couples in Paris that was only a pop concoction in the first place. But the music is quite another matter. It is easily the most enduring element of the whole undertaking.

Old hands at turning popfare and even the lowest pulpfare into fine art, and no doubt also out of a deeply ingrained habit of performing at the same level of enthusiasm and authenticity in an obscure roadside joint or dance hall as in the grand ballrooms and auditoriums, Ellington and Armstrong proceeded as if they had simply been provided yet another occasion to play the kind of marvelous good-time music that keeps the blues at bay in the very process of acknowledging that they are ever present.

Paris Blues opens with a trumpet note that is the exact duplication of a European locomotive whistle. It turns out to be the introduction to *Take the A Train,* Ellington's theme, written, however, not by Ellington himself but by Billy Strayhorn, his protégé, assistant, and arranger.

The actual A train, a subway on the Eighth Avenue Independent Line in New York City, had no such whistle, to be sure. But even so, as Ellington's theme it becomes yet another extension, elaboration, and refinement of the traditional down-home railroad sounds that are so unmistakable in the guitars and harmonicas of the old folk blues musicians. Moreover, in the original recording, Ellington's piano intro rings the departure bell; the calling woodwinds and responding brass shout as if in an all-aboard announcement of destination, as the 4/4 percussion thumps onward, and in this case, homeward.

Most other blues-oriented musicians seem to use the basic railroad onomatopoeia of the folk blues guitar player as unconsciously as they proceed in terms of such idiomatic devices as, say, vamps, riffs, breaks (and pickups), eight-, twelve-, and sixteen-bar choruses and call-and-response patterns, among other things, including the syncopation and special nuances in timbre. To them the stylized sounds of locomotive whistles, bells, pistons, steam, and so on seem long since to have become such natural or conventional elements of their musical grammar, syntax, and vocabulary that they are for the most part as unnoticeable as if they were only so many dead metaphors that go to make up the denotative verbalization of everyday discourse. But not only did Ellington almost always proceed with an awareness of the folk derivation of the blues idiom expression comparable to that of an etymologist, he also had a very special attachment to trains and railroads per se as subject matter. And yet his *Daybreak Express*, which is if anything even more precise in programmatic detail than Honegger's *Pacific 231*, is no less abstract in its purely musical cacophony and dissonant voicing. *Happy Go Lucky Local* is no less literal, no less abstract, nor any less symbolic than the trains in the traditional folk blues lyrics, in the spiritual and in Afro-American folklore that reaches all the way back to the underground railroad of the antebellum South.

He created two new trains for *Paris Blues*. One, *Wildman Moore*, brings Armstrong into Gare St. Lazare; and the other is the boat train that pulls out of Gare St. Lazare, separating the lovers at the end of the story. The first comes in on a festive beat that is also suggestive of a New Orleans Mardi Gras parade. As for the other one, at another point in the story is the also and also of the blues in Paris more evident than in the sound of the departing locomotive (which Ellington scored in terms of the rattle and clatter specific to European railroads).

Everything in the outchorus up to the last somewhat un-European shout of the departing whistle is every bit as heartrending as any of the old folk guitar blues lyrics about train number so-and-so done took my baby away from me. But even so, as the ongoing percussion gains momentum and heads for the *banlieue* and the open country and the transatlantic steamer, the atmosphere of lamentation and yearning is overridden by suggestions of continuity and expectation.

Ellington's train compositions following *Paris Blues* include "The Old Circus Train; Turn Around Blues"; *LOCO MADI*, which was the final section of the *U WIS* [University of Wisconsin] *Suite*; and a one-minute, fifty-eight-second gem called *Track 360*, which features drummer Sam Woodyard.

III

No composer ever approached an assignment to do a background score better prepared and more habitually disposed to represent the spirit of place, time, and circumstance in music than was Ellington when he came to Paris that autumn.

He had written *A Tone Parallel to Harlem*, a concert piece commissioned by Arturo Toscanini for the NBC Symphony Orchestra some ten years earlier. But long before that there were such standard Ellington dance-hall and nightclub numbers as *Harlem Speaks, Echoes of Harlem, Uptown Downbeat, Harmony in Harlem, I'm Slappin' Seventh Avenue with the Sole of My Shoe*, and "Harlem Airshaft," that were also unexcelled evocations and celebrations of life in uptown Manhattan. Nor was the cacophonous hustle and bustle of midtown Manhattan, with its urgent horns and motors and neon lights and twinkling skyline, ever more compellingly rendered in than in *Mainstem*, his special arrangement of a finger-snapping, foot-tapping tone parallel to Broadway.

Harlem Airshaft, incidentally, provides a handy example of how stylized railroad sounds function as the musical equivalent of dead metaphors. The train whistles, bells, chomping drive rods, hissing steam, and much of the rest are all there as surely as they are there in the obviously down-home rural atmosphere of *Happy Go Lucky Local*. But not as such. They are simply a part of the language (ensemble choruses, solos, call-and-response patterns, riffs, breaks, and so on) now used to tell the story at hand. But then, as Ellington was perhaps even less likely to forget than the traditional folk blues guitar player, the old whistle-blowing engineers (and their bell-ringing fireman) were bearers of tidings and tellers of tales, tall and otherwise, in the first place. It is entirely consistent with the nature of the idiom that the main strains of the trombone player's work in progress in the film becomes a train's sound in the final scene in Gare St. Lazare, for by so doing it suggests, however fleetingly, the end of yet another blues tale told by a train whistle.

Ellington's extensions, elaborations, and refinements of the basic idiomatic particulars of blues idiom vocabulary, grammar, and syntax were not attempts to go beyond the form, but rather were efforts to take it as far as it would go. He was one on whom very little, if anything, was ever lost, and whatever became a meaningful part of his personal experience was likely sooner or later to be processed into music—Ellington music, dance music that was also all-purpose music.

He was neither a folk nor a provincial musician on the one hand, nor was he a pretentious one on the other. When his first performances in England and France back during the early thirties moved critics to hail him as a contemporary master and to discuss his work in context with such highly regarded composers as Debussy, Ravel, Ibert, and Delius, he was surprised, delighted, and even flattered, but the overall effect was to expand his functional frame of reference. Even as it increased his awareness of deeper and broader implications of what he was doing, it also encouraged him to proceed in *and on* his own terms, which he had evolved from King Oliver, Jelly Roll Morton, Sidney Bechet, and Armstrong, among others, with a good deal of help from such immediate forerunners as Lucky Roberts, James P. Johnson, Willie "the Lion" Smith, and crucial advice from Will Marion Cook, whose Southern Syncopated Orchestra toured Europe following World War I, and Will Vodery, musical director for Ziegfeld and bandmaster for General Pershing in postwar Germany and musical director of Cotton Club shows.

Unlike the American musician played by Paul Newman in *Paris Blues*, whose great ambition is to write a composition that measures up to the standards of a French critic, Ellington was not nearly so impressed by Auric, Durey, Honegger, Milhaud, Poulenc, and Tailleferre (also known as *Les Six*) as they, to the consternation of ever so avant-garde U.S. critics, quite frankly were by him. Not that he was not deeply touched by such serious and prestigious admiration, but he took it all, and Paris as well, in his stride, and returned home no less preoccupied with, or excited by, the challenges of the nightclub, dance hall, and theater circuit and the likes of Fletcher Henderson, Fats Waller, Don Redman and McKinney's Cotton Pickers, Chick Webb, Earl Hines, Jimmie Lunceford, and Art Tatum, with Count Basie in the wings.

IV

In its original and literal sense, the expression "the second line" refers to all those music lovers who go along with the parade through the streets of New Orleans as if they can't bear to go in the opposite direction from a bass drum. Sometimes they dance and prance along the sidewalks; and sometimes, when there is room enough, they share a side of the street itself. Armstrong once remembered them as "guys just following the parade, one suspender down, all raggedy, no coat, enjoying the music. 'Course they had their little flasks, but when the parade stopped to get a taste in a bar, the second line held the horses or the instruments for the band. . . ." Over the years their outrageous costumes, which sometimes included the umbrella regardless of the weather, their high jinks and irrepressibly high spirits and earthy cavorting have become as much a part of the marvelous tradition of the New Orleans street parade as the legendary bands themselves.

But in another sense, the second line refers specifically to those totally dedicated young New Orleans musicians who used to march along beside one special band to be near that particular and very special instrumentalist whose style and manner they preferred above all others, that master musician who was not only their model but also their household god. For quite a number of trombone players, for example, it was Kid Ory. For some reedmen, it was Johnny Dodds or Sidney Bechet. For Armstrong, it was Joe Oliver, the star of the Onward Brass Band—"he was the nearest thing to Buddy Bolden to me. When he went into a bar to yackety with the guys—he didn't drink—or when he'd be parading and not blowing, I'd hold his horn so all he had to do was wipe his brow and walk."

So in a third sense, the second line is an idiomatic reference to an apprenticeship to any given master. Obviously, the source of the image is the parade. But perhaps from the very outset, it also applied to musicians who did not play in marching bands. Piano players, for instance, had their second liners, as did banjo players, trap drummers, and so on. If Tony Jackson or Jelly Roll Morton was your model, it was not a question of marching, to be sure, but when as a devoted but underage youngster you sneaked into the honky-tonk, hid yourself as close to the piano as you could get, or, as was perhaps often the case, hung around outside listening from the sidewalk and the back alleys, you were in Jackson's or Morton's second line nonetheless. Banjo and guitar players did the same for, say, Johnny St. Cyr as did string bass players for Pops Foster. After all, the brass and woodwind apprentices also spent far more time in the second line outside the honky-tonks and dance halls than they spent in parades.

By further extension, the second line image also suggests a deliberate choice of mentors, role models, functionals and hence *true* fathers (and what the poet W. H. Auden once referred to as the real ancestors), ancestral imperatives, or mission in life. Not only did Armstrong almost always refer to King Oliver as *Papa Joe*, he always addressed him as such. Then he, in turn, came to be called Pops by instrumentalists of all kinds and vocalists as well as all over the world. Everywhere he went he was greeted in effect as the culture hero (bringer of fundamental equipment for living) that in fact he was.

Among those in the second line upon his rearrival at Gare St. Lazare that October was none other than Ellington himself, who was to pay him permanent tribute some nine years later with *A Portrait of Louis Armstrong*, Part III of his *New Orleans Suite*, the sixth segment of which is appropriately titled "The Second line." Incidentally, there is much in his early work to suggest that although Ellington did not grow up marching alongside your Joe Oliver in the Onward Brass Band, somewhere along the way he did spend a significant amount of time in the metaphorical second line of King Oliver's Creole Jazz Band, among others, nonetheless.

V

What almost always seemed to count for most in Armstrong's estimation was not the architectural splendors or even the historical grandeur of a place, but the quality and quantity of the fun to be found there, whether upon arrival or in due course, as in some unheard-of, out-of-the-way stop on a tour of one-night stands.

But then he never seems to have been one of your wide-eyed and ever-so-eager young men from the provinces come to seek fame and fortune in the great metropolis anyway ... not even when he arrived in Chicago as a twenty-two-year-old journey-man from New Orleans. He had been sent for by King Oliver, the master himself; and he took the great city by storm long before he had time to be dazzled by it. He went to New York at the insistence of Fletcher Henderson, another maestro of national standing, and his impact on older and younger musicians alike was hardly less than that of the Pied Piper on the children of Hamelin. Not only was the reception the same everywhere he went, but his phonograph recordings had made him a great celebrity in all of the cities of Europe years before he set foot in London and Paris at the age of thirty-three.

It was as if Armstrong had been born knowing that the blues was nothing if not good-time music. Certainly he was conditioned from infancy by postfuneral music that celebrated life in the very face of the finality of death. In any case, even before he began his apprenticeship in Storyville, the Mardi Gras fetes, the dance halls, and the riverboats, he was already proceeding as if the basic social and, yes, existential function of the blues musician was to conjure up or otherwise generate an atmosphere of revelry, jubilation, and earthly well-being, and so also of affirmation and celebration. Nor was any of the exuberant slapstick and mockery of Armstrong the Entertainer any less a means of dispelling gloom and putting banality to riot than was the incredible elegance of his scintillating trumpet.

Armstrong enjoyed being in Paris not only because of the high critical esteem in which he was held there, but because it was a good-time town, not unlike the New Orleans of his youth. As for the Parisians, they knew that whenever he rolled into town (always as if atop the Glad Wagon), the blues would be held at bay (stone frozen in place not unlike the gargoyles at Notre Dame), at least for the time being.

VI

An Ellington composition is the product of a musician who was an extraordinary embodiment, if not archetype, of the artist as playful improviser. It is in overall shape, and specific detail as well, the happy consequence of a very imaginative and highly skillful playfulness that achieves that measure of elegance that can take even the most functional activity to that special level of stylization known as fine art.

Not that the basic dynamics of the Ellington method were unique. On the contrary, the skillful playfulness so characteristic of blues idiom musicians like Ellington the Orchestrator and Armstrong the Soloist may well be the indispensable condition of the creative process as such. For in painting, literature, dance, drama, or music, it is precisely through ever more skillful playfulness or playful skill that literal reproduction (representation, reenactment, even onomatopoeia) is subordinated to considerations of design and ornamentation, and that the raw material of everyday experience is processed into aesthetic statement.

In the case of Ellington, such play was also likely to be a matter of *interplay*, not only with the musicians on hand, as in a jam session, but also (on occasion) as if in an ongoing dialogue with the also and also of the entire idiom. "This is my this year's stuff," he could have well said to Armstrong as they rehearsed *Wild Man Moore* and *Battle Royal*, "that I got from your that year's stuff that you got from King Oliver's Buddy Bolden stuff back when."

Ellington's *Echoes of Harlem, Boy Meets Horn, Are You Sticking?, Warm Valley,* and *Concerto for Cootie* were not derived from the European concerto form but from playing around with the orchestral implications of the solo emphasis that Armstrong had brought into the forefront of the idiom even before his landmark performances on *Potato Head Blues* and *West End Blues*. Ellington's solo showcase compositions retain all of the spontaneity of a jam session while providing a consistently richer and more precise context. Showcase indeed.

VII

Those critics who presume to make fundamental distinctions between pure music and programmatic or descriptive music also tend to consign programmatic music to a lower order of aesthetic endeavor and achievement. But to Ellington, who was no less a performer and maestro than a composer, such categories were more academic than pragmatic. Along with all of their details evocative of uptown Manhattan, in *Echoes of Harlem* and *Harlem Airshaft*, for instance, were also idiomatic concertos for trumpet star Cootie Williams, and they were written to be played in dance halls and nightclubs far more often than in vaudeville theaters, not to mention concert halls.

Nor was *Wild Man Moore*, with all of its locomotive beat and terminal station atmosphere, any less a functional concerto than was *Battle Royal*, with its purely musical jam session–like play and interplay on the progression of *I Got Rhythm*. In *Wild Man Moore* the legendary trumpetmaster engages in a solo/ensemble call-and-response exchange with disciples assembled to greet him at the train station. In *Battle Royal* he playfully invades a nightclub and precipitates a musical free-for-all, in and out of which he soars as if from a perch somewhere on Mount Olympus.

The concertolike structure of Ellington's compositions provided precisely what was needed to feature Armstrong in both episodes of the film. But when the same two numbers were used sometime later in a recording session with Ellington's orchestra combined with Count Basie's, neither was performed as a concerto. Both were used as a framework for a series of purely musical exchanges by outstanding soloists from each orchestra.

Ellington's scenic numbers for the soundtrack were *Birdie Jungle, Autumnal Suite, Nite,* and *Paris Stairs,* all of which are as playful and artful as they are atmospheric. *Birdie Jungle* has tongue-in-cheek dance beat. *Autumnal Suite* gives the signature strain a cozy medium tempo statement. *Paris Stairs* is a waltz for what in effect is the *pas de quatre* that the two couples' movements add up to during an afternoon outing.

Guitar Amour, which is used in the film as a number performed in a Paris nightclub, perhaps inevitably evokes memories of the late Django Reinhardt, the widely admired French Gypsy guitar player who made several records with some of Ellington's musicians during the orchestra's second visit to Paris in the spring before the outbreak of World War II and who also made a brief concert tour with Ellington in the United States shortly after the war. In point of fact, while he was in Paris working on the film, Ellington was not only in contact with Reinhardt's cousin, also a guitar player, he also playfully voiced phrases from his work in progress. In the film, however, the role of the Gypsy guitarist is played by Serge Reggiani, who in real life is an outstanding guitar player and also a very popular singer.

On the set, Ellington not only double-checked the suitability of the music for each episode but also, as was his usual practice, carefully voiced special passages for the instrumentalists, including Aaron Bridges, who played piano on camera, and the celebrated French drummer Moustache. Ellington seldom finished scoring his music until he had heard it played back not only on the appropriate instrument, but also by the individual musician he had in mind. With him it was always more a matter of getting it ear-perfect rather than note-perfect.

VIII

When the sequences in which Armstrong appeared had been filmed, he and his all-star sextet went on to the next stop on his heavily booked European concert tour. Ellington remained in Paris until all of the major work on the scenes shot on location there were finished. Then, having also done background music for another production, *Turcaret*, a classic French play by Lesage last performed in 1709, he came back to New York to complete the parts of the score that he had agreed to record for the sound-track and also for a United Artists record album (UAL 4092) with his own orchestra.

What he actually did, of course, was to play each composi-tion into the desired shape and texture during rehearsal. It was not a matter of drilling the musicians on each passage until each section of the orchestra could play its assignments in the new score to his complete satisfaction, as was the case with most other composers. It was rather a way of continuing the process of cre-ation and orchestration that he had begun on the piano some time before. Each musician was provided with a score, to be sure, which each could read and play expertly at sight if necessary. But Ellington, who was always as sensitive to his sidemen's musical personalities as a choreographer is to the special qualities of each dancer's body in motion, always preferred to leave himself free to take advantage of the options that opened up during rehearsal and also during the performance itself.

As others have said, the whole orchestra was no less a per-sonal instrument to Ellington than was the piano. In a sense, the same is obviously true of all conductors, but not in the same way and to the same extent as with Ellington. The control he exer-cised from the piano as a performing composer as well as con-ductor using the comp was much more complete than even a

Toscanini could achieve with a baton. He not only set tempos, moods, and voicing as if the various sections of the orchestra were physical extensions of the keyboard, but he also inserted riffs and dictated phrasings, shadings, and even revisions.

He actually played the orchestra from the piano. His control was such that the voicing, phrasings, the interplay of soloist with ensemble and of soloists with each other, and the overall sound and inimitable beat usually seemed so organic that the precision of the musicianship was often likely to be obscured by the very effect it created. Nor was this achieved at the expense of the individuality of his musicians. The invention of the idiomatic concerto was only his most obvious device for showcasing their distinctive identities. The individuality, spontaneity, and inventiveness were no less intact and in evidence on such tightly constructed three-minute compositions as in *Harmony in Harlem, C-Jam Blues,* and *Mainstem,* in which each solo participant fulfills a role that is as immediately distinguishable as is a character in a story.

The remarkable evolution from excellent but not yet exceptional musicians into world-famous musical identities of such unmistakable and indelibly Ellingtonian sidemen as Johnny Hodges, Cootie Williams, Barney Bigard, Harry Carney, Lawrence Brown, "Tricky Sam" Nanton, Rex Stewart, Jimmy Blanton, Ben Webster, Ray Nance, and others, including Cat Anderson, Paul Gonsalves, and Jimmy Hamilton, should make it quite clear that the Ellington process did not reduce musicians to robots. It brought the very best they had in them. Indeed, in almost every instance, the musician found himself being featured before he himself realized that he had something special to offer beyond recent improvement in his craftsmanship.

The inspiration, no less than the discipline that came from working alongside Ellington the performing composer, conditioned his sidemen to use their solo space to make meaningful statements as if in the context of a discussion rather than as simply a chance to display their extraordinary technical virtuosity per se, as is often the case in jam sessions and in bands that use arrangements that are closer to jam session routines than to composition.

Not that such displays (which to be done well require every bit as much improvisational resourcefulness as technical facility) were not also a part of the Ellington repertoire. After all, he did work primarily in the world of show biz and entertainment that included the floor show, the vaudeville stage, the minstrel and specialty acts predating the *commedia dell'arte.*

So when the occasion called for it, he seldom hesitated to parade his superb lineup of soloists across the stage as if they were so many dazzling musical acrobats, jugglers, and tumblers. But even as Ellington the Entertainer waved them into the spotlight like an ever-charming ringmaster, Ellington the ever alert composer often sat at the piano during the next rehearsal and said, "Hey, how does that little thing you did during the second show last night go? Like this? How about this and then this?" But then, sometimes the same thing would happen to a purely technical run overheard as the musicians were warming up backstage. Sometimes he would simply play it and call out the name of the musician he was quoting and then go on playing around with it as a point of departure of a jam session, to which other members of the orchestra made contributions sometimes at his specific prompting and sometimes gratuitously, but always because by one means or another he stimulated them into participation.

Nor did his use of such material in a carefully wrought composition preclude its further use as a gimmick to display intensity as such, as in the case of *Wild Man Moore* and *Battle Royal,* used on the soundtrack of *Paris Blues* on the one hand and in his joint recording session (Columbia ACL 1715) with the Count Basie orchestra on the other. Both approaches were acceptable forms of making music, which is nothing if not a form of play in the first place. Some play, no matter how artful and elegant, is primarily for sheer entertainment. Another kind adds up to an extension, elaboration, and refinement of the rituals that reenact the basic technologies of survival of a given people in a given time, place, and circumstance. This, of course, is the primordial function of fine art, which attenuates into banality and sterility when overextended, overelaborated, and overrefined.

IX

The blues-idiom soundtrack for every day goings-on in the United States (and by extension, the contemporary world) that the work of Armstrong and Ellington over the years adds up to is the musical approximation of the representative anecdote in literature. Indeed its special use of the break, for instance, not only reflects but embodies an attitude toward disjuncture that is no less affirmative than that of the explorers, frontiersmen, and early settlers facing the unknown. Nor is the processing of mundane onomatopoeia, workaday cacophonies and pop inanities, among other things, into no less elegant than soulful melodic and orchestral statement adequate to the emotional needs of the times, entirely unrelated to the miraculous erection of storybook castles or great American metropolitan areas—or, for that matter, the orchestration of a veritable jam session of dissonant colonial voices into a constitutional democracy. *E pluribus unum,* human nature permitting.

Moreover, the Armstrong/Ellington soundtrack not only provides the context but also prompts the choreography to condition any Dramatis Personae to the ongoing and yet somehow also ever recurring ride cymbal *also and also and so on* of contemporary actuality through resilience and evermore refined but never overrefined improvisation.

PART FIVE

THE VISUAL EQUIVALENT
TO BLUES COMPOSITION

BEARDEN PLAYS BEARDEN

I

As striking as the figurative and thematic dimensions of most of the paintings and collages of Romare Bearden so often are, the specific forms as such—however suggestive of persons, places, and things and even of situations and events, actual or mythological—are by his own carefully considered account always far more a matter of on-the-spot improvisation or impromptu invention not unlike that of the jazz musician than of representation such as is the stock in trade of the portrait painter, the illustrator, and the landscape artist of, say, the Hudson River School.

Not that there is ever anything casual, random, or merely incidental about his choice of subject matter. Except for his completely nonobjective works of the late 1950s and early '60s, the raw materials he processes into aesthetic statement either come directly from or in some way allude to or otherwise reflect historic, geographic, or idiomatic particulars of Afro-American experience. Nor is it at all unusual for works in any given one-man exhibition to be so closely and deliberately interrelated in subject matter as well as style as to constitute a series, or even a sequence, that is undeniably not only narrative and anecdotal in nature but also intentionally so.

But even when a series or sequence comes as close to illustration as the twenty collages in the exhibition titled Odysseus, the images as such, for all their evocation characters and episodes of a long-established and well-known story line, were seldom pre-conceived. More often than not they began simply as neutral shapes with contours that were simply what they happened to be. What each original shape eventually became was always determined only as each collage evolved.

Sometimes, as in the case of the autobiographical suite of twenty-eight collages titled Profile/Part I: The Twenties, the theme of childhood recollection was agreed upon in advance. But even so, the specific reminiscences that now seem so integral to each picture actually came only after each composition began to click into focus as an aesthetic statement. It was, he reports, more a matter of saying this looks like a garden, so why not Miss Maudell Sleet's garden, rather than saying now I'm going to re-create Miss Maudell's garden.

Of course, once such a painting is completed an artist can say any number of interesting and essentially literary things about it (as Bearden has done on request on not a few occasions). But although sometimes he may talk as if about an illustration, what he is referring to is a painting, a system of organized forms; and in the process of pulling it together he was far more concerned with such aesthetic elements as decorative and ornamental effect than with narrative or dramatic impact. Indeed, as charming as such remarks can be, the picture as a painting would not be changed one bit if he called Maudell Sleet Miss Emily Ellison and reminisced about how after her husband died she used to bury her savings in an Alaga syrup bucket. In the case of *Farewell Eugene*, Bearden tells a touching and informative anecdote about a boyhood friend in Pittsburgh and about how Eugene, who taught him how to draw, used to make pictures of houses in which the interior activities could be seen from the street. *But the painting does not tell that story at all!*

Each of his paintings is evolved out of what the juxtaposition of the raw materials at hand brings to mind as he plays around with them in much the same as, say, Duke Ellington in search of a tune or in the process of working up an arrangement or composing a fully orchestrated blues sonata begins by playing around with chords, phrases, trial runs, and potential riff patterns on the keyboard. The exact imitation of nature is irrelevant to the aesthetic statement Bearden wishes the picture to make. That statement, however, is altogether dependent upon the ornamental and decorative quality achieved.

"You have to begin somewhere," he has said. "So you put something down. Then you put something else with it, and then you see how that works, and maybe you try something else and so on, and the picture grows in that way. One thing leads to another, and you take the options as they come, or as you are able to perceive them as you proceed. The fact that each medium has its own special technical requirements doesn't really make any fundamental difference. My point is that my overall approach to composition is essentially the same whether I'm working with the special problems and possibilities of the collage, or with oils, watercolors, or tempera. As a matter of fact I often use more than one medium in the same picture."

"Once you get going," he has also said, "all sorts of things begin to open up. Sometimes something just seems to fall into place, like the piano keys that every now and then just seem to be right where your fingers happen to come down. But there are also all those times you have to keep trying something over and over and then when you finally get it right you wonder what took you so long. And of course there are also times when you have to give it up and try something else. But sometimes it turns out just great as the beginning of another, totally different picture. By the way, this sort of thing is much more likely to have to do with how something fits into the design or ornamental structure of the painting than with its suitability as subject matter."

Nor is Bearden unaware of the relationship of his procedures to those of jazz musicianship. He is conscious not only of beginning by vamping as if till ready for the downbeat and the first chorus of each composition, but also of hitting upon and playing around with details of both color and form as if with visual riff phrases. Nor is he any less aware of working in terms of relating sololike structural elements to ensembles, sometimes as call-and-response patterns, sometimes as in jam session leapfrog sequences and sometimes as in full band interplay of section tonalities (trumpets with or against trombones, reeds, or piano, and so on).

That he learned to work in his own way with the separations between colors and with the different values of a given color by studying the expressive use of interval in the piano style of Earl Hines is a matter of record. And he has also said that his application of what he learned from Hines led him to appreciate the visual possibilities of Ellington's absolutely fantastic use of blues timbres, down-home onomatopoeia, urban dissonance, and cacophony in numbers such as "Daybreak Express" and "Harlem Airshaft"; to Chick Webb's accentuations on "Stomping at the Savoy"; to rhythmic extensions of Count Basie's deceptively simple abbreviations of ragtime and Harlem stride; to the instantly captivating distortions and disjunctures of Thelonious Monk, and in due course also to the realization that his basic orientation to aesthetic statement had been conditioned by the blues idiom in general and jazz musicianship in particular all along.

Nor was anything more consistent with his background as an Afro-American who came of age between 1914 and 1935. His background in point of historical fact is hardly distinguishable from that of the great majority of the outstanding blues idiom musicians of his generation and of the preceding generation as well. He spent his early years in the bosom of the church, as the old folks in the pews used to say, down home in Mecklenburg County, on the outskirts of Charlotte, North Carolina; and in a transplanted down-home neighborhood in Pittsburgh, Pennsylvania, where he, exactly like those destined to grow up to become leaders and members of the great orchestras that conquered the world for American music, heard and absorbed the spirituals, the traditional hymns, gospel songs, and amen corner moans in context and conjunction with the prayers, sermons, shouts, testifying shuffles, and struts that make up the service or ritual that gave rise to them in the first place. As he also imitated and in some instances choreographed for playground purposes the work chants, railroad rhymes, and field hollers that, along with the music of the kitchen, the washplace, the fire circle, the street corner, the honky-tonks and the dance halls, were the secular complements to church music.

Not even the New Orleans of young Louis Armstrong himself during the first and second decades, or the Kansas City of young Charlie Parker during the 1930s was dominated more definitively by music and musicians than was the Harlem that was Bearden's briar patch and stamping ground as a schoolboy and young adult. He spent his puberty and adolescence in the very Heart of Harlem, as the incurably square ofay radio announcers back during that time, which was the heyday of the uptown cabarets, used to say. The legendary rent party sessions, for instance, were regular, though informal, neighborhood events that were so much a part of his childhood awareness that he took them for granted much the same as if they were church suppers and socials, or even sandlot baseball games.

Such celebrated stride time piano players as James P. Johnson, Willie "the Lion" Smith, and Lucky Roberts, among others, were not only immediately recognizable as everyday figures on the sidewalks of the neighborhood, but were in most instances also instantly identifiable by the personal nuances that were their signatures as artists. Fats Waller, as a matter of fact, was a very close friend of Bearden's family. And so among many others was Flournoy Miller of the famous Miller and Lyles vaudeville team, whose reputation was comparable to that of Williams and Walker, and Sissle and Blake. The performers working in such smash hit Broadway revues of the period as *Shuffle Along, Chocolate Dandies, Hot Chocolates,* and *Lew Leslie's Blackbirds* were inseparable parts of the musical life of the neighborhood.

As were such headliners from the Columbia, Keith, and T.O.B.A. circuits and/or the world of phonograph records as Ethel Waters, Alberta Hunter, Mamie Smith, Lucille Hegeman, Perry Bradford, John Bubbles, and so many others. The stage entrance to the Lafayette Theatre was just across the street from the Bearden apartment on 131st Street. The main entrance was around the corner, on Seventh Avenue. The Lincoln Theatre was only a few blocks away, on 135th Street off Lenox Avenue. Before Florence Mills, the star of *Blackbirds,* became the sensation of Broadway and London, she had established her reputation at the Lincoln as well as the Lafayette; and when she died suddenly at the very peak of her triumph, all Harlem grieved as if for a most darling member of the household, and as the funeral procession slowly wound its way through the streets, young Bearden was among the hundred and fifty thousand mourners who are said to have lined the streets while thousands more waved farewell from windows and rooftops, and he also remembers that people came back from the burial talking about how one airplane flew over the ceremony and released a flock of blackbirds and another came scattering roses.

When the Savoy Ballroom opened at 140th Street on Lenox Avenue, about ten blocks away Bearden was not quite twelve years old. But even before that, the patterns of sound coming from such not faraway spots as the Renaissance Casino, Small's Paradise, and the Nest Club were no less a part of the local atmosphere than were the voices of the woofers and jive shooters and tall tale tellers and signifiers in the various neighborhood lunch counters, poolrooms, and barbershops.

Then almost as if overnight the big orchestras of Fletcher Henderson, Duke Ellington, Chick Webb, Cab Calloway, Charley

Johnson, Claude Hopkins, Jimmie Lunceford, McKinney's Cotton Pickers, and the Savoy Sultons had either evolved on the scene, or had come to Harlem from elsewhere. Thus, during the time of the now-epical battles of the great bands and jam sessions, Bearden was a very curious, gregarious, and devilishly mannish adolescent of good standing in most social circles in Harlem; and not only was impeccable musical taste an absolute requirement for growing up hip, urbane, or streetwise, but so was the ability to stylize your actions—indeed, your whole being—in terms of the most sophisticated extensions and refinements of jazz music and dance.

"Regardless of how good you might be at whatever else you did," he has said more than once, "you also had to get with the music. The clothes you wore, the way you talked (and I don't mean just jive talk), the way you stood (we used to say stashed) when you were just hanging out, the way you drove an automobile or even just sat in it, everything you did was, you might say, geared to groove. The fabulous old Harlem Renaissance basketball team, like the Globetrotters that succeeded them, came right out of all that music at the Renaissance Casino." Nor were the Globetrotters unrelated to the fox trotters at the Savoy Ballroom. Incidentally, when Ellington's *It Don't Mean a Thing if It Ain't Got That Swing* came out, Bearden was eighteen and very much the fly cat about town and on campus as well.

II

But obviously he did not learn to paint by listening to music. He learned to paint by looking at and responding to many paintings. Even when he listens to music on the radio while at work in his studio, his specific objectives and procedures are exclusively those of a painter, and accordingly his efforts are best understood and most fully appreciated in terms of and in the context of the works of the visual artists, not the musicians he admires and attempts to extend, elaborate, and otherwise refine, and those he rejects either in part or on the whole, and so ignores or feels compelled to counterstate.

Each painting, that is to say, is a visual statement that is a reference or allusion to another or other paintings, to which in effect it either says yes and also and also and perhaps also; or it says no or not necessarily or on the other hand or not as far as I for one am concerned. Not that musicians don't do exactly the same thing. Ellington's unique voicings, for example, began by saying yes in some instances and no in others to King Oliver, Jelly Roll Morton, Fletcher Henderson, and even the likes of Paul Whiteman and the saw fiddle Tin Pan Alley extensions of George Gershwin. Such, after all, are the dynamics of the creative process. But the point is that as visual artists, painters must proceed in terms of existing *visual* statements. It is precisely thus that they participate in the ongoing dialogue that makes their métier what it continues to be.

Indeed, as should surprise no one, it was a painter who made Bearden realize, as only a painter could have, that elements of blues idiom musicianship could be applied to visual composition. During the days when he was still a young journeyman, so to speak, he used to visit the studio of Stuart Davis, an American master of post-Cubist persuasion, who had studied in Paris, and in the course of discussions about the approaches of Picasso, Matisse, Braque, and Juan Gris, among others, Davis, who had a large collection of jazz records, kept coming back to the music of Earl Hines and kept trying to make him see visual devices in terms of the way Hines did things on the piano. Davis, who was no less deeply involved with native U.S. techniques, raw materials, and attitudes than with avant-garde experimentation, also told him that the subject matter of painting includes the materials of expression.

. But his friendship with Davis, who, by the way, was not native to the blues idiom, came not at the beginning of Bearden's career as an artist, but (as stated above) a few years later. It was not what motivated him to become a painter. It was rather advice from an older and more accomplished fellow professional, and it gave him new insight into, and eventually a greater facility with, the ideas and techniques he had already acquired in the normal course of his apprenticeship to visual expression. As his earliest works show, he was already trying to process raw material from the blues territory, as it were, into art long before he met Davis. What Davis said made him realize that the jazz aesthetic itself was applicable to visual statement.

At the outset of his career as a serious painter, there was George Grosz at the Art Students League. "It was during my period with Grosz," he has written, "under whom I began studying several months after graduating from New York University, that I began to regard myself as a painter rather than a cartoonist. The drawings of Grosz on the theme of the human situation in post–World War I Germany made me realize the artistic possibilities of American Negro subject matter. It was also Grosz who led me to study composition through the analysis of Brueghel and the great Dutch masters, who in the process of refining my draftsmanship initiated me into the magic world of Ingres, Dürer, Holbein, and Poussin."

His apprenticeship at the league also put him in an environment where his fellow students and his instructors lived in terms of visual art much the same as so many of the people among whom he had grown up in Harlem lived with, by, and for music. It was through them and their dialogues, debates, enthusiasms, and put-downs that he was to come to know and frequent the great midtown galleries and museums and also the small galleries and certain ateliers in Greenwich Village as young jazz musicians used to know and frequent the Harlem nightclubs, dance halls, practice rooms and showcase theaters. Young painters at the league and at parties shared their excitements over the ongoing explorations and achievements of Picasso, Matisse, Braque, Klee, and so on to Hans Hofmann with the same sense of direct involvement, even if not quite with the same degree of sophistication, as he was used to hearing in uptown hangouts where musicians registered their responses to the latest output of Armstrong, Ellington, Lunceford, and Basie, or discussed the basis of their personal sense of identification with Art Tatum or Teddy Wilson, Lester Young, or Coleman Hawkins, and so on.

In college (majoring in mathematics) he had drawn cartoons influenced at first by E. Simms Campbell, Ollie Harrington, and Miguel Covarrubias, and then also by Daumier, Forain, and Käthe Kollwitz. His initial attempts at serious painting began with tempera. Then came watercolor and then oil. About which he has written as follows: "My temperas had been composed in closed forms, and the coloring was mostly earthy browns, blues, and greens. When I started working with watercolor, however, I found myself using bright color patterns and bold, black lines to delineate semiabstract shapes. I never worked long on a painting with this method or made many corrections. I had not yet learned that modern painting progresses through cumulative distructions and new beginnings.

"When I started to paint in oil, I simply wanted to extend what I had done in watercolor. To do so, I had the initial sketch enlarged as a photostat, traced it onto a gessoed panel, and with a thinned color completed the oil as if it were indeed a watercolor."

Then he goes on: "Later I read Delacroix's *Journal* and felt that I, too, could profit by systematically copying the masters of the past and of the present. Not wanting to work in museums, I again used photostats, enlarging photographs of works by Giotto, Duccio, Veronese, Grünewald, Rembrandt, de Hooch, Manet, and Matisse. I made reasonably free copies of each work by substituting my own choice of colors for those of these artists, except for those of Manet and Matisse, when I was guided by color reproductions."

Still later, after he began to play with pigments as such "in marks and patches distorting natural colors and natural objects as well," and found out that tracks of color tended to fragment his composition, he went back to the Dutch masters once more. To Vermeer and Pieter de Hooch in particular, he says, and then adds that it was then that he "came to some understanding of the way these painters controlled their big shapes, even when elements of different size and scale were included within these large shapes. I was also studying at the same time the techniques which enable the classical painters to organize their areas, for example: the device of the open corner to allow the observer a starting point in encompassing the entire painting; the subtle ways of shifting balance and emphasis; and the use of voids, or negative areas, as sections of 'pacivity' also perhaps 'sections of reduced tension' and as a means of projecting the big shapes.

"As a result, I began to paint more thinly, often on natural linen, where I left sections of the canvas unpainted so that the linen itself had the function of a color. Then in a transition toward what turned out to be my present style, I painted broad areas of color on various thicknesses of rice paper and glued these papers on canvas, usually in several layers. I tore sections of the paper away, always attempting to tear upward and across on the picture plane until some motif engaged me. When this happened, I added more papers and painted additional colored areas to complete the painting."

Such in brief is Bearden's natural history as a painter; and appropriately—nay, inevitably—it reflects his personal involvement with the so-called Museum Without Walls, that imaginary collection or world anthology of art reproductions that enables a contemporary artist to proceed as if the art of all the ages in the world at large were coexistent (as indeed it is in the truly contemporary sensibility). Moreover, by the same token it reveals the specific nature of his personal dialogue or argument with the ongoing tradition of visual expression. Each statement of his own intentions as an artist coincidentally affirms some elements in the work of some painters and counterstates some elements in others, even sometimes not only in the same painter, but in a given painting.

The juxtaposition of paintings in Bearden's purely functional museum does not make any concessions to differences between historical periods. Only the aesthetic statement is relevant: "Some observers have noted that the apparent visual basis of my current (1969) work, the use of overlapping planes and of flat space, is similar to Cubism. In actual practice, however, I find myself as deeply involved with methods derived from de Hooch and Vermeer, as well as the other masters of flat painting, including the classic Japanese portrait artists and the pre-Renaissance Sienese masters, such as Duccio and Lorenzetti. What I like most about the Cubism of Picasso, Braque, and Léger is its primary emphasis on the essentials of structure. Nevertheless, I also find that for me the Cubism of these masters leads to an overcrowding of the pictorial space. This accounts for the high surface of the frontal planes, so prevalent even in some of the most successful early works of the Cubists. In fact, such exceptions as the collage drawings of Picasso in which emptier areas are emphasized only point up what is otherwise typical. Much of the agitation in Juan Gris's *Guitar and Flowers*, for instance, is the result of the violent diagonal twist of his planes away from the stabilizing rectangle of the surface. Even the early Cubism of Mondrian, who was in many ways a descendant of de Hooch and Vermeer, contains a number of small bricklike rectangular shapes, which strike me as being more a concession to the manner of the time than essential to his austere conception of space and structure." Still it is the Cubists who provide the contemporary context for his work. The Cubists, far from painting cubes or cubicals, are nothing if not flat-surface painters.

Other specifics of his museum dialogue, as it were, are spelled out with textbooklike precision and classroom-type demonstration in *The Painter's Mind: A Study of the Relations of Structure and Space in Painting*, which he wrote in collaboration with his longtime friend and colleague, the late Carl Holty, one-time member of the famous Creative Abstraction group in pre–World War II Paris, who also taught at the Art Students League. *The Painter's Mind* is a treatise on flat painting beyond everything else. In it, outstanding examples from the whole worldwide museum that is the heritage of all present-day painters are in effect reinterpreted in light of the twentieth-century emphasis on flat-surface painting as opposed to the life-like representation and nineteenth-century misconceptions of the classical ideal and Renaissance perspective.

It was Bearden's early orientation to flat painting that led to his special interest in Stuart Davis. Indeed, it was in the very process of discussing decoration, ornamentation, and design as the primary objectives of contemporary painting that Davis, whose preoccupations were no less vernacular than avant-garde, began talking about Earl Hines and about how his own use of color intervals had been influenced by the way Hines used space as statement in building structures of sound on the piano. "Earl Hines' hot piano and Negro jazz in general," he once wrote, "were among the things which have made me want to paint, outside of other paintings." Remembering all the way back to the epochmaking Armory Show of 1913, in which he was represented by five watercolors, Davis also wrote, "I was enormously excited by the show, and responded particularly to Gauguin, van Gogh, and Matisse, because broad generalization of form and the non-imitative use of color were already practices within my experience. I also sensed an objective order in these works which I felt was lacking in my own. It gave me the kind of excitement I got from the numerical precision of the Negro piano players in the Negro saloons, and I resolved that I would quite definitely have to become a 'modern' painter."

At first Bearden didn't really know what to make of the fact that Davis, who had a large record collection to be sure, so often insisted on making a connection between painting and jazz. He had already had to endure more than his share of pseudo sophisticated ofays showing off how hip they were to the uptown jive, and there was always another one of those perhaps well-intentioned but boring do-gooders determined to talk about something you know about so as to make you feel comfortable in the great white world outside of Harlem. But as Davis went on to clarify his conception of the roll jazz played in *predetermining an analogous dynamics in design,* Bearden was able to see just how fundamental all of Davis's points about jazz were. He was talking about how one was *disposed,* or rather predisposed, to process *any raw material* into aesthetic statement.

What Davis made him realize as never before was the workaday relationship of all of his formal training and apprenticeship, of all the abstract formulations and theoretical concerns to his basic idiomatic conditioning. "And from then on," he said, "I was on my way. I don't mean to imply that I knew where I was going. But the more I just played around with visual notions as if I were improvising like a jazz musician, the more I realized what I wanted to do as a painter, and how I wanted to do it.

"I must say I was not just impressed but also deeply moved by the fact that Stu Davis, who so far as I was concerned was one of the best American painters around, felt that it was so crucially important and worked so long and deliberately to acquire something that, as he pointed out, I had inherited from my Afro-American environment as a matter of course. I had gone to him to find out more about the avant-garde, and he kept trying to make me appreciate the fact that so far as he was concerned the aesthetic conventions of Harlem musicians to which so many of my habitual responses were geared, were just as avant-garde as Picasso, Braque, Matisse, Mondrian, and all the rest. By the way, jazz, especially boogie-woogie, was the main thing Mondrian wanted to talk to Davis about during the several times they met."

III

The Painter's Mind is in a very real sense a book about how to see the aesthetic statement in pictures in spite of the subject matter, or in any case, whatever the subject matter, and also in spite of, or whatever the stylistic convention. It is a book about structure and space with primary emphasis on design, decoration, and ornamentation as the indispensable fundamentals of visual expression. It does not discuss color, which as charcoal drawings and sketches and as black-and-white reproductions show, is a *dispensable* fundamental; but the implication is that color, like form, is to be used not in imitation of nature, but for decorative, ornamental, and design values.

According to *The Painter's Mind,* perspective and illusion are not essentials, only conventions, while structure is always necessary in any work of art. "Many things are revealed to us as we look at a work of art with its multiplicity of images. Not all who look will see the same thing; some people, for instance, will be pleased by a particular image, others depressed—each according to his temperament, his imagination, and his spiritual needs. But whatever the image, the only reality present is structure. There is no face, no ship, no landscape, no real depth. These are illusions; the structure that purports them is not."

Such contentions are entirely consistent with Bearden's orientation to flat painting, the use he makes of Byzantine painting and African art, his deliberate violations of scale, and his arbitrary use of color. (Obviously, his use of jet black as a color for human beings is not meant to be naturalistic.) Perhaps not so obvious is the fact that even when black functions as a symbolic reference to so-called black people of Africa and the United States, it is not the reference that is of paramount importance but the design: how the black shape works with other shapes and colors.

Moreover, black may or may not say Afro, but inevitably says silhouette, and almost always has the effect of a cutout in a collage, perhaps the flattest of flat painting.

Everything in *The Painter's Mind* is predicated upon the definitive assumption of twentieth-century artists that the painter should dominate his subject matter rather than be dominated by it. His talent is not at the service of description. What counts is how what is said is said. It is a process of stylization. Even when the examples under discussion are such classic classical representations of religious subject matter as Duccio's *The Marys at the Sepulchre* or Giotto's *The Resurrection*, or Tintoretto's *The Baptism*, or Rembrandt's *Bathsheba*, what the authors concern themselves with are the particularities of technique that enable each master to make the painting his individual aesthetic statement beyond all else.

Only about his complete nonfigurative works, however, is Bearden likely to go so far as to say what Georges Braque, for instance, once said about the subordination of subject matter: "When you ask me whether a particular form in one of my paintings depicts a woman's head, a fish, a vase, a bird, or all four at once, I cannot give a categorical answer, for this 'metaphoric' confusion is fundamental to the poetry. . . . It is all the same to me whether a form represents a different thing to different people or many things at the same time, or even nothing at all; it might be no more than an accident or a 'rhyme'—a pictorial 'rhyme,' by the way, can have all sorts of unexpected consequences, can change the whole meaning of a picture—such as I sometimes like to incorporate in my compositions."

Indeed, Bearden is convinced that Braque's statement is clearly an exaggeration. The subjects in a Braque painting are more denotative than his declaration would lead you to expect. Whatever else they may be, any layman can see that his still lifes are made from tables, bottles, glasses, musical instruments, and so on. Bearden feels that Braque is closer to actual practice when he goes on to say: "Objects do not exist for me except insofar as a rapport exists between them and between them and myself. In other words it is not the objects that matter to me but what is in between them; it is this in-between that is the real subject of my pictures."

In practice, Bearden's position is closer to what Stuart Davis seems to have had in mind when in reference to one of his paintings done in 1924–25 he said that they were based on a generalization of form in which the subject matter was conceived as a series of planes, and the planes as geometrical shapes—a valid view of the structure of any subject—these geometrical shapes were arranged in direct relationship to the canvas as a flat surface." In some paintings, Davis goes on to say, "the large forms were established on the flat-surface principle, but the minor features were still imitative."

It is generally accepted that twentieth-century painting does not have to tell a story and does not have to depict anything. Its figures can be shapes that mean nothing. Nevertheless, Braque's declarations seem to be somewhat modified, if not contradicted by his use of such titles as *Bottle and Glass, Man with Guitar, Bottle of Rum, Violin and Pipe, Still Life with Guitar, Painter and Model.* It is no doubt true that these are only shapes that tell no story. It is also true that no very special meaning is attached to these objects per se, that, in effect, they have been neutralized so that they exist primarily as elements in a picture not concerned with factual description. But it is likely to be less true that it would have made no difference to Braque if viewers saw cats and dogs instead of bottles and glasses and two generals instead of the painter and his model—although Braque could have made pretty much the same pictorial statement with two generals. Perhaps it is more to the point to say that bottles, glasses, guitars, violins, pipes, and even painters and models were not used to record, suggest, or symbolize anything about liquids, music, tobacco, and so on, rather only because they were ordinary, familiar three-dimensional objects, and as such could be used to emphasize the fact that the painter is working in terms of flatness and not perspective. Similarly, when letters are used in a Léger or Davis painting, whatever they may or may not spell, they function as two-dimensional ornamental shapes, and they also serve to keep the surface as flat as, say, a Mondrian.

But all the same, Bearden, who is nothing if not an exponent of the flat surface, sees no reason why his pictures should not tell a story so long as the narration and depiction do not get in the way of the painting as such. In his view, a painting does not have to say anything either literal or symbolic, but it can if it wishes. Of course, it must always avoid unintentional counterstatement or detrimental empathy. On the other hand, there can be no question of any violation of scale, perspective, or nonrealistic color destroying the illusion in a flat painting, since description is always subordinate to design.

Bearden is convinced that doctrinaire artists who would rigorously exclude all descriptive elements from all of their work are placing unnecessary restrictions on themselves. He sees no reason why aesthetic statement cannot be multidimensional. Certainly there is no inherent reason why a mural, for example, cannot be narrative without compromising its function as an ornament. Bearden, who has done both figurative and nonfigurative murals for interior as well as exterior walls, claims that he is aware of a preference only after the composition of a given project is already under way.

In any case, although the figurative shapes in his painting are almost always a matter of improvisation, and are completely subordinate to the most fundamental requirements of design, decoration, and ornament, once they come into existence as realistic objects, even as they fulfill their indispensable function as elements in the composition they acquire powers of suggestion and illusion that may be very strong indeed. Sometimes they stimulate associations with concrete objects, places, and events, and sometimes they become symbolic evocations by the same token. In other words, unlike Braque's neutralized bottles, glasses, guitars, painters, and models, Bearden's flat-surface musicians, train cutouts, his rural and urban landscapes with their farmers and apartment dwellers are not only meant to be taken as representations of very specific examples of reality, they may be deliberately symbolic at the same time, as in the case of *Carolina Shout,* for instance. What the figures suggest is an ecstatic high point in a down-home church service. At the same time, however, the title, made famous by a Harlem Stride piano composition, implies that the movements and gestures are not unrelated to the dance hall, the jook joint, the honky-tonks, and the barrelhouse. So even as the figures evoke the Sunday morning service, there are also overtones of the Saturday night function referred to in *Mecklenberg County Saturday Night.*

The evocations and associations in Bearden's works are indeed so strong, and so deliberately and specifically and idiomatically either down-home rural or up-north urban, that perhaps it is not too much to say that his preoccupation with imagery from a special American context, which he uses in much the same way as Picasso, and especially Miró, uses Spanish imagery, is surpassed only by his commitment to the aesthetic process that will give his painting the "quality of a flat surface decorated by hand"—and also gives him the option to use any raw material whatever, or no identifiable subject matter at all.

But the fact is that once his arbitrary shapes and photo cutout details become figures in paintings, what they suggest very often reflects some aspect of the idiomatic particulars of Afro-American life. In other words, in spite of the obvious fact that he does not work primarily in terms of illusion, the trains, for example, that are present in so many of his pictures are meant to be taken as real-life railroad trains. As such, however, they connote as well as denote, as do the locomotives in the old guitar and harmonica folk blues. And as do those in Ellington's *Daybreak Express,*

Way Low, Happy Go Lucky Local, The Old Circus Train Turn Around Blues, Loco Madi, and so on and on inbound and outbound. They are also not only the northbound limiteds and specials that down-home folks used to take or dream of taking up the country or the southbound ones bringing tidings and/or visiting relatives, or "my baby back to me," but are sometimes also symbolic of the totally imaginary vehicles in the spirituals and of the ever so metaphorical, but no less boardable, underground railroad of the fugitive slaves.

Perhaps the most distinctive, if not the definitive feature of Bearden's treatment of the figurative elements in his paintings is the pronounced emphasis that is almost always given to the ceremonial dimension of each scene and event. Even in his portraits, whether of individuals, couples, or groups, the people not only seem to pose for the occasion exactly as folks used to get themselves up to watch the birdie for the photographer of yesteryear, with his view camera on a tripod, his black cloth, and rubber-ball plunger. They also seem posed not only for the occasion, but also as if for some special occasion. There are few candid shots. Even when, as in the series of black-and-white *Projections* (1964), there are unmistakable evocations of newsprint and movies, it is the choreographic movement of the old silent films that comes to mind (along with the old newspaper *stills*), not the documentary Technicolor of *National Geographic* magazine.

Nor is there any contradiction between the compelling impact and hence importance of Bearden's subject matter as such, and the assessment of what is relevant and irrelevant in visual art given in *The Painter's Mind.* For, as should be obvious enough to anyone with even a slight familiarity with Byzantine, Romanesque, and African art, it is precisely by working primarily in terms of ornamentation and decoration that he generates the strong ceremonial and ritualistic associations that some reviewers refer to as mythic overtones. The ornamental emphasis also frees the evocative dimension of his work from sentimentality and provincialism. Compared to the ceremonial dignity of Bearden's radiant still lifes, Degas's great "snapshots" of ballet dancers, for example, look almost as genre as Millet's peasants. By contrast, not only are Bearden's North Carolina cotton pickers anything but genre, his folk and jazz musicians are depicted with a ritual formality that suggests characters in a ballet.

The ornamental and ritual emphasis also serves to counterstate the pathetic (as it does in the case of the agony in the highly stylized representations of the Crucifixion). As is to be expected of an artist who began as a political cartoonist and remains an enthusiastic admirer of Grosz, Goya, Daumier, Forain, and Kollwitz, Bearden sometimes, especially in his urbanscapes, creates configurations that may be taken as social commentary. But even so, the overall impact of *The Block, The Street, Evening Lenox Avenue, The Dove, Rocket to the Moon,* and *Black Manhattan,* for example, is, as he intended, much closer to such Ellington tone parallels and celebrations as *Uptown Downbeat, Echoes of Harlem, I'm Slapping Seventh Avenue with the Sole of My Shoe, Drop Me Off in Harlem,* and *Harlem Airshaft* than to any of the Welfare Department tear-jerk rhetoric so habitual among so many mostly cynical spokesmen (and persons!) and so readily accepted and repeated by the world's champion one-upmen (and persons!) become do-gooders.

Incidentally, having grown up in close contact with such prominent Afro-heritage figures of the so-called Harlem Renaissance, New Negro movement as Arthur Schomburg, Langston Hughes, Countee Cullen, Claude McKay, and Aaron Douglas, Bearden has always had a special interest in African art. But it was not until he began working in terms of the assumptions underlying *The Painter's Mind* that he discovered the pragmatic aesthetic relevance of African art—along with that of Byzantine, Japanese and Chinese art—to Cubist and post-Cubist painting. Before that he, like so many other U.S. Negro artists, attempted to identify with African art racially, or in any case politically (and also in its entirety), only to have his images come out looking exactly as if they were derived from the Mexican images of Diego Rivera and Miguel Covarrubias, and from one Winold Reiss, to whom as a matter of fact they were infinitely closer in spirit, and intention as well, than to Ife, Dogon, Fon, Senufo, or Benin. He learned to apply certain devices of stylization appropriated from African art but, needless to say, he could not use African devices as if he were an African, because, for all his ancestral bloodlines, he could not be idiomatically African, not being native to African experience. He could not be idiomatically Spanish, Dutch, or French either. He could only be idiomatically American, and most specifically, blues idiom American. And that, it just so happens, is quite enough, because as a twentieth-century American he not only can but also must synthesize everything in the world as a matter of course—and feed it back to the world at large as a matter of course.

In all events, Bearden has made it clear that his actual use of African art is based on aesthetic, not political, and certainly not racial considerations. Accordingly, the very strong African-like elements in his work are derived not nearly so directly from the African artifacts on display in the Schomburg library in his old neighborhood as from such Cubist adaptations as, say, Picasso's *Demoiselles d'Avignon*. Moreover, it is on Picasso's terms, as it were (not to mention prices) that Bearden clearly intends his own appropriations to be judged.

IV

Of far more fundamental significance than any question of how much of the art of ancestral Africa is discernible in the work of Romare Bearden is the blues idiom. It is the aesthetics of jazz musicianship that has conditioned him to approach the creative process as a form of play and thus disposes him to trust his work to the intuitions that arise in the course of creating it, which, in turn, also enables him to make the most of the fact that the primary emphasis of contemporary painting is on design, decoration, and ornamentation.

It is also his blues idiom orientation to vamping and riffing and otherwise improvising (as classic African artists were forbidden by custom to do but as frontier Americans were required by circumstances to do) that leads him to dominate his subject matter precisely as the jazz musician does. Any musical subject matter whatsoever is only raw material to be processed into King Oliver music or Jelly Roll Morton music or Louis Armstrong music. A traditional twelve-bar blues progression becomes *Parker's Mood.* A thirty-two-bar popular standard titled *Please Don't Talk About Me When I'm Gone* is transformed by Thelonius Monk into *Four in One* as if it were only a folk ditty.

Nor is such domination merely in the interest of a romantic proclamation of individuality per se. Far from being egotistical in any conventional sense, it is rather a matter of just such free enterprise as is to be expected in an open and ever-changing society, as opposed to closed ones that are rigidly restricted by tribal taboos, or by despotic rulers. But even more than that, it represents the artist's participation in an ongoing dialogue with tradition and his never-ending struggle in the void. What it is mainly concerned with is not so much the individual as with human existence as experienced by an individual. At any rate, when the blues-oriented listener hears only a few bars of music on the radio or a phonograph and says Ole Louis or says Ole Duke or says Ole Count or says That's Yardbird or That's Monk or That's Miles or says I hear you Trane or I hear you Ornette, he has said it all. Moreover, he has spoken with the same sophisticated awareness of art as a playful process of stylization as that which qualifies the art critic to take only a glance at a picture and say: a Picasso or say a Matisse or say a de Kooning, Motherwell, Hans Hofmann, and so on. He is identifying the essence of the musical statement not by subject matter and title but by how it is played, as the art critic does with a picture when he tells how it is together simply by acknowledging the name of the artist.

Whatever Ellington played became Ellington, as whatever Picasso painted became a Picasso beyond all else. And the same is true—and has been for some time now—of Romare Bearden. When one looks at his paintings one sees more than the subject matter. Ultimately it is not only Bearden's North Carolina or Bearden's Harlem or Bearden's musicians or Bearden's Odysseus, but also a Bearden stylization of an attitude toward human existence, a Bearden statement/counterstatement and thus that which stands for Bearden himself, and hence a Bearden *(which, incidentally, one is probably much more likely to see in real life after rather than before seeing in a frame)*.

And what finally is a Bearden if not design or ornament or decoration for a wall, where it hangs not primarily as a record but as an emblem or badge or shield or flag or banner or pennant, or even as a battle standard and existential guidon. And of what is it emblematic if not that in terms of which the fundamental rituals of the blues idiom condition one to survive (with one's humanity, including one's sense of humor, intact, to be sure). What indeed if not flexibility become elegant improvisation not only under the pressure of all tempos and not only in the response of all disjunctures, but also in the face of ever-impending nothingness. Yes, it is precisely in doing this that a Bearden wall ornament functions as a totemistic device and talisman for keeping the blues at bay, if only intermittently.

PART SIX

THE STORYTELLER
AS BLUES SINGER

ERNEST HEMINGWAY SWINGING

THE BLUES AND TAKING NOTHING

I

Ernest Hemingway was a man of active goodwill. He was also a man of practical action. He was, that is to say, a man whose personal commitment to what he once referred to as "society, democracy, and the other things" always went beyond parlor games and the light picketing stage. He was indeed a man well aware of his fundamental involvement in the welfare of mankind, and his response to the issues and movements of his time is not only a matter of biographical fact; it is also reflected in everything he wrote. But the much-quoted Hemingway statement about writers being forged in injustice was never intended as an argument for the literature of sociopolitical protest.

Hemingway never separated the world of fiction from the everyday actualities of life around him, but neither did he confuse the ends and means of aesthetics with those of politics. "The hardest thing in the world to do," he once declared and repeated in substance time and again, "is write straight honest prose on human beings. First you have to know the subject; then you have to know how to write. Both take a lifetime to learn and anybody is cheating who takes politics as a way out. It is too easy."

He believed that all the outs were too easy and that the thing itself was extremely hard to do. "But you have to do it," he went on, "and every time you do it, those human beings and that subject are done and your field is that much more limited." He was, as will be seen, always very much preoccupied with all of the things that affect the art of serious fiction, especially those that make it so everlastingly difficult.

He considered some of these things in *Death in the Afternoon*, continued with others in *Green Hills of Africa*; and *A Moveable Feast* is in part a review of some of the key working principles of his early apprenticeship. He also wrote a number of articles and letters on the subject. As a matter of fact, quite a bit of Hemingway's nonfiction is basically concerned with the aesthetics of narration.

In "Old Newsman Writes," a correspondence-article that he did for *Esquire* in 1934 during the heyday of the "social consciousness" movement in U.S. literature, he was specifically apprehensive about the writer's involvement with politics as such. A writer, he was convinced, could make himself a nice career by espousing a political cause and working for it, making a profession of believing in it, and if it won he would be very well placed. All politics, he said, is a matter of working hard without reward, or with a living wage for a time, in hope of booty later. "A man can be a Fascist or a Communist and if his outfit gets in he can get to be an ambassador or have a million copies of his books printed by the government or any of the other rewards the boys dream about."

Twenty-four years later, when George Plimpton, interviewing him for the *Paris Review* series on the art of fiction, asked him to what extent he thought a writer should concern himself with the sociopolitical problems of his times, he replied that everyone had his own conscience and that there should be no rules about how a conscience should function. "All you can be sure about a political-minded writer," he went on, "is that if his work should last you will have to skip the politics when you read it." He then added that many so-called politically enlisted writers change their politics frequently and that this is very exciting to them and to their politicoliterary reviews. "Sometimes they even have to rewrite their viewpoints—and in a hurry. Perhaps it can be respected as a form of the pursuit of happiness."

As the old newsman he had applied the same principle to

Tolstoy and *War and Peace* in the *Esquire* article. Read it, he suggested, "and see how you will have to skip the big Political Thought passages that he undoubtedly thought were the best thing in the book when he wrote it, because they are no longer true or important, if they ever were more than topical; and see how true and lasting and important the people and the action are."

He had also had a few things to say about politicoliterary criticism in the *Esquire* article. "Of course, the boys would be wishing you luck," he said sarcastically; "but don't let them suck you in to start writing about the proletariat, if you don't come from the proletariat, just to please the recently politically enlightened critics. In a little while these critics will be something else. I've seen them be a lot of things and none of them was pretty. Write about what you know and write truly and tell them where they can place it. They are all really very newly converted and very frightened, really, and when Moscow tells them what I'm telling you, then they will believe it."

He then went on to say that books should be about the people you know, that you love and hate, not about the people you study up about. True writing about such things, he always insisted, would automatically have all the economic implications a book could hold. No serious writer, he was convinced, could ever allow himself to be deceived about what a book should be because of what is currently fashionable. Books, good books, at any rate, were always about what you really feel rather than what you are supposed to feel, and have been taught to feel.

He accused "recently enlightened" and "converted" writers of abandoning their trade and entering politics because they wanted to do something where they could have friends and well-wishers, and be a part of a company engaged in doing something instead of working a lifetime at something that will only be worth doing if one does it better than it has been done before—and for which, he might have added, there are no guarantees. He never withdrew this accusation, and as for converted critics, he rejected their laudations as well as their damnations, along with their sincerity. "Not a one will wish you luck," he quipped, "or hope that you will keep on writing unless you have political affiliations in which case these will rally around and speak of you and Homer, Balzac, Zola, and Link Steffens. You are as well off without these reviews."

On one occasion he spoke of declining enlistments (such as those under which Frederick Henry in *A Farewell to Arms* had served time for society, while quite young) and making oneself responsible only to oneself—exchanging "the pleasant comforting stench of comrades" for the feeling that comes when one writes well and truly of something and knows objectively that one has done so "in spite of those who do not like the subject and say it is all a fake." The same feeling comes, he went on, when one does something that people do not consider a serious occupation and yet one knows, in oneself, that it is as important and has always been as important as all the things that are in fashion.

The man who made these statements, it should be remembered, did not lack any concern for the plight of his fellowmen. He did not wish to live in an Ivory Tower indulging in Art for Art's sake. It is true, of course, that he did have a consuming interest in sports, that he spent a lot of time fishing and hunting, but his participation in such activities was neither frivolous nor decadent. It was not only a universally recommended form of healthful recreation but was, as such stories as "Big Two-Hearted River" and "The Short Happy Life of Francis Macomber," among others, indicate, quite obviously a highly rewarding extension of his profound preoccupation with the basic disciplines of human existence. Nor was there anything at all even questionable about his very special but completely serious enthusiasm for bullfights. He did not regard the bullfight as a form of casual amusement but as a ritual drama that had direct relevance to his personal sense of life and to the form as well as the content of his fiction. Violent death was for him neither a matter of cold-blooded indifference nor of degenerate fascination. It was something he wanted to write about because he had come to believe that it had fundamental literary significance; and his response to it in bullfighting was entirely consistent with long-established notions of epic poetry and tragic fiction and drama. Violence is not indispensable to literature, to be sure, but no one can deny that without it the tragic heroism in *Medea* and *Macbeth* and the epic heroism of the *Iliad*, the *Nibelungenlied*, and *Beowulf* would be something else altogether.

It is also true that in *Death in the Afternoon* Hemingway advises writers to let those who want to save the world do so "if you can get to see it clear and as a whole." But then there is also good reason to assume that the implication is that those who do not "see and hear and learn and understand" are not likely to be the ones to save it anyway. He was not referring to saving the earth from interplanetary disaster but those who join crusades. He was referring once more to writers who enlist, and he was to spell out some of his misgivings about them in "Old Newsman Writes." But the author of *A Farewell to Arms* already knew that more confusion and destruction than salvation frequently came from people who were too busy saving the world to find out what it was about. That, few will deny, is reason enough to admonish writers to stick to the task of writing as well as possible.

Perhaps those who found evidence in *To Have and Have Not* that Hemingway had changed or was changing his mind about the role of the writer in society were more impressed by some of his personal political gestures than by what was actually in the novel itself. It is true that Harry Morgan, the protagonist of *To Have and Have Not*, comes to realize that one man alone does not have a very good chance the way things are. It was not at all difficult to hear overtones of social consciousness in his dying words to that effect in the 1930s. But it is Richard Gordon the novelist, not Harry Morgan, who is the writer in the story. Morgan is a smuggler. Richard Gordon is not at all the product of Hemingway's alleged hard-boiled anti-intellectualism that so many critics have made him out to be. What he really represents is Hemingway's response to literary opportunism and corruption. He writes "social consciousness" novels, of course, but he himself is really a "middle class" social climber, a slick literary opportunist who is not only ignorant of the people whose cause his books are supposed to serve, but he also has no real artistic integrity and is even deficient in personal competence. His "enlistment," as his wife makes clear, is part and parcel of his personal corruption. It is exactly the sort of thing the "old newsman" had in mind when he spoke of those who take the easy way out of the difficulties inherent in writing straight honest prose on human beings.

The scene, the world, the dramatic context of the action in *To Have and Have Not* is obviously and quite intentionally political. It is in a very literal sense a story about life in the United States during the Depression of the 1930s; and it is written in terms of, that is to say, in *the terms* of such political problems as unemployment, crime, socioeconomic exploitation, and revolution. But those who overemphasize Harry Morgan's conversion to the brotherhood of man while overlooking the implications of Richard Gordon's personal corruption seem to be more concerned with making political applications of fictional materials than with Hemingway's total fictional statement. Hemingway was not opposed to interpretations that indicated the political implications of his work, but he himself seems always to have been concerned with human problems that go beyond political issues as such.

It is true that he was already actively engaged in the Spanish Civil War even before *To Have and Have Not* reached the bookstores, but it should also be remembered that while this "novel about the Depression" was still in progress, he wrote "The Short Happy Life of Francis Macomber" and "The Snows of Kilimanjaro," two of his best short stories, both of which are extensions of the nonpolitical themes underlying the Richard Gordon episodes. Both are about personal corruption in the sophisticated world of money and leisure. Richard Gordon, whose fascination for this world (into which Francis Macomber was born) is his undoing, is deficient in personal and artistic integrity, in personal competence, and in moral and physical courage. Francis Macomber, a rich playboy who lives the life that both Richard Gordon and the writer in "The Snows of Kilimanjaro" ruin themselves to become a part of, does not until a few happy minutes before his wife kills him have that which is required to fulfill his manhood—and the role of the hero. He is, that is to say, a *have* who *has not.* One could also say that the writer in "The Snows of Kilimanjaro" compromises his talent *to get* only to find that he *has got* nothing.

Indeed, one can reverse the point of view and read *To Have and Have Not* as an extension of the themes in "The Short Happy Life of Francis Macomber" and "The Snows of Kilimanjaro," which, after all, are more fully realized as works of art. In this context Harry Morgan becomes the figure on the positive side of a coin, the negative side, which is a composite of Richard Gordon, Francis Macomber, and the writer in "The Snows of Kilimanjaro," whose name is also Harry. But in either case the double plot of *To Have and Have Not* suggests the dynamics of pastoral at least as strongly as it suggests those of revolutionary agitation. Either way one looks at the juxtaposition of episodes, Harry Morgan, the lowly fisherman, is the common man who personifies essential virtue and nobility, whereas Richard Gordon and those of higher social status are embodiments of human shortcomings. Harry may be poor, the pastoral poet might say, but he is the better man and he leads a better life, which from one political point of view might well indicate the need for revolution because society is upside down. But from another it could be regarded as the irony of fate: The have-nots really *have* while the haves have *not!*

William Empson refers to pastoral as being a puzzling form that looks proletarian but is not. In *Some Versions of Pastoral*, he also points out that the essential trick of this genre is to imply a beautiful relation between rich and poor. But then he goes on to observe that the pastoral poet is traditionally class-conscious *but not conscious of a class struggle as such* (emphasis added). "Pastoral is a queerer business," he says, "but I think permanent and not dependent on a system of class exploitation. Any socialist state with an intelligentsia at the capitol that felt itself more cultivated than the farmers could produce it." Empson also believes that good proletarian art is usually "covert pastoral." And then he makes another observation, which should help to clear up much of the confusion that surrounds most committed, enlisted, or "social consciousness" writing. "To produce a pure proletarian art," he says, "the artist must be at one with the worker; this is impossible, not for political reasons, but because *the artist never is at one with any public*" (emphasis added).

What the writer wants to be one with is the great enduring traditions of literature. This holds as true for a writer like André Malraux, whose raw material is the very stuff of social consciousness, as it does for Ernest Hemingway, who never stopped insisting that the writer's primary job was to see and learn and write. Earlier, in *Some Versions of Pastoral*, Empson had already used Malraux as an example of the writer who had avoided the usual traps of proletarian literature. The heroes of *Man's Fate* "are communists," he begins, "and are trying to get something done, but they are very frankly out of touch with the proletariat; it is from this that they get their pathos and dignity and the book its freedom from propaganda."

When *Man's Hope*, the first major literary effort to come out of the Spanish Civil War, was published, *Time* magazine reported that Malraux had written it on the battlefield. "Between battles," a caption under his picture in the cover feature review-article ran, "impassioned prose." The article called the novel a new kind of book, one that combines vivid journalistic observation with extraordinary imaginative flights. "Largely written in Spain between July and November 1936, it was turned out diary fashion while Malraux was leading the Loyalist Air Force. After flights over Franco's territory, he shut himself up in Madrid's Hotel Florida, wrote in five- or six-hour spurts, making few corrections."

Hemingway, as is well known, wrote the play *The Fifth Column* in the same hotel in 1937 under similar conditions. Hotel Florida was struck by more than thirty high-explosive shells while composition was in progress. "So if it is not a good play perhaps that is what is the matter with it," he said. "If it is a good play, perhaps those thirty some shells helped write it. When you went to the front at its closest it was fifteen hundred yards from the hotel, the play was always slipped inside the inner fold of a rolled-up mattress. When you came back and found the room and the play intact you were always pleased."

The Fifth Column was the work of a man of action *in* action. But not even *The Fifth Column*, for all its newsprint atmosphere of immediacy, was turned out as agitation propaganda, impassioned, calculated, or any other kind. Hemingway was willing to risk his life for the cause but he did not deliberately compromise his aesthetic principles for political ends. What he wrote in the Introduction to the play when it was published in *The Fifth Column and the First Forty-nine Stories* is entirely consistent with what the old newsman had written about art and politics: "Some fanatical defenders of the Spanish Republic, and fanatics do not make good friends for a cause, will criticize the play because it admits that fifth column members were shot. They will also say and have said, that it does not present the nobility and dignity of the cause of the Spanish people. It does not attempt to. It will take many plays and novels to do that, and the best ones will be written after the war is over. It was," he said, "only a play about counterespionage in Madrid," and it had the defects of having been written in wartime, "and if it has a moral it is that people who work for certain organizations have very little time for home life."

The Fifth Column did have political relevance, of course, and given the subject matter, it was immediate relevance at that; but this in itself could never have been enough for a man who was always trying to write prose that would have five dimensions. And besides, it should never be forgotten that Hemingway was both clearly and finally convinced that political immediacy as such was an element that would always fall away and leave a story flat. *The Fifth Column* was not a very successful work by any yardstick. But if it had to stand on its political relevance it would probably be of very little significance whatsoever. As it is, however, it at least stands as an interesting finger exercise in preparation for the major novel that followed.

There was also immediate political relevance in *For Whom the Bell Tolls*, but Hemingway was also very much concerned about the relevance of the color, contours, and textures of the terrain and the smell and taste of food and drink and so on, none of which does political relevance any harm. After all, he believed that one should always write as well as possible, and besides, there is no law that has ever required a writer to work harder to describe the chronological development of a worthy cause, a good crop, or a conversion of a sinner than he would to describe anything else—say, the sheen on a freshly hooked trout or the beads of sweat on a chilled bottle of Pouilly-Fuissé.

The military material in *For Whom the Bell Tolls* is so accurately rendered that much of it was actually used by the U.S. Army in courses in the tactics of guerrilla warfare. But so far as Hemingway the novelist was concerned, it had to be written that way because it was that kind of story. There were political issues and military materials because these things had been completely assimilated as natural personal involvements and were ordinary elements in his literary imagination. As for the operational accuracy of his rendition, which, it should be remembered, was equally true of the fishing, hunting, prizefighting, and bullfighting sequences in any of his other stories, that was no doubt one of the dimensions he was referring to when he talked of going beyond the tricks of journalism.

For Whom the Bell Tolls was a work of art. As far as the specific political and economic elements in the story are concerned, nobody ever had to remind Ernest Hemingway that there things should not be left out. He had been talking and writing about that sort of thing ever since he had started trying to write fiction. Everything you know should be there, he began insisting in Paris in the 1920s, and never stopped. Sometimes it showed and sometimes it didn't. But it was there like the underwater seven eighths of the iceberg, sustaining the one eighth one sees. His was a never-ending effort to comprehend the world in all of its complexity so that anything he wrote well enough about would represent life as a whole. He also liked to say that one could leave out the things one knew enough about. But he always went on to say that these things would be there anyway. And he did not mean to imply that they would be there by chance either. But the relative proportion of elements or of emphasis in a work of art is determined not by political significance as such but by the writer's sense of form.

Political significance is inherent in all stories. Political details, however, are something else. Like all other details, they were included in *For Whom the Bell Tolls* or omitted from it, on the principle of the iceberg. "Anything you know," Hemingway assumed, beginning back in the days of his apprenticeship and was still maintaining in the *Paris Review* interview in 1958, "you can eliminate and it only strengthens your iceberg. It is the part that does not show. If a writer omits something because he does not know it then there is a hole in the story." On the other hand, that which was omitted on the principle of the iceberg, he wrote in *A*

Moveable Feast, could actually "make people feel something more than they understand." To which he added, "But they will understand the same way they always do in painting."

It is the "enlisted" writer who insists that the political significance be spelled out in no uncertain terms. But it is often in the very process of doing just this that such a writer is most likely to leave out other things, the omission of which can only make his fiction essentially thin, hollow, of limited interest and application—and all too ephemeral, no matter what initial impact it makes. Some writers leave out almost everything that does not serve their immediate political purpose. Many consider complexity of circumstances and motives to be precious indulgences that can wait until a better world has been achieved. There are those who do not hesitate to suppress details that run counter to, or do not contribute directly to, the social doctrines and objectives to which they are currently committed.

Beyond all political considerations, immediate or otherwise, the man who had not been able to make *Death in the Afternoon* enough of a book and who had declared in *Green Hills of Africa* that carrying prose as far as it would go was the most important thing a writer could do, wanted *For Whom the Bell Tolls* to contain as much of his sense of life as possible, "the good and the bad, the ecstasy, the remorse and sorrow, the people and the places and how the weather was." The awareness of the involvement in mankind and of one's possibilities for self-fulfillment and grandeur were also elements in that sense of life, as was one's consciousness, whether sharp or intuitive, of the relativity and ultimate absurdity of actuality and the objectivity and finality of death.

The writer's problem does not change, he had told the Marxist-oriented Second American Writers' Congress on a trip to New York after two active months in Spanish combat zones. "It was always how to write truly and having found out what is true to project it in such a way it becomes part of the experience of the

person who reads it." Several years earlier he had expressed the
same point of view as the old newsman, and in "Monologue to
the Maestro" he had outlined his working assumptions and procedures; and his sample list of required reading had encompassed
the entire range of prose fiction. Among the standards that he
suggested to young writers to aim at were *Tom Jones* and *Joseph
Andrews; The Charterhouse of Parma* and *The Red and the Black; Sentimental Education* and *Madame Bovary; War and Peace* and *Anna
Karenina; A Portrait of the Artist as a Young Man* and *Ulysses; The
Brothers Karamazov, Buddenbrooks, Huckleberry Finn, The Turn of the
Screw, The American, Midshipman Easy,* and *Peter Simple.* His list of
writers also included Turgenev, Maupassant, Kipling, Stephen
Crane, W. H. Hudson, and Conrad. And to the objection that
reading so many great books might discourage the apprentice,
Hemingway replied that if such were the case he ought to be dis-
couraged, that unless he runs against the clock like a miler "he
will never know what he is capable of attaining."

What he was obviously trying to attain when he wrote
For Whom the Bell Tolls was that which the best works of fiction
always add up to: a representative image of life in the contemporary world. It was a story about an American engaged in guerrilla
operations among Spanish partisans of the Loyalist cause; but
to the extent that Hemingway was successful, his efforts to tell
how it really was make it infinitely more important as a commentary on the predicament of man than as the document of the
Spanish Civil War that some had expected in spite of the speech
at the Second Writers' Congress. Hemingway had not intended
to write a melodrama about the salvation of mankind through enlightened comradeship. His sense of life was not dialectical but
dramatic, and what he wrote in this instance was tragedy. The
story begins with the hero aware of his involvement in mankind
but in the end he dies, and his death is that separate peace that all
men must make with the world and must find within themselves.

II

He almost always worked for a surface simplicity, but completely dedicated to the fundamental aims of literature as he was, Ernest Hemingway was never any less concerned than were, say, André Malraux and Thomas Mann with creating fiction that would reflect an image of man consistent with contemporary insights into the complexities of human experience. Malraux was stating his most definitive conception of the function of fiction and indeed of all artistic expression when he pointed out that *The Conquerors* was not only a story about political revolution but was first of all a presentation of the human situation. And, of course, Mann makes it quite obvious that such a presentation is the basic objective of *The Magic Mountain.* No less mistakable, however, are the implications of the title, the tone, and the content of *In Our Time,* and when Hemingway insists that the adequately informed and accurately rendered *part* can be made to represent the *whole,* he is (as with his remarks about the iceberg principle of omission) not only reiterating the same objective but is also reconciling (for himself, at any rate) the comprehensive scope of his aspirations with the frequently misunderstood simplicity of his procedure.

What Malraux and Mann express in terms of general cultural and political considerations, Hemingway seems to have preferred to approach as the problems involved in the development of the individual writer as artist. Thus in *The Voices of Silence* and *The Metamorphosis of the Gods* Malraux has elaborated a comprehensive theory of all art as a revolt against man's destiny of nothingness. What lies before us is everything and nothing, and what is the past except everything and nothing. Likewise the political essays that Mann collected in *Order of the Day* along with the literary opinions in *Essays of Three Decades* add up to his definition of the New Humanism, a whole theory of human nature and conduct.

On the other hand, in such books as *Death in the Afternoon, Green Hills of Africa,* and *A Moveable Feast* and in such magazine articles as "Old Newsman Writes" and "Monologue to Maestro" Hemingway articulates his assumption about the craft of fiction only in terms that relate to the background conditioning and orientation of the individual writer, his literary aims, his competence as craftsman, and his imagination.

Nevertheless, Hemingway's notions about the significance of disorientation and isolation in the lives of individual writers have essentially the same philosophical implications as the cataclysmic and apocalyptic images of man's absurdity that enable Malraux to proclaim that art is man's means of humanizing the world. Hemingway and Malraux, differences in emphasis notwithstanding, are also in remarkable agreement with the process that Mann almost always associates with human refinement. *Buddenbrooks* in the end turns out to be a story about the emergence of artistic sensitivity against the breakdown of an erstwhile solid family. *The Magic Mountain* goes to great lengths to show how disease makes Hans Castorp a more complete man; and predictably the mistreatments and dislocations that Joseph suffers in *Joseph and His Brothers* are the specific means by which he improves his perspective on the contradictory elements of human brotherhood.

When George Plimpton asked about the remark he had once made about great writing and injustice, Hemingway replied that a writer without a sense of justice and injustice would be better off editing the yearbook of a school for exceptional children than writing novels. "The most essential gift for a good writer," he then went on to say, "is a built-in shockproof shit detector. This is the writer's radar and all great writers have used it."

He had made the original statement about writers and injustice in *Green Hills of Africa.* At one point during a dull stretch on safari, after reading in *Sevastopol,* an early novel by Tolstoy, he had begun ruminating about the importance of the experience of war on the development of writers like Tolstoy and Stendhal, and the influence of the revolution and the Commune on Flaubert and had not only decided that war, especially civil war, was an irreplaceable experience for a writer, but also that "writers are forged in injustice as a sword is forged." He had also suggested that the experience of prison in Siberia had made Dostoyevsky, who was already a good writer, a better one, and then he had speculated about the effect such an experience might have on a writer like Thomas Wolfe.

Indeed, what Hemingway had to say about Wolfe is of its very nature a refutation of those who would quote his statement about writers and injustice out of context and then accuse him of not reflecting enough concern about injustice. Hemingway's basic assumption is not that the experience of injustice makes for political commitment, but that the realization that human life is contradictory and mysterious should make for aesthetic discipline. What he wondered was if sending Wolfe to Siberia or to the Dry Tortugas would "give him the necessary shock to cut the overflow of words and give him a sense of proportion."

He said nothing that implies that writers should be turned into weapons or instruments of social reform because of injustice. When he says forged as a sword is forged he is referring to the tempering of metal. The sensibility of the writer must be prepared to withstand the shocks and distortions inherent in human existence even as the blade must hold its edge in the clang and clash of battle. Metal that has been properly forged will hold up. The literary sensibility that has been exposed to human existence in the raw, so to speak, will maintain the sharp edge of its artistic integrity when confronted with complexity.

Hemingway did not express any concern at all about Wolfe's social and political affiliations. He didn't even mention them. What he was concerned about was Wolfe's prose. What bothered him was Wolfe's lack of an adequate sense of proportion, his lack of discipline, his overuse of words. He did not wonder if rugged blood and guts experience in Siberia or the Dry Tortugas would make him a better man and citizen; he wondered if it would make him a better novelist. A writer, he had already said in *Death in the Afternoon*, must always pay a certain nominal percentage in experience to be able to understand and assimilate what he inherits and what he must in turn use as his own point of departure. It is clear enough that he doubted that Wolfe had paid the minimum percentage in the sort of personal experience that builds in the required shockproof detector which is the serious writer's protection against sentimentality, among other things. *Look Homeward, Angel* and *Of Time and the River* make that all too obvious. The overflow of words that Hemingway wanted to cut was a rhetoric based not on hardheaded insight but on enthusiasm, and on academic sentimentality. "Didn't Hemingway say this in effect," wrote F. Scott Fitzgerald in his notebook, "if Tom Wolfe ever learns to separate what he gets from books from what he gets from life, he will be an original." The point is well taken, but the statement in *Green Hills of Africa* indicates that Hemingway was not so much concerned about Wolfe's originality as with his verbal sobriety. As was Wright Morris in *The Territory Ahead*.

"What we have," Morris complains after quoting one of Wolfe's outbursts, "is a man with his eyes closed, his pores open, whipping himself into a state of intoxication with what is left of another man's observations. The rhetorical flow, lyrical in intent, is unable to keep up with the flow of the emotion, the verbal surge of clichés, of scenic props." Instead of Whitman's closely and lovingly observed artifacts, Wolfe, Morris continues, produces "a river of clichés, nouns, and soaring adjectives. He may be in love with life but he woos her with books, and looks through another man's eyes and uses another man's language." "The presence of raw material, real raw, bleeding life—the one thing that Wolfe believed he got his big hands on—is precisely what is absent from his work. He begins and he ends with raw material clichés."

The misgivings that Hemingway had about the effects of undigested reading and that have often been mistaken along with his interest in the so-called manly arts, as an indication of anti-intellectualism, was already very much in evidence as early as the time of *The Sun Also Rises*. In a very fundamental sense most of Robert Cohn's troubles in that story grow out of the stubbornness with which he clings to ideas he has gotten only from books. "He had been reading W. H. Hudson," Jake Barnes, the narrator, relates, "that sounds like an innocent occupation but Cohn had read and reread *The Purple Land*. *The Purple Land* is a very sinister book if read too late in life. It recounts the splendid imaginary amorous adventures of a perfect English gentleman in an intensely romantic land, the scenery of which is very well described. For a man to take it at thirty-five as a guidebook to what life holds is about as safe as it would be for a man of the same age to enter Wall Street direct from a French convent, equipped with a complete set of the more practical Alger books. Cohn, I believe, took every word of *The Purple Land* as literally as though it had been an R. G. Dun report. You understand me, he made some reservations, but on the whole the book to him was sound."

Robert Cohn, significantly enough, was also a writer. The implications, however, are as personal and practical as they are aesthetic. They are also obvious. Cohn, like Thomas Wolfe (who was to come later, of course), did not have a built-in detector to spot the stuff and nonsense. He was thus likely to be more enthusiastic than informed, more bookishly romantic than really and truly reliable. When at one point he persists in his Hudson-inspired fantasy about going to South America, Jake Barnes tries to shift his attention to British East Africa. When he refuses to budge, Jake tells him, "that's because you never read a book about it. Go read a book all full of love affairs with the beautiful shiny black princesses."

Perhaps at least a large measure if not most of the essentially academic confusion about his apparent resistance to intellectual elaboration is a result of the failure to realize that Hemingway himself was nothing if not intellectual. All serious writers are inevitably intellectuals. They write for people who like books, not for people who think books are unimportant. No matter how much they may wish to save the world, they really write not for "the people" but for "the readers." Many for whom fiction is the primary mode of expression, however, are frequently more functional intellectuals than nominal ones—and would not have it otherwise.

Hemingway was one of these. He was first of all an image-maker and storyteller, and those who accuse him of not being sufficiently intellectual obviously ignore the specific nature of his intellectual commitment. But even so, they must concede that most of his nonfiction could only have been addressed primarily to other intellectuals, since they could hardly believe that the passages on the art of fiction in *Death in the Afternoon, Green Hills of Africa*, and the *Esquire* articles were written for the edification of big-game hunters, bullfighting fans, and *Esquire* hipsters. But then perhaps they also ignore or dismiss his nonfiction altogether. And yet, volume aside, not even Thomas Mann has left a more careful documentation of his intellectual position, and few writers since Henry James have written so much to explain their literary point of view.

The reply that he addressed to Aldous Huxley, who had accused him of writing as if he were ashamed of being thought of as intelligent and cultured, is a basic statement of what was actually Hemingway's longstanding working conception of the fiction writer as intellectual. A good writer, he wrote in *Death in the Afternoon*, should know as much as possible. "A great enough writer seems to be born with knowledge, but he really is not; he has only been born with the ability to learn in a quicker ratio to the passage of time than other men and without conscious application, and with an intelligence to accept or reject what is already presented as knowledge." But he was firmly convinced that a writer who made people in his stories talk about such things as painting, music, letters, and science when they wouldn't naturally do so or who did so himself to display his knowledge or used fine but unnecessary phrases was "spoiling his work for egotism."

But in spite of all the unmistakable clues that Hemingway provided, some of his most incisive observations are frequently misconstrued as obvious evidences of his *anti-intellectualism*. Nevertheless, few philosophical analyses of the modern temper reflect a more profound sense of responsibility than the "nothing sacred" recollections in which the narrator-protagonist of *A Farewell to Arms* registers his reactions to easy sentiment, enthusiastic lip service, and high-sounding abstractions. "I was always embarrassed by the words, sacred, glorious, and sacrifice and the expression, in vain," says Frederick Henry, remembering a wartime comrade whom he describes as being patriotic. "We had heard them sometimes standing in the rain almost out of earshot, so that only the shouted words came through, and had read them, on proclamations that were slapped up by bill posters over the other proclamations. Now for a long time, and I had seen nothing sacred, and the things that were glorious had no glory and the sacrifices were like the stockyards at Chicago if nothing was done with the meat except to bury it. There were many words that you could not stand to hear and finally only the names of places had dignity. Certain numbers were the same way and certain dates and these with the names of the places were all you could say and have them mean anything. Abstract words such as glory, honor, courage, or hallow were obscene beside the concrete names of the villages, the numbers of roads, the names of rivers, the numbers of regiments, and the dates."

What the built-in automatic shockproof stuff and nonsense detector was spotting and rejecting in this instance was not the Gettysburg Address itself, of course, but rather the cynical exploitation of its realism by enlistment propaganda technicians, who slapped posters over other posters. *A Farewell to Arms* is among other things a story about a young man who serves time for a great cause, becomes disenchanted, and declines further idealistic enlistment. It is a drama about his discovery of the bewildering absurdity of the human condition. The contradictions of human nature would seem to be bad enough, but on top of that, natural accidents turn out to be very natural indeed. It is, in this sense, also the story about a man who thinks he has enlisted to become a hero in a melodrama only to discover that he has always been involved in *the* eternal tragedy, who is a hero because he is not quite defeated and is wiser and therefore better prepared to confront future adventures, whose latent stuff-and-nonsense detector has been activated and calibrated and better secured to help him withstand the inevitable shocks to come.

The words that Lincoln spoke at Gettysburg were motivated by a profound sense of human life as a tragic struggle and by a commitment to that struggle in full awareness of human weakness. Lincoln, the embattled commander in chief, was talking about the realization of human possibilities through courage and hope. Reduced to platitudes and slogans, his words, as Hemingway's hero heard them several generations later in Italy, were being used to mislead naïve crusaders to expect melodramatic miracles in situations in which epic tenacity and endurance were hardly enough to keep hope itself alive. It was the overeager enlistee, not the cause, whom Hemingway was rejecting when he declared his willingness elsewhere to let those who want to save the world do so. There never was a time when he himself refused or did not volunteer to fight for the possibility of human freedom as defined by Lincoln at Gettysburg. But neither was there ever to be another time in which he would oversimplify the issues, the circumstances, and minimize the natural exasperations that are part and parcel of the best intentions in the world.

He was also to write that he "could only care about people a few at a time." But in view of his lifelong performance in the field, those who misinterpret this as a callous expression of a hard-boiled antisocial point of view can do so only by ignoring the fundamental complexity, to say nothing of the honesty involved. Nor does it contradict his status as a lifelong man of active good will. People love themselves and those intimates they hold most dear, they like their friends, hate their enemies and are more or less indifferent to the rest of mankind, until circumstances (and suddenly enlightened self-interest) force them to cooperate to ward off some common danger or to come by some benefit that cannot be secured in any other way. People who are forever protesting their love of mankind are seldom taken at their word by mankind, not even by their closest relatives, who, knowing them as they do, are likely to find them downright incredible. They themselves never expect to be taken at their word by bank clerks and policemen, for instance, who incidentally spend quite a lot of time protecting mankind whether they love it or not.

But if Hemingway's idealism was rugged, he was not given to easy and superficial cynicism either. His commitments remained firm because they were based on realistic estimates of the situation in the first place. Perhaps, as with all combat intelligence reports, the most immediate social value of his writing is to be found in its unflinching accuracy. In person, however, for all his shockproof calibration, he represented the kind of heartwarming support all movements are not only lucky to have but also cannot sustain themselves without.

Hemingway's goodwill is steadfast. But, as with Malraux and Mann, so was his artistic integrity. Nor was it ever an integrity kept carefully away from exposure. In the preface to *The Fifth Column and the First Forty-nine Stories*, he extended the image of the sword being forged. "In going where you have to go and doing what you have to do and seeing what you have to see, you dull and blunt the instrument you write with. But I would rather have it bent and dulled and know I had to put it to the grindstone again and hammer it into shape and put a whetstone to it and know I had something to write about, than have it bright and shining and nothing to say, or smooth and well-oiled in the closet, but unused."

He was not always successful. No writer ever was. That was another fact of life. "Am trying to be a good boy," he remarked twenty-some years later, in another context, "but it is difficult trade. What you win in Boston you lose in Chicago." But he never stopped trying, and most of his nonfiction represents a never-ending effort to keep the fundamentals in focus. The old newsman in "Old Newsman Writes" editorialized about the literary risks involved in fulfilling one's political obligations. The monologist in "Monologue to the Maestro" was trying to spell out the essentials of good craftsmanship in everyday working terms, and twenty-three years later the interviewee was spelling out the very same essentials for a latter-day "maestro" from the *Paris Review*. The defender in "Defense of Dirty Words" counseled accuracy with details and advised against moral condescension and false propriety. And so on it always went. The huntsman stalking kudu in *Green Hills of Africa* was also seeking prose with five dimensions. The aficionado did not go to the arena to have "publishable ecstasies" about death in the afternoon, for even as he responded to the bullfighter's grace under pressure, the writer was working on the perpetual problem of how to render the actual thing that produced the emotion he was experiencing.

There was his conception of what straight honest prose on human beings was, and he tried to maintain what he once called "an absolute conscience as unchanging as the standard meter in Paris, to prevent faking." He was not always successful at that, either, of course. But the built-in radar was always on red alert against easy outs and was constantly feeding back useful information about life as well as letters. "Really good writing very scarce always," he wrote in response to a *Time* magazine inquiry about the literary state of the nation in the late summer of 1947. "When comes in quantities everybody very very lucky." He was somewhat flippant as he sometimes was when he did not want to sound like a bloody owl, but he was never really kidding about these matters. As for his achievement, that was a matter of talent and luck, and he had no delusions about that either. "Madame," he said to the little old lady in *Death in the Afternoon* who was disappointed because "A Natural History of the Dead" was not like *Snowbound.* "I'm wrong again. We aim so high and we miss the mark." But that was never any reason for him to stop hunting the green hills, nor was it enough to make him stop fishing the Gulf Stream—or trying to write fiction that would have five-dimensional accuracy.

And yet—as Ernest Hemingway was no less aware than were André Malraux and Thomas Mann—the bard, the gleeman, the scop, the minstrel have always agitated and propagandized for the cardinal virtues and against the deadly vices. The great ones, however, as Mann came to realize and as Malraux seems to have been born knowing, have always gone against official policies on excellence and evil whenever in their considered opinion such policies were in conflict with the deepest, richest, and most comprehensive interests of human existence, even in the process of extolling official feats at functions of state.

Indeed, the very existence of the great epics suggests that long before constitutional provisions for freedom of the press, the ancients were aware, as contemporary totalitarians—whether of the right or the left—apparently are not, that fundamental human ideals and aspirations are best served not by routinizing the writer's subject matter and prescribing his areas of emphasis but by giving attention to the implications of his ambiguities—if only as even tyrants give ear to the wisdom of fools.

The great epics, the heroes of which always represent personal qualities that are unconventional but that are recommended for nationwide emulation, also suggest that while dissent and protest are perfectly natural and often inevitable concerns of the writer, they are still only incidental to his ultimate ceremonial function, *celebration.* For even as bards, gleemen, and scops chanted in praise of heroic achievement, were they not at the very same time updating the heroic context and the ongoing necessity for heroic endeavor?

III

When Ernest Hemingway declared that all bad writers were in love with the epic, he was not expressing disdain for epic heroism. Nor was he repudiating the epic as a fundamental category of literary expression. He was objecting to overwritten journalism and pointing out that the injection of *false* epic qualities into such writing did not transform it into literature. He was condemning pretentious elaborations and fake mysticism. Thus he was reemphasizing his preference for the clear-cut statement, or, as he puts it elsewhere, "straight honest prose on human beings."

He was also expressing once again his definitive conviction that the universal in art is achieved through the particular. What he wanted to create was a prose style that would have five dimensions, and his extraordinary artistic discipline was always geared to that aspiration. But his actual procedure was based on the assumption that the adequately informed and accurately rendered incident becomes the representative anecdote with epic as well as economic, political, and all the other implications fiction is capable of communicating. Moreover, he was equally convinced that the suggestiveness of such communication was always enhanced when certain obvious details were omitted on what he called "the principle of the iceberg"—a procedure that may not have had as much to do with the deliberate use of the device of understatement as such as with the scrupulous avoidance of overstatement.

Perhaps his practice of omitting that which, like the unseen seven eighths of the iceberg, is already implicit (and need only be suggested anyway) also accounts for his characteristic avoidance of summaries. Perhaps he assumed that details were supposed not only to speak for themselves but also add up in such a way as to make generalizations unnecessary. At any rate, he seems never to have been so much concerned with abstract definitions of literature as a fine art as with the functional requirements of the process by which raw experience is transformed into style. In articles such as "Old Newsman Writes" and "Monologue to the Maestro," in numerous interviews, and in such books as *Death in the Afternoon, Green Hills of Africa,* and *A Moveable Feast,* almost every observation he made about art was specifically and immediately applicable to his special conception of the mechanics of stylization.

Kenneth Burke has described literature as symbolic action and has defined symbolic action as "the dancing of an attitude." Hemingway might well have employed the same concept if only to insist that the writer see to it that the dance be consistent with the music of actuality. Indeed, it was for the express purpose of protecting the writer against any involvement with inauthentic choreography that Hemingway required the writer to develop a built-in shockproof stuff and nonsense detector. (Incidentally, the remarks he made in *Death in the Afternoon* about the "bedside mysticism of such a book as *Virgin Spain*" indicate that he was also alert to the fact that bad choreography only adds up to unintentional farce.)

Hemingway seems never to have consciously affiliated himself with any literary movement. The obviously ambitious and completely sincere young apprentice in *A Moveable Feast* assimilated whatever he could from Gertrude Stein, Ezra Pound, James Joyce, and every other source available to him in Paris during the 1920s; but whenever he sat down to write he seems always to have been entirely on his own. "All art," he was to contend in *Death in the Afternoon,* "is only done by the individual. The individual is all you ever have and all schools only serve to classify their members as failures." Nevertheless, the working principles he evolved in the process of coming to terms with his own individual technical problems as an artist (not unlike those that emerge from the no less personally oriented prefaces of Henry James) are as valid for other writers as for himself.

Indeed, what they add up to is a fundamental contribution to the poetics of contemporary fiction. Much if not most of the so-called Hemingway influence, however, almost always seems to be based on certain obvious aspects of his fiction itself rather than on the principles that underlie it. The principles acknowledge tradition and provide for influence, but of their very nature they preclude imitation in favor of individuality. Hemingway himself, it should be remembered, preferred to regard the Hemingway influence as "only a certain clarification of the language"; and what he had to say about imitation was entirely consistent with his misgivings about schools and movements in art. "Anybody can write like somebody else," he wrote in "Notes on Life and Letters," another of the articles he did for *Esquire*, "but it takes a long time to get to write like yourself and then what they pay off on is having something to say."

Perhaps the most fundamental Hemingway principle, and certainly a good one for any serious craftsman to begin with, is the one that requires writers to know what they really feel rather than what they are supposed to feel or have been taught to feel. This distinction, as simple and as obvious as it sounds, is extremely difficult. Nevertheless, it is indispensable to the writer who is working for an accurate projection of what really happens in action, who is trying to record the sequence of motion and fact that stimulates his emotional response to an experience and is therefore for him the essential truth of that experience.

Some writers violate the stimulus-reaction principle as a matter of course because they are committed to the objectives of social and political agitation and propaganda. Such writers almost always manipulate stimulus-response patterns to present a specific case for a given sociopolitical program. Thus if they are engaged in promoting racial integration in the United States, for example, they systematically reduce stimulus-response sequences to oppressor-oppressed formulas and deliberately overemphasize all effects in terms of victimization in order to show the inhumanity of segregation. Sometimes such writers become so overzealous in the interest of a cause that they actually change virtues into shortcomings in order to blame them on oppression. On the other hand, writers defending segregation manipulate the stimulus-response pattern to show how "existing" shortcomings (regardless of what caused them) make some Americans unfit for integration. In order to prove that so-called blacks are unqualified to exercise their inherent rights as native citizens, these writers show that they are incapable of making the "normal" response to "normal" stimuli. But then, many pro–civil rights writers also present the stimulus-response pattern as abnormal, in order to promote the need for rehabilitation programs!

Writers who become overimpressed with research data from the behavioral sciences almost always seem to assume that they already know what normal stimulus-response patterns are. They seem to have convinced themselves that there is a scientific key to human conduct and that this key will enable them to write more accurate fiction based on more reliable information about human nature. What they forget, however, is that categories and formulations do not necessarily add up to dependable information and more precise insights. Somehow or other they also seem to overlook the fact that the description of stimulus and response in the novels of Henry James, Edith Wharton, and Joseph Conrad remain for the most part valid, while hardly any scientific treatise on the nature of human nature and conduct written during the same period can be read today without fundamental reservations. Not only is this the case, but the scientist himself would be the first to insist on such reservations—in light of his subsequent "findings." It was never necessary for Thomas Mann to revise

Buddenbrooks, for example, but Sigmund Freud was forever revising and supplementing basic assumptions underlying earlier "findings."

Indeed, it is precisely that fiction that is based most directly on scientific "information" about human nature that seems to date or "go bad afterward" most rapidly. Perhaps one reason for this is the fact that such information is always based on some assumed absolute, whereas any practical approach to human nature should probably be relative. Writers who forget this also seem to forget this even more crucial fact: As necessary and as natural as scientific procedure is, and as indispensable as scientific information is, so far as the creative process is concerned such information is only raw material for the imagination—real toads for Miss Marianne Moore's imaginary garden, as it were.

On the other hand, those writers whose primary discipline is literature are also aware of still another fundamental fact: Science, no matter how richly human or even humanitarian its ultimate goals, *dehumanizes* experience in the very process of coming to terms with it. Whereas literature, by direct contrast, always humanizes or dramatizes experiences. Literature is always concerned with how things feel to the human being. Such, as a matter of fact, is an objective of all art. "A work of art," writes Suzanne K. Langer, "expresses a conception of life, emotion, inward reality. But it is neither confessional nor a frozen tantrum; it is a developed metaphor, a nondiscursive symbol that articulates what is verbally ineffable—the logic of consciousness itself."

Thus when Hemingway begins with the problem of knowing and describing what one really feels, he is concerning himself with the most fundamental of all literary requirements. And when he renders the beads of sweat on a cold pitcher of beer in a darkened room in Valencia, or the shooting of six cabinet ministers in a rain-puddled courtyard in the early morning, or the dust rising and powdering the leaves of trees as the troops march by a house in a village that looks across the river and the plains to the mountains, he is proceeding on the firm, even if unstated, assumption that what he is writing is art to the extent that it communicates the essence of subjective experience.

There is, for whatever the juxtaposition may be worth, no essential difference at all between Suzanne Langer's definition of art in *Problems of Art* and what Hemingway had already said about the nature of literature some twenty-two years earlier in "Old Newsman Writes." Hemingway's observations were written for *Esquire* magazine. Miss Langer's were originally part of a series of lectures dealing with the pivotal concepts in the philosophy of art. "A work of art," she stated, "is an expressive form created for our perception through sense or imagination, and what it expresses is human feeling."

She then went on to point out that feeling as she uses it includes "everything that can be felt, from physical pain and comfort, excitement and repose, to the most complex emotions, intellectual tensions, or the steady feeling-tones of a conscious human life." What Hemingway had already told *Esquire* readers was a pivotal concept in the philosophy of the art of fiction. "All good books," he wrote, "are alike in that they are truer than if they had really happened," and after one finished reading one, "you will feel that all that happened to you and afterward it all belongs to you; the good and the bad, the ecstasy, the remorse and sorrow, the people and the places and how the weather was. If you can get so you can give that to people, then you are a writer."

Thus did he reveal the roles of his poetics. Thus did he state his functional definition of literature; and if its relationship to the prefaces of Henry James seems far-fetched, its affinities with Joseph Conrad, for whose resurrection Hemingway once declared his willingness to make sacrifice of a ground and powdered T. S. Eliot, does not. Moreover, Conrad is perhaps the best possible evidence that Hemingway's principles do not restrict other writers to Hemingway's personal style.

"My task which I am trying to achieve," wrote Conrad some

two years before Hemingway was born, "is by the power of the written word to make you hear, to make you feel—it is above all to make you see. That and no more, and that is everything. If I succeed, you shall find there according to your deserts: encouragement, consolation, fear, charm—all you demand—and, perhaps, also that glimpse of truth for which you have forgotten to ask."

Another Hemingway working principle, closely related to the first, applies to the material the writer uses. It requires the writer to utilize the things he is really involved with and knows and cares about. "Books," he said, "should be about the people you know, that you love and hate, not about the people you study up about." Nor should the serious writer ever be misled about what a book should be because of what is currently in fashion.

Hemingway was convinced that the writer who develops sufficient insight into his own firsthand experience and achieves sufficient accuracy in describing it can create stories about it that will represent the whole of human experience. By this he did not in any way imply that the writer should limit himself to the knowledge at hand or even to the knowledge of the experience at hand. Nobody ever knew any better than he that the writer has to learn to see the world as a whole before he can make his part represent that whole; but he always warned the writer not to show off his knowledge as such, and even insisted that the writer could leave out things precisely because he knew enough about them.

Perhaps some writers violate the principle of materials selection simply because they are overambitious, or perhaps they just simply do not know their own limitations. Many, however, are guilty of the fallacy of subject matter significance. These assume that some things are inherently more significant than others. As a matter of fact, some things obviously are, but, as matter for fiction, the importance or significance of things, places, events, and people depends on the quality of the writing. Most people would probably concede that coronations and presidential inaugurations are more important events than the crowning of a homecoming queen or the installation of a president of a campus fraternity. Nevertheless, an incompetent writer can turn an insignificant story even about suicide, while a good writer can create a masterpiece about a bauble. The blisses of the commonplace no more nor less than the thunder of peasants in revolt become exciting or dull depending upon the writer's insight, his sensibility, and his craft.

But perhaps along with its other misconceptions the subject matter significance fallacy confuses subject matter and theme at the very outset. On the other hand, the primary application of Hemingway's principle of selection is not to theme but to raw material. In this connection, Hemingway's basic assumption is that whatever his theme, the writer will have a better chance of realizing it if he works with the raw material he has a real feeling for and with which he is intimately familiar.

The writer works in terms of his raw material. That is to say, whatever his story is, he creates it out of or in the terms of some experience that presumably interests him, just as the painter composes his pictures in the terms of that which becomes his model, as it were, whether that model be a person, countryside, or skyline, an event or some trifling object that strikes his fancy. Georges Braque, for example, was forever painting still lifes that included tables and bottles. Matisse painted odalisques for years on end, and at one time Picasso painted picture after picture that included a musical instrument, while during another period there were sea urchins in almost every picture, and so on. Hemingway, as has been noted, frequently worked in terms of sports. There has always been a great deal of misunderstanding among some critics about the fact that he also worked in terms of war experience; but nothing seems to have caused more pretentious confusion than his use of raw material from sporting activities. This has even caused some to express doubts about his sincerity and among most Marx-Freud intellectuals the official word seems to be that he is not only frivolous but also unadult.

And yet it is all but impossible to imagine any of these same critics and intellectuals questioning the fact that Goya used the raw materials of war and bullfighting. Nor do they reject Degas for all his dancing girls or Toulouse-Lautrec because he haunted nightspots, whorehouses, and sporting events and used such material in his pictures. Serious writers should be able to see the snobbishness of superficial critics and shortcut intellectuals for what it really is, and should also realize that such superficiality in matters of art also betrays something else: Many intellectuals do not really know very much about just plain ordinary everyday life in the first place. And besides, it is seldom those who belong to the intellectual establishment who are forever protesting their commitment to the high-minded, the classy, the dignified, profound, and educational anyway. It is almost always the newcomer, the ambitious peasant, the pretentious son of a shopkeeper, the status seeker who learned or read or heard about it all in books at school.

Certainly no writer who has even the slightest contact with, or appreciation for, brownskin folks from down home can afford to allow himself to be misled by "intellectuals" whose own first-hand experience outside the world of books is so limited that they are unaware of the fundamental importance of sports in human society. Indeed, Hemingway's lifelong involvement in sports is in itself a good enough reason for so-called black writers to take him seriously, what with all the raw material all around them. Perhaps through Hemingway they will someday come to realize that their traditional involvement with figures such as Jack Johnson, Joe Gans, Sam Langford, Sugar Ray Robinson, Jesse Owens, Jackie

Robinson, Willie Mays, Jimmy Brown, and Michael Jordan, with hunting and fishing and so on, has as much literary significance as anything else has.

Moreover, those who still insist that the subject matter or raw material itself must have profound philosophical implications to begin with, have only to realize that in spite of the three hundred years in which so-called black Americans have been the victims of human slavery, oppression, and unrelenting foul play, the so-called black athlete has displayed a sense of fair play and has achieved a reputation for sportsmanship that will stand beside that of any gentleman to the manner or manor born. Intellectuals will look long and hard before they find a more compelling manifestation of the transcendent dignity and nobility of man than that.

Still another fundamental working principle is involved when Hemingway maintains that fictional experience is not described but is made up. This does not contradict his requirement for descriptive accuracy. A story is invented, created, not recorded or simply reported. The writer makes it up, *but he must make it up the way things actually happen in life.* In other words, gardens in fiction are as imaginary as they are in Marianne Moore's poetry, but the toads that inhabit them must be every bit as believable as she required her metaphorical toads to be.

Nor did Hemingway ever confuse the writer's quest for the fable in the flesh with the detection and revelation of some traditional figure already existing beneath the surface obscurity of the carpet of human experience. The fable, he seems to have known from the very beginning, is that which the writer himself fabricates out of his sense of flesh-and-blood actuality. It is not something that the writer is supposed to find because he has been taught it is there. It is that which he makes of what he really and truly does find. The act of fiction is an art of configuration.

"If it was reporting," Hemingway wrote in "Monologue to the Maestro," "they would not remember it. When you describe something that has happened that day the timeliness makes people see it in their own imaginations. A month later that element of time is gone and your account would be flat and they would not see it in their minds or remember it. But if you make it up instead of describe it you can make it round and whole and solid and give it life. You create it for good or bad. It is made, not described."

Sometimes he referred to it as inventing from knowledge. "If a man is making a story up," he said also in "Monologue to the Maestro," "it will be true in proportion to the amount of knowledge of life that he has and how conscientious he is; so that when he makes something up it is as it would truly be. If he doesn't know how many people work in their minds and actions his luck may save him for a while, or he may write fantasy. But if he continues to write about what he does not know about he will find himself faking. After he fakes a few times he cannot write honestly anymore."

When "the maestro" wanted to know how the imagination fitted into the creative process, Hemingway told him that nobody knows anything about it except that it is what one gets for nothing. "It is the one thing besides honesty that a good writer must have," he went on. "The more he learns from experience the more truly he can imagine; if he gets so he can imagine truly enough people will think that the things he relates all really happened and that he is just reporting."

Perhaps blues-oriented writers will relate some of Hemingway's other notions about the process of literary creation to what they themselves have already learned about the improvisation from musicians. It should be easy enough for them to see a practical connection between what Hemingway once said about making up stories and what Duke Ellington, for instance, does when he begins a phrase or two and ends up with *C-Jam Blues* or *Mainstem*. Referring to *The Old Man and the Sea*, Hemingway told

Robert Manning, "I knew two or three things about the situation but I didn't know the story. . . . I didn't even know if that fish was going to bite for the old man when it started smelling around the bait. I had to write on inventing out of knowledge." He rejected everything that was not or could not be completely true. "I didn't know what was going to happen for sure in *For Whom the Bell Tolls* or *Farewell to Arms.* I was inventing."

In the 1958 interview for the *Paris Review* series on the art of fiction, Hemingway reiterated and expanded some of the notions he had expressed in "Monologue to the Maestro" in 1935. When George Plimpton asked about changes in conception, theme, plot, and character, Hemingway replied, "Sometimes you know the story. Sometimes you make it up as you go along and have no idea how it will come out. Everything changes as it moves. That is what makes the movement which makes the story. Sometimes the movement is so slow it does not seem to be moving. But there is always change and always movement."

And then at the end of the interview, when Plimpton asked him why the creative writer was concerned with representation of fact rather than fact itself, Hemingway echoed "Old Newsman Writes" as well as "Monologue to the Maestro." "Why be puzzled by that?" he began. "From things that have happened and from things as they exist and from all things that you know and all those you cannot know, you make something through your invention that is not a representation but a whole new thing truer than anything true and alive and you make it alive. That is why you write and for no other reason that you know of." And then he concluded as if winking at the whole thing, "But what about all the reasons that no one knows?"

Unlike William Faulkner, who frequently wrote about racial interrelationship, Ernest Hemingway for the most part seems to have concerned himself with Negroes as subject matter even in

Green Hills of Africa, only in passing, so to speak. Also, whereas Faulkner, who was always deliberately and sometimes fiercely southern, worked with raw material that involved the so-called black people of his immediate region of the United States, Hemingway, as one hardly needs to point out, wrote about Africans of various tribes and nations and Cuban Negroes as well as U.S. "black" people both northern and southern. He was never any less vernacular for being as cosmopolitan as he was, however, and U.S. "black" writers will find his work, whatever its raw material, no less relevant than that of Faulkner to the fundamental problems involved in the forging of Americans and the making of American literature.

Sometimes Faulkner wrote as if he were really an ambivalent self-searching Mississippi mulatto who was officially "white" because he grew up in the home of his "white" relatives but who always either knew or had reason to believe that he was kith and kin to some of the Negroes around him—some of whom had fundamental human qualities that he not only admired but found largely missing in many of the white people he knew. His intimacy with his "black mammy" and the Negro playmates of his childhood seems to have been far too complex for him to refer to himself as an honorary Negro, as Kenneth Tynan reports that Hemingway did one night in a bar in Havana, but although he often wrote as if he regarded himself as being an honorary confederate colonel, he also wrote as if he had been as much influenced by his listening to some Mississippi Uncle Remus lying and signifying as by what he had learned from books and from listening to the planters and lawyers and businessmen and rednecks in the mansions, in the courthouse square, and at the crossroads stores.

It was Ernest Hemingway the Midwesterner-become-cosmopolitan, however, not William Faulkner the race-oriented Mississippian, who wrote fiction that always expresses essentially the same fundamental sense of life as that which underlies the spirit of the blues. Hemingway, needless to say, did not write in terms of the blues, but what he wrote was the literary equivalent to blues music. Much of what Faulkner wrote not only includes blues idiom, wit, and wisdom; in some instances it also appears to be conscious extensions of Negro folklore. But as richly interwoven with Negro idiom as his highly distinctive rhetoric so frequently is, and as close to the feeling of some Negro spirituals as he comes from time to time, the fundamental sense of life that his fiction represents is always more closely related to the conventional Greco-Roman tradition of tragedy, comedy, and farce—of destiny, the fateful curse, doom, of honor, hubris, and outrage than to the blues tradition of pragmatic American existentialism.

Hemingway, for all his honorary Negrohood, wrote far more about Spanish bullfighters than about "black" U.S. athletes and next to nothing about "black" U.S. musicians. Nevertheless, not only was his sense of actuality closer to the blues tradition than to anything in Spain (except Goya, perhaps), his celebrated prose style, which has direct historical connections with Kansas City, also has astonishing even if incidental similarities to—and aesthetic affinities with—the instrumental blues style of the Kansas City jazz musicians.

The simple, direct, concrete declarative statements that are so characteristic of Hemingway's essentially coordinate prose style create a descriptive and narrative pace and precision, the affirmative effect of which is actually comparable to that created by the steady but infinitely elastic and inclusive 4/4 rhythm of the now classic Kansas City blues score. There is no one-to-one relationship between music and prose composition, to be sure; and in this instance far more significant than any question of direct influence, whether through derivation, imitation, or even adaption, is the implied affinity of sensibilities.

Whatever the reason, which could have as much to do with being midwestern as with anything else, it was as if the editors under whom Hemingway worked as an apprentice on the *Kansas*

City Star and the Kansas City Negro bandleaders, arrangers, and sidemen somehow or other represented two different aspects of the same fundamental orientation toward communication. Had young Count Basie, for instance, gone to work as a reporter for the *Star,* he would have found that its style sheet for prose writers was in complete agreement with his own basic conception of making statements on the piano. "Use short sentences," the very first rule ran. "Use short first paragraphs. Use vigorous English. Be positive, not negative."

Perhaps it is enough to say that by the 1930s Kansas City musicians had evolved a style of blues orchestration that was grounded on principles of brevity, vigor, and positive accentuation equivalent to those that Hemingway had picked up at the *Kansas City Star* in 1917; and that Kansas City sidemen such as Lester Young, Jo Jones, and Buck Clayton were if anything even more scrupulous about clichés, about being florid on the one hand or becoming mechanical on the other, than were the editors of the *Star;* and that, in any case, the fiction of Ernest Hemingway, by the very nature of its emotional authenticity, its stylized precision, its flesh-and-blood concreteness, and the somehow relaxed intensity of its immediacy, qualifies not only as the blues but as classic Kansas City blues.

So much having been implied, however, perhaps it is also permissible to add (if only to provoke those with overprecious literary taste) that the resemblance between Hemingway and a Kansas City musician such as Count Basie (who, incidentally, like the well-known man of letters Edmund Wilson was born in Red Bank, New Jersey) becomes more striking and suggestive on closer juxtaposition. Not only do both work primarily with blues material, which they usually turn into solidly pulsating no-nonsense celebrations of human existence in all its complexity, both also have a clean-cut surface simplicity that belies the multiple dimensions beneath and that actually seems more casual or natural than slice-of-life realism. Both are also lyric, but neither is given to oversentimentality and neither can tolerate elaborate structural embellishments. Indeed, the traditional Basie method of blues orchestration and the Hemingway system of omitting known details on what he referred to as the principle of the iceberg are one and the same, nor is that all: Count Basie's piano solo riffs, which are his instantly recognized trademark, resemble nothing in the world any more than they do the neatly stripped precision of a typical Hemingway passage of quoted dialogue.

And, incidentally, even more obvious in his dialogue sequences than elsewhere is the Hemingway equivalent to the Kansas City riff. In all probability, Hemingway actually derived his technique of repeating key words and phrases from the early experiments of Gertrude Stein, but what he achieved in the process of assimilating and refining (also influenced by Ring Lardner) was a very special rhetorical device not only for stating and repeating themes but also for playing and improvising on and around them as a Kansas City musician might do.

Thomas Mann sometimes spoke of themes in his fiction in terms of a "dialectic orchestration" that was based on the principles of sonata composition, and sometimes he also employed a prose version of the Wagnerian leitmotif. Similarly, Hemingway, who frequently spoke about what he had learned about writing description from his visits to art museums, also on at least two occasions spoke of his deliberate use of musical technique. "I should think," he said in his *Paris Review* interview, "what one learns from composers and from the study of harmony and counterpoint would be obvious." And elsewhere he told Lillian Ross of *The New Yorker* that he had used the word "and" consciously over and over in the first paragraphs of *A Farewell to Arms* "the way Mr. Johann Sebastian Bach used a note in music when he was emitting counterpoint."

But even as the reference to Bach is in itself somewhat more like jazz than like German, so perhaps is Hemingway's actual use of musical forms. Moreover, in spite of the traditional U.S. provincial overemphasis on European taste in U.S. music programs, Hemingway's ear, like that of most other U.S. writers, including Henry James, was more indigenously American than impressively classical. His fine literary ear for the music in the Spanish language, for instance, was obviously more American than Iberian. What he heard in Spain was almost always translated into comprehensive American in *For Whom the Bell Tolls* as Italian was translated in *A Farewell to Arms* and *Across the River and into the Trees*. At any rate, when Jake Barnes and others in *The Sun Also Rises* repeat words such as enjoy, joke, utilize, fiesta, irony, and pity, to name only a few, they actually play conversational riffs with them; and when Jake as narrator states, repeats, and rhymes hot with bright with sharply white in the same paragraph near the very end of the book, he plays nonconversational riffs. The narrator of *Death in the Afternoon* (Hemingway himself) organizes the entire final chapter or outchorus sequence of that book on a series of riffs. He begins with, "If I could have made this enough of a book," and improvises for seventeen paragraphs, playing with should have, would have, could have, should, would, could, if it were more of a book it would have, among others, such as "There is nothing in this book about . . . nor does it tell." Then he ends with "no, it is not enough of a book, but still there were a few things to be said. There were a few practical things to be said."

IV

Many intellectuals reject the image of man that the fiction of Ernest Hemingway represents. Some flatly dismiss the typical Hemingway hero as an inauthentic projection of little more than boyhood fantasy. Others, who accuse him of operating within a system of values so codelike that it amounts to a cult, insist that his involvements are so extremely circumscribed that his fiction has very little connection with the ordinary everyday obligations of human society, that he is not a hero but a zero.

A typical expression of this point of view is an article that Delmore Schwartz, a very intellectual New York poet, wrote for *The Southern Review* following the publication of *To Have and Have Not*. "There is a definite code," Schwartz declares, "by which characters are judged and by which they judge each other and which often produces the basis of the conversation. It is important to recognize that the code is relevant, and only relevant, to a definite period of time and to a special region of society. Courage, honesty, and skill are important rules of the code, but it is these human attributes as determined by a specific historical context. To be admirable, from the standpoint of this morality, is to admit defeat, to be a good sportsman, to accept pain without outcry, to adhere strictly to the rules of the game, and to play the game with great skill. To be repugnant and contemptible is to violate any of these requirements. It is a sportsmanlike morality, or equally, the morality of sportsmanship. It extends its requirements into the region of manners and carriage, and one must speak in clipped tones, avoid pretentious phrases, condense emotions into a few expletives or deliberately suppress it—noble, to borrow a pun from William Carlos Williams, equals no bull."

Several pages later Schwartz assesses *To Have and Have Not* as "a stupid and foolish book, a disgrace to a good writer, a book which should never have been printed." His own article, however, can hardly be regarded as a credit to a responsible intellectual. Hemingway's fiction has absolutely nothing to do with *requiring* people to speak in clipped tones or to condense emotion into a few expletives; not even the specific guidelines that he suggested to other writers make any such requirements, and of course nobody actually recommends pretentious phrases. Hemingway, it is true, did write about a world that requires heroic action. It may be said to be a world of tragic and epic action. But nowhere has it ever been reduced to any definite code by which characters are judged and by which they judge each other. It would be not only irresponsible but downright ridiculous to imply that Nick Adams, for instance, who figures in a number of Hemingway's most important short stories, is being initiated into a cult that is based on the belief that life is a game to be played by the rules of the sportsman or that Hemingway seeks to give the impression that Nick will be among the blessed if he can only master some "definite code" of conduct.

Wouldn't it be far more accurate to say that Nick's various initiations have to do with the fact that Hemingway seems convinced that life is extremely complex for everybody, initiated or not, that things are never necessarily as they seem, and that the best equipment is none too good? Can even the most casual reader of *A Farewell to Arms* seriously contend that the disastrous outcome of that story was in any way related to the fact that the hero and/or heroine did not measure up to some definite code?

Nevertheless, Schwartz, whose misreadings of Hemingway may have often been equaled but have seldom been surpassed, persists. "Examples," he asserts, "are in fact, too plentiful. Cohen [*sic!*] in *The Sun Also Rises* is a prime example of one character who violates the code again and again. He does not play the game, he discusses his emotions at great length, he does not admit defeat with the lady whom he loves, and when he is hurt, he lets everyone know about it. Thus he must be one of the damned." Nonsense. Almost everybody else in the book may be damned, but Robert Cohn's main problem is that he is a bloody bore.

None of Hemingway's critics ever suggest any reasons why anybody should be expected to put up with Cohn's eternal whining about his personal affairs—least of all why, given his own disabilities, Jake Barnes should. And yet Jake is Cohn's most patient friend. There is something to be said for that; and there is also something to be said for the fact that Jake, who has far greater personal troubles than Cohn, never burdens his friends with them. What can anybody do to help Jake? On the other hand, there is very little evidence that Cohn ever really is considerate of anybody but himself.

It is extremely difficult to believe that anybody prefers, accepts, or willingly endures people who are repugnant, contemptible, and unsportsmanlike, who have no courage, honesty or skill, and who complain all the time and try to evade the responsibility for everything. And yet young Saul Bellow, for example, did seem to be recommending the point of view expressed by the central figure of his early novel *Dangling Man*. Bellow's hero could hardly be referring to anybody other than Hemingway in the following statement from the opening section of that book: "Today, the code of the athlete, of the tough boy—an American inheritance, I believe, from the English gentleman—that curious mixture of striving, asceticism, and vigor, the origins of which some trace back to Alexander the Great—is stronger than ever. Do you have feelings? There are correct and incorrect ways of indicating them. Do you have an inner life? It is nobody's business but your own. Do you have emotions? Strangle them. To a degree, everybody obeys this code. And it does admit of a limited kind of candor, a closemouthed straightforwardness. But for the truest candor, it has an inhibiting effect. Most serious matters are closed to the hard-boiled. They are unpracticed in introspection, and therefore badly equipped to deal with opponents whom they cannot shoot like big game or outdo in daring.

"If you have difficulties, grapple with them silently, goes one of their commandments. To hell with that. I intend to talk about mine, and if I had as many mouths as Siva has arms and kept them going all the time, I still could not do myself justice."

The dangling man refuses to feel that any of this represents self-indulgence. Nor does he seem to mind in the least that he may be imposing all of it on other people without so much as a by your leave, as it were. He proceeds as if he has an inalienable right to do so, never even pausing to ask himself why the hell anybody else should give one good goddamn about what happens to him. The dangler seems to be satisfied with the case he makes, and perhaps he is also satisfied with his compensations. But let him look to his manners, since (as Thomas Mann demonstrates so well in *Joseph and His Brothers*) it is not only the sheerest folly but sometimes downright dangerous to expect other people to love you more than they love themselves, there *are* correct and incorrect ways of indicating your feelings. There are wise and there are foolhardy ways of doing so. Etiquette, after all, goes far beyond being nice because it is pretty. It is always a matter of refined self-interest, even at the table. There is such a thing as altruism, to be sure, but nobody has the right to *demand* it of anybody else.

The dangling man makes much of the fact that he is keeping a journal; and he is forever talking about the blue ribbon books he is reading, and he engages in deliberately profound postgraduate debates with himself. Most serious matters, he scoffs, are closed to the hard-boiled who, he contends, are unpracticed in introspection. But what he overhastily overshoots is the very real possibility that the closemouthed may well be much more given to introspection than the blabbermouth. And furthermore, his journal does not back up his claim to superiority. What his essentially academic notes reveal about his dangling life is not more introspective than what one gets from Jake Barnes or Frederick Henry. The dangler may be considerably more bookish and theoretical about himself and life in Chicago. But Jake and Frederick exercise infinitely more poetic sensitivity in dealing with themselves and life in France and Spain and wartime Italy. *The Sun Also Rises* and *A Farewell to Arms* being first-person narratives qualify as introspective journals, too. Moreover, not only are they memoirs and confessions by virtue of the specific stylistic convention employed, but also Hemingway made every effort to keep the tone and imagery consistent with the narrators' sensibilities. Indeed, in each case the rhetoric is a significant part of the first-person hero's characterization.

The facts just simply do not support those intellectuals who charge Hemingway with being preoccupied with the hard-boiled nonreflective hero anyway. Nick Adams is definitely not hard-boiled by any standards—except, of course, those of bookworms and incurable cowards (and there are such people), but they hardly count in such matters. Nick is constantly being hurt, shocked, scandalized, and even numbed by what he has to undergo and witness. His response to experience is not at all that of the tough guy, but of someone of delicate sensitivity and poetic imagination. As much as he represents anything else, and as much as it has been ignored, Nick is Ernest Hemingway's portrait of the artist as a very sensitive young man; nor does this separate him from Jake, Frederick, or Robert Jordan.

It is not really accurate to describe any of Hemingway's protagonists as hard-boiled, except Harry Morgan in *To Have and Have Not*. Perhaps Harry, the writer in "The Snows of Kilimanjaro," does come close. He is dying of gangrene, and feels that he has compromised his talent, is undeniably hard, bitter, and cruel. But even so, the flashbacks show him to be far too much involved with loneliness and introspection and far too concerned about the nuances of literary expression to qualify as hard-boiled. As a matter of fact, it is extremely difficult for any of Hemingway's writer-characters to qualify. As for Hemingway himself, what's a big fat tough guy doing carrying on like that about landscapes and architecture and paintings and fine food and vintage wines and all, in *Death in the Afternoon* and *Green Hills of Africa?* And as if that were not enough, what's he doing honing his phrases like that?

As for Harry Morgan, the smuggler in *To Have and Have Not*, as rugged as he is, there is much more to be said for him as an example of Hemingway's descriptive consistency than offended intellectuals can use against him as a member of the cult of the hard-boiled. To begin with, he has to be tough in the line of work he has been forced into—and as things turn out, he is not actually tough enough! And he is not a typical Hemingway hero anyway. It is easy enough to imagine Nick Adams becoming Frederick Henry, Jake Barnes Robert Jordan, and even Harry the writer, but not Harry Morgan. There is perhaps still much of Nick in beat-up old Colonel Richard Cantwell in *Across the River and into the Trees*, but hardly any in Harry Morgan, although Nick would have been happy to be his friend and go fishing with him and would have been fascinated by his practical skill, his ruggedness, and his courage, and would never have made the mistake that Richard Gordon, the writer of the left-wing intellectual novels, made about Harry's wife, Marie.

It would be perfectly natural for Nick Adams to go to Spain to see the bullfights and the great art museums and write *Death in the Afternoon*. He would like the Spanish people not because they were hard-boiled (because they're not) but because they have great dignity and style in the face of death and are serious about life, but not sad and not cold, and liking them, he would become a sincere student of their language and literature. He would celebrate their food and wine and the national glories of their country because he always was lyrical about things like that. Given the chance, the boy from *Big Two-Hearted River* would also go on safari (although hysterically afraid of snakes) and write *Green Hills of Africa*. He could not possibly regard the bullfight and big-game hunting as preoccupations that preclude introspection and intellectual seriousness because *Death in the Afternoon* and *Green Hills of Africa* are as intellectual and even scholarly as they are anything else.

But then Nick the writer (not unlike Flaubert, Henry James, Proust, and Joyce) would rather be identified as a novelist than as an intellectual anyway. And as for that special breed of self-righteous intellectual whose humanity somehow aligns them with the Miura bull against the man, and who complain because the fish can't hook fishermen and the wild animals can't shoot back at the huntsman, an essentially nice fellow like Nick would brush questions of their insanity aside and simply regard them as library tough guys whose strong-arm tactics are probably mostly verbal.

For his own part, Nick would not hesitate to claim that hunting, fishing, and his interest in the bullfights not only enhance his life and his feeling for life but also his feeling for fiction—and could always point to stories like "The Undefeated," "Now I Lay Me," and "The Short Happy Life of Francis Macomber" to prove it. Nick Adams may or may not have dictated "Remembering Shooting-Flying" to Ernest Hemingway. Either could have written the following passage: "When you have loved three things all your life, from the earliest you can remember, to fish, to shoot, and, later, to read; and when, all your life, the necessity to write has been your master, you learn to remember and, when you think back you remember more fishing and shooting and reading than anything else and that is a pleasure."

But finally, in all the intellectual epithet-slinging and chicken-house forensics, the most specific and perhaps the most significant statement Hemingway himself ever permitted any of his characters to make on the subject of being hard-boiled never seems to get mentioned—not even in passing. The nada passages from *A Clean, Well-Lighted Place* and the insomniac theme in "Now I Lay Me" are often referred to (and usually misinterpreted as the obverse side of the "cult of sensation"). But nobody ever seems to remember what Jake Barnes says about his own conduct in *The Sun Also Rises*. Jake does not go around begging for sympathy, like Robert Cohn, but sometimes lies awake at night thinking about himself and CRIES (!): "It is awfully easy to be hard-boiled about everything in the daytime," he says, "but at night it is another thing."

Even Malcolm Cowley, one of the first intellectuals to regard Hemingway as a haunted and nocturnal writer in the tradition of Poe, Hawthorne, and Melville, seems either to have overlooked

or, worse still, underestimated the significance of Jake's self-reve-
lation. But Cowley's oversight notwithstanding, no statement or
gesture in any of Hemingway's fiction (or nonfiction) seems more
indicative of Hemingway's own sensibilities or is a more fundamental clue to the conduct of any of his characters, rugged, tender, or insomniac. In one statement, Jake, who knows what
bullfighters are like without their costumes, reveals the all-too-
human knight without his shining armor and in so doing defines
the essential nature of Hemingway's conception of heroic action.
The Hemingway hero is not as hard as nails and fearless. He is a
man who can pull himself together and press on (through the
night as well as the daylight) in spite, or even because of, his fears
and weaknesses.

Jake, who also knows that the sun will rise again and again
and assumes the earth will abide with or without him, has already
accepted the dreadful conditions of his existence. He does not
submit to them, however. Nor does he simply struggle with them.
It is not for nothing that he admires the bullfighter's grace and
dignity. He makes the most of his restrictions. And in the process,
as Hemingway makes very clear, he goes beyond them. Jake the
cripple is a more admirable man and certainly a far less anxious
one than Robert Cohn, who, when he is not wailing about his bad
luck, uses his excellent if somewhat bull-like physical endow-
ments as if a man can be more powerful than a dragon—as if
might makes right after all.

Perhaps in spite of themselves, some intellectuals are frequently more interested in substantiating their own theories than
in coming to terms with actuality. If so—and the evidence that
Thurman Arnold offers in *Symbols of Government* and *The Folklore of
Capitalism* is as sobering as it is convincing—then many will go
right on accusing Hemingway of being head shaman of a cult of
hard-boiled primitivism and zeroism. But even the most zealous
defenders of the pieties of civilization against the forces of re-
gression will be hard put to find any truly viable textual evidence

to prove that Ernest Hemingway ever preferred the charges of a nine-hundred-pound Miura bull to the capework, the footwork, and the calmly and exquisitely executed faenas of an always vulnerable but seldom desperate man!

Many who agree with Malcolm Cowley's contention that Hemingway was a haunted and nocturnal writer whose images are symbols of an interior world do so apparently because they are already convinced that the interior world involved is itself the inherent source of the code of hard-boiled conduct they find so utterly deplorable. They almost always describe it as a world devoid of intellectual and spiritual insight and purpose and therefore doomed to an endless round of pointless violence relieved only by equally endless and pointless rounds of physical self-indulgence. In other words, they concede that Hemingway was haunted and then either state or smugly imply that his nightmare only reflects his own personal limitations. This puts all self-dedicated intellectuals one up on Ernest Hemingway for cocktail party purposes, of course, but the validity of the Hemingway image of life remains inseparable from the undeniable impact his fiction has always had on most readers, even the outright hostile ones.

There are also intellectuals who regard Hemingway as a writer whose images are symbols of man as victim, as if the people in his fiction have already been maimed by world-withering dragon flames and now numbly subsist in a nightmarelike domain of ruins imprisoned by an invincible reign of dragon terror. Those who focus from this point of view emphasize the prevalence of violence in all his work. They elaborate the implications of Jake's wound, Frederick's star-crossed romance, the "casual" brutality and perversion surrounding Nick Adams, and so on. They generalize, usually in terms Marxian, Freudian, or Spenglerian, about the oppressive condition of man "in our times" and the absence of human values in the modern world; and then somehow or other they, too, seem to blame it all on Hemingway's own shortcomings.

Even those who praise him for his reportorial objectivity and accuracy seem compelled to accuse Hemingway of a fundamental failure of sensibility. Indeed, many intellectuals, including those who acknowledge the fact that his style represents a highly sophisticated literary achievement, seem to have convinced themselves that his fiction is inadequate because his ideas are not as complex and as significant as their own. They express condescending opinions time and again about his "preoccupation" with violence and physical sensation, as if there would actually be less violence to be involved in (or to be haunted about) and less need for the gratification of physical appetite if only his intellectual interests were more elevated and more comprehensive!

What with all the gory deeds in Homer, Aeschylus, Sophocles, Euripides, Virgil, Dante, and Shakespeare and all the blood-stained pages in the *Charterhouse of Parma*, *The Brothers Karamazov*, *War and Peace*, *Great Expectations*, *Sentimental Education*, and *Moby-Dick*, one can only question the sincerity of anybody who implies in any way that peril, violence, and ruin are abnormal and even extraordinary preoccupations for literature. It would seem that anybody with even a minimum familiarity with epics and fairy tales would know better than that; and yet it is precisely the implication (or even insinuation) most intellectuals make when they encounter such things in the fiction of Ernest Hemingway.

But, except when matters involve so-called black Americans of course, at no time do U.S. intellectuals become more confused about fundamentals or more ensnarled in pretension and nonsense than when they express their reactions to the relish with which Hemingway wrote about "the pleasures of sensual experience." Intellectuals who normally insist on the keenest appreciation of the most subtle nuances in works of art somehow or other suddenly find it highly questionable that Hemingway created characters who can enjoy the firsthand experience of natural phenomena and life itself. Some accuse him outright of being insensitive to higher cultural values and of reducing human life to the aboriginal level of animal-like gratification of physical appetite. Others regard him as decadent and consider his enthusiasm for the sensual as a clear-cut manifestation of his pathological condition. His involvement with actual things and people, for them, strangely enough, becomes an escape from reality—a sinking into nature, a desperate compensation for something else. They never indicate what else.

Even the most intramural of anti-Hemingway intellectuals must know that savoring vintage wines and delicately blended foods has nothing at all to do with primitive behavior and is indeed the very opposite of desperation. Hemingway's heroes do not slake their thirst at any and every pond, nor do they tear at their food with murderous claws, and nothing could be more contrary to desperation than the way they hunt and fish. Contemporary American literary intellectuals, no matter how conditioned by Marx-Freud clichés, surely must realize that the terrain, the waters, the vegetation, and other life forms of the earth, in addition to the sustenance they provide, can also give delight that is sufficient unto itself simply by being there—and that sexual bliss is at least as worthy of celebration as political concepts, scientific discoveries, or a Bach fugue, and no less relevant to the well-being of mankind. And yet it is not at all uncommon for intellectuals who reject Hemingway to imply that there are human involvements, values, and benefits for which these things are only desperate substitutes!

When these same intellectuals read about the delights of physical existence in the well-established academic classics, however, their response seems to be quite different. They do not seem to find the celebration of physical gratification questionable at all when they read *Gargantua and Pantagruel*, *War and Peace*, *Tom Jones*,

Wilhelm Meister, or *Buddenbrooks.* Nor do they ever seem to find it necessary to accuse the great poets of wishing to return mankind to savagery because some of their poems are odes to the elements and some rhapsodize the vigor and simplicity of buxom country wenches. Those who admire Thoreau, for example, become blissful and sentimental, with never a thought of compensation, at the mere mention of *Walden* and *A Week on the Concord and Merrimack Rivers.*

Hemingway, on the other hand, was for his part always ambivalent about nature. He knew too much about its complexity to become oversentimental about it. "An Alpine Idyll" is a definitive and unmistakable representation of this essential ambivalence. It shows that a holiday in the mountains is good for the two foreign skiers but that permanent residence there has had a shockingly opposite effect on a local peasant. The skiers are returning to the workaday world brown, healthy, and "glad there are other things beside skiing." The snowbound peasant, however, has become as brutally inhuman as nature itself. All winter long, every time he has gone to the barn, he has hung the lantern in the mouth of his wife's frozen corpse (which he has propped against the wall). The implications are clear enough. An idyllic landscape is as complicated as any other. Those who think of it only as a place of escape obviously do not know what is going on there. In the opening scene, at the very moment that it is impossible for the two skiers to realize that anybody can be dead on such a beautiful morning, they are witnessing the peasant relieving the sexton at the graveside—"spreading the earth as evenly as a man spreading manure in a garden."

Unlike Thoreau at Walden Pond, but very much like Jake and Bill at Burguette, Nick Adams is only a man on vacation at Big Two-Hearted River, a man taking time out for recreation. He is a man doing something that he happens to like to do very much. Thoreau, on the other hand, was a man trying to prove a point. He went into the (nearby) woods to get away from the complexity of society. His two-year residence in the thickets was part experiment and part protest demonstration and he spent most of that time reading, puttering about, theorizing, behaving for all the world like a decadent intellectual dabbling in petit trianon primitivism. Thoreau was a Harvard boy playing scout games—as if the whole country had already been settled and overcivilized. In 1845!

Nick Adams does not spend his time speculating and theorizing about man and nature. He is lucky enough to be where he wants to be and doing something he enjoys very much and he has put the need to think and write behind him for the time being. At no time, however, is it even remotely implied that he wants to make freshwater fishing a way of life. As with skiing in "Cross-Country Snow," it is something he likes to do when means and circumstances permit. He neither confuses it with other things nor tries to substitute it for them. He regrets the fact that a companion on a similar outing a long time ago, having come into wealth, has apparently become too involved with other things; but nowhere does Nick himself ever reject or even complain about "other things." He clearly does not agree with Bill in "Three-Day Blow" that marriage ruins men; nor can it be said that he concurs when George in "Cross-Country Snow" laments that life is hell because Nick's becoming a father is going to curtail their skiing. Not only does Nick (in one story or another) accept social responsibility, including military service, he is also, without ever making too much self-certifying noise about it, an incurable book lover. In "Big Two-Hearted River," for example, as soon as he catches his first two trout and stops to eat his sandwiches, he begins wishing for something to read.

Books are also a part of the fun for the huntsman and fisherman in *The Sun Also Rises*, *Green Hills of Africa*, and "Three-Day Blow." Of course, none of these characters works at his books while on holiday. He enjoys them. The huntsman in *Green Hills of Africa* whose main objective is to write as well as he can and to learn as he goes along, who feels that he must write a certain amount in order to enjoy the rest of his life, flatly states that he likes hunting kudu in Africa as much as he likes going to see the pictures in the Prado in Madrid. "One is as necessary as the other," he says when asked if one were not better than the other; and then he adds: "There are other things, too."

It was Thoreau, not Hemingway, who seemed to forget that there are other things. "I went to the woods," Thoreau declared in *Walden*, "because I wished to live deliberately, to confront only the essential facts of life, and see if I could not learn what it had to teach, and not, when I came to die, discover that I had not lived." As much as Hemingway liked the woods, he always knew that the essential facts of human life also include many things that people do in families, communities, cities, and nations. Jake Barnes, for instance, could have had fun at Walden Pond for a while. The fishing trip to Burguette is evidence of this. But extended residence on the outskirts of Concord can hardly be suggested as a solution to his problems. One can only wonder what Thoreau would have made of Jake's predicament; and one must also wonder what advice he would have given young men, like the one in "God Rest You Merry Gentlemen," who wants to be castrated because he does not know that what he keeps feeling is an essential part of life. Hemingway could have told him that monks and pet cats feel the same thing.

Hemingway regarded the gratification of physical appetite as a fundamental and indispensable dimension of human fulfillment, but, his detractors notwithstanding, he never suggested that sensual experience was the only reality. If he had really believed that, he probably would have written guidebooks, if anything—certainly not novels and short stories as highly polished and as subtle as he could possibly make them.

Nor did he ever imply that the sensual is anti-intellectual. Quite the contrary. It is a part of the intellectual. It is as much a part of civilization as anything else. What he said about drinking,

for instance, has nothing at all to do with "sinking into nature."
"Wine," he wrote in *Death in the Afternoon*, a book about refinement and style, "is one of the most civilized things in the world
and one of the natural things of the world that has been brought
to the greatest perfection, and it offers a greater range for enjoyment and appreciation than, possibly, any other purely sensory
thing which may be purchased. One can learn about wines and
pursue the education of one's palate with great enjoyment all of a
lifetime, the palate becoming more educated and capable of appreciation and you have constantly increasing enjoyment and appreciation of wine even though the kidneys may weaken, the big
toe become painful, the finger joints stiffen, until finally, just
when you love it the most you are finally forbidden wine entirely.
Just as the eye, which is only a good healthy instrument to start
with becomes, even though it is no longer so strong and is weak-
ened and worn by excess, capable of transmitting constantly
greater enjoyment to the brain because of knowledge or ability to
see that it has acquired. Our bodies all wear out in some way and
we die, and I would rather have a palate that will give me the
pleasure of enjoying completely a Château Margaux or a Haut-
Brion, even though excesses indulged in the acquiring of it has
brought a liver that will not allow me to drink Richebourg, Croton, or Chambertin, than to have the corrugated iron internals of
my boyhood when all red wines were bitter except port and
drinking was the process of getting down enough of anything to
make you feel reckless. The thing of course is to avoid having to
give up wine entirely just as, with the eye, it is to avoid going
blind. But there seems to be much luck in all these things and no
man can avoid death by honest effort or say what use any part of
his body will bear until he tries it."

Nor do any of the sentiments of the huntsman who wrote
"Remembering Shooting-Flying" have anything at all to do with
despair. They are the sentiments of a man who knows something
about having a good time. The woodcock, he says at one point, is

easy to hit because he has a soft owl-like flight and you also get two chances at him. "But what a bird to eat flambé with armagnac cooked in its own juice and butter, a little mustard added to make the sauce, with two strips of bacon and pommes soufflé and Croton, Pommard, Beaune, or Chambertin to drink."

Many birds were fine to shoot and wonderful to eat. "There were lots of partridges outside of Constantinople and we used to have them roasted and start the meal with a bowl of caviar, the kind you never will be able to afford again, pale gray, the grains as big as a buckshot and a little vodka with it, and then the partridges, not overdone, so that when you cut them there was the juice, drinking Caucasus burgundy and serving French fried potatoes with them and then a salad with Roquefort dressing and another bottle of what was the number of that wine? They all had numbers. Sixty-one I think it was." There were also other birds in other places but none to beat the sand grouse, the lesser bustard, and the teal for pan, griddle, or oven.

"I think they were all made to shoot," he concludes, "because if they were not why did they give them that whirr of wings that moves you suddenly more than any love of country? Why did they make them all so good to eat and why did they make the ones with silent flight like woodcock, snipe, and lesser bustard, better eating than the rest?

"Why does the curlew have that voice, and who thought up the plover's call, which takes the place of noise of wings, to give us that catharsis wing shooting has given men since they stopped flying hawks and took to fowling pieces? I think that they were made to shoot and some of us were made to shoot them and if that is not so well, never say we did not tell you that we liked it."

Nor did his all-consuming enjoyment of terrain ever turn him away from the glories of landscape painting. The two things always enhanced each other. As did his enthusiasm for bullfighting and his appreciation of Goya. Nothing ever turned Hemingway away from painting or any other art. His reading enhanced his living and his writing; and his living enhanced his reading and his writing. "For we have been there in books and out of books—and where we go, if we are any good, there you can go as we have been."

Sooner or later everything comes around to his commitment to art. "A country finally erodes," he wrote in *Green Hills of Africa*, "and the dust blows away, the people all die and none of them were of any importance permanently except those who practised the arts, and these now wish to cease their work because it is too lonely, too hard to do, and is not fashionable. A thousand years makes economics silly and a work of art endures forever, but it is very difficult to do and now it is not fashionable."

The sentiments of a typical Hemingway hero, like those of Hemingway himself, are almost always those of a man involved with the *refinement* of experience. It is inaccurate to define any of his actions in terms of desperation, and downright ridiculous to classify them as escapism and substitution. It is also misleading to define them as the actions of a man in search of value in a naturalistic world. Nick Adams, Frederick Henry, Harry Morgan, Harry the writer, and Robert Jordan certainly are not looking for something to live for; they all proceed on the pragmatic values they already have. "I didn't care what it was all about," says Jake Barnes, "all I wanted to know was how to live in it. Maybe if you found out how to live in it you learned from that what it was all about."

But apparently once certain kinds of intellectuals have convinced themselves that the Hemingway hero is a man in despair because he cannot discover the essential meaning and values in a world of violence and chaos, they no doubt find it natural enough to think in terms of frustration and compensation and assume that anyone having fun must be a member of a cult devoted to hedonism. It is not at all difficult to see how this neat but hasty and pretentious and not unfatuous assumption could lead them to insist that there is a Hemingway code and to complain that it represents a fundamental evasion of intellectual responsibility.

The Hemingway hero, in point of fact, however, is not evasive at all. On the contrary, he is almost always a man who functions in terms of confrontation. He is too persistently pragmatic to be evasive and too thoroughly individualistic ever to be confined to a cult. He is a man of form, discipline, and courage, of course; but his behavior is much too realistic and far too flexible to conform to any conventional code of conduct. Nor does his rejection of the speculations, theories, and rationalizations of most contemporary intellectuals make him either nonintellectual or antiintellectual. If anything, it indicates that he is all too intellectual. Nonintellectuals do not take issue with intellectuals. When they do not ignore them, they are likely to be overimpressed by them. Perhaps because they do not understand them. Hemingway not only understood the issues but was also convinced that only fiction was complex enough to deal with them.

No one can seriously accuse the Hemingway hero of not using his head. With the exception of Harry Morgan, the typical Hemingway hero is almost always not only a thinking man but also a reading man and frequently a writing man. He does not indulge in academic abstractions and intellectualized clichés and slogans but neither does he rely on tribal instinct, superstition, magic, or hand-me-down rules of thumb. He proceeds on concrete information, his discipline being that of the empiricist who responds in terms of what he personally knows and feels rather than what somebody else has decided he should know and feel. His movements, even in moments of crisis, are seldom desperate because, like those of the bullfighter, the huntsman, the fisherman, the soldier, and, yes, the scientist, they are based on his objective, practical, and operational estimate of the situation. Robert Penn Warren once wrote that the Hemingway hero was becoming aware of nada. Perhaps one might add that he is someone who has the blues (is bedeviled by blue devils) because, like Ecclesiastes, he has confronted the absurdity of human existence and knows that each moment and each experience count.

Blues-oriented writers should find it easy enough to recognize the pragmatic hero of the fiction of Ernest Hemingway as a man whose personal tradition of confrontation, discipline, and self-realization is in many essentials very much like their own. Ralph Ellison, in fact, has already done so. Indeed, for Ellison, everything Hemingway wrote "was imbued with a spirit beyond the tragic with which I could feel at home, for it was close to the feeling of the blues, which are, perhaps, as close as Americans can come to expressing the spirit of tragedy."

When Ellison on another occasion pointed out that the blues "express both the agony of life and the possibility of conquering it through sheer toughness of spirit," he was only reminding his idiomatic relatives of something that he knew very well they had every reason in the world to have known all their lives. He was, that is to say, articulating something that most live in terms of though they may never stop to think about it—or ever be able to define it. As a matter of fact, there are those who live in terms of the blues tradition and then not only accept but also repeat and even propagate clichés of outsiders whose firsthand contact with and information about the idiom even at its best tend to be extremely limited and often are actually questionable.

One such writer was Richard Wright. Ellison, who had a profound awareness of the process by which the blues move beyond the painful facts of life in the very act of acknowledging their existence, noted that the lyrical prose in Wright's autobiography "evokes the paradoxical, almost surreal image of a black boy singing lustily as he probes his own grievous wound." Wright himself, however, seemed to ignore the lustiness of the blues idiom in music as well as the traditional toughness of spirit exemplified by so-called black Americans spirit. Nor is this undeniable toughness to be confused with being hard-boiled. William

Faulkner, for example, thought of it in terms of human endurance and celebrated it precisely because its humanity was seemingly unvanquishable!

It was as if Wright heard only the words and did not respond to the music at all. But the words, as magnificently poetic as they can sometimes be, are only a part of the statement of the blues pattern. The spirit of the music is something else again. The lyrics almost always have tragic implications. They tell of disappointments, defeat, disaster, death, of trials, tribulations, mistreatments, losses, separations, frustrations, and miseries. The music, however, does not create an atmosphere of unrelieved suffering, wailing, wall lamentation, chest-beating, and gnashing of teeth by any means. There is always an element of regret and sobering sadness that life should be this way, to be sure, but the most characteristic ambiance generated by the sound and beat of blues music as such is not despondency but earthiness and a sense of well-being. The verbal response to a blues vamp, whether in a ramshackle honky-tonk or a swanky midtown New York nightspot, is not "Alas" or "Alack" but rather some expression equivalent to "Hey now" or "Yeah now" or "Lord, am I born to die." At such a time "Lord, have mercy" means "Lord, enable me to endure the good time that this music is already generating." Indeed, once the music gets going, the words may be mumbled, jumbled, or scatted.

Incidentally, this intermingling of tragic and comic elements in the blues is often as complex and as outrageously robust as the tragicomic texture of Elizabethan drama. Gilbert Murray points out that "the peculiar characteristic of classical Greek drama is the sharp and untransgressed division between tragedy and comedy. The two styles are separate and never combined. No classical author is known to have written in both."

Not only did Elizabethan playmakers write in both, they often combined the two in the same script, alternating serious passages with comic or comic-relief passages. *In a fully orchestrated blues statement, it is not at all unusual for the two so-called elements to be so casually (and naturally) combined as to express tragic and comic dimensions of experience simultaneously!*

Sometimes, as in the now-classic Kansas City–style shout, stomp, shuffle, and jump, the very beat of the music actually belies or in effect even denies the words. Even as the singer spills out his tale of woe, the music in the background not only swings, stomps, jumps, and shouts irrepressibly, but often has comic capers and even mocking laughter among the trumpets, insistent bawdiness among the trombones, and at times the moaning and groaning in the reed section becomes almost unbearably seductive! Sometimes, as a matter of fact, the singer's own movements suggest dionysian revelry more than anything else.

Moreover, those conditioned by the idiom have always used the blues as *good-time music.* Social welfare–oriented technicians seem to regard the blues as an expression of despair. But in Sunday sermons, down-home and down-home-derived preachers of all denominations have traditionally (and knowingly) referred to it as music of worldly and devilish temptation.

The female singer of blues, for instance, is never regarded as an old witch, a sad Cassandra, or a foreboding old hag from a Greek chorus. She is not primarily the bearer of bad or sad tidings at all; on the contrary, she is one of the queens of the earth. She is the big mama, the great consort, the all-embracing female principle, and even when she is not personally good-looking in any conventional sense, she is still responded to as a highly desirable woman. When such blues dive divas as Ma Rainey, Bessie Smith, and Dinah Washington complained that they were laughing to keep from crying and had empty beds, there were always men in the audience who eagerly offered to comfort them—the offers implying that the men had heroic qualifications, it being fully understood at the outset that Big Mama has an empty bed not because there is none who is willing but because by her standards a good man is always hard to find.

As for the male blues singer, his role is almost always that of the combination of dashing sweet man and ever-ready stud male that women stand in line to touch as he passes. Even as a singer such as the Falstaffian Jimmy Rushing used to kid himself publicly about being five by five, as wide as he was tall, the women in his audiences responded as if he were the most irresistible phallic figure in the world.

But just as there are those who continue to insist that the good-time elements in the world of Ernest Hemingway are only manifestations of despair or even dehumanization, nevertheless there are many who are all too easily convinced, mostly by psychopolitical theories, that down-home and down-home-derived folks who find enjoyment in the blues can only be running away from the frustrations of oppression and regressing to sensual abandon as a means of escape, or else are just simply too completely victimized to realize what the obvious facts of life actually are and therefore doing jungle dances in a fool's juvenile paradise.

Most so-called black Americans know only too well that this is nonsense, and so does anybody else who knows the difference between what art reflects or is compounded of and what it expresses—or anybody who has ever really listened to music and felt the natural need to dance to it. And so should U.S. "black" writers. Nor should these writers fail to note the similarities between the indictments that U.S. intellectuals bring against Hemingway and the smug but provincial assumptions that allow them to condescend to so-called black expression as if most other U.S. expression were endlessly fructifying. It is not. And what is more, only a minimum understanding of rat race dynamics is required to enable such writers to see the cultural deprivation and intellectual bankruptcy, not to mention the all too obvious personal fear of physical inadequacy, behind such pretension. For one thing, those who condemn sensual gratification, whether in response to elements in the fiction of Ernest Hemingway or in the blues idiom in music, are never quite able to free themselves of envy. For another, they almost always overstate their charges in ways that are not only spiteful but that also betray an appalling disregard for simple ordinary everyday facts.

Only a willful obtuseness or something worse would allow anybody who has read the descriptions in the first chapter of *To Have and Have Not* to charge that even Harry Morgan represents any playing down of sensibility. And anybody who introduces even the sleeping bag sequences in *For Whom the Bell Tolls* as evidence that Hemingway was out to reduce the world to the gratification of the sex urge would be as intellectually irresponsible as those who describe so-called black Americans as childlike simple creatures of sensual abandon. An outsider—say, a blonde from the jet set—who comes into a down-home-style hall and pulls off her shoes, lets her hair down, and begins stomping and shaking and jerking and grinding in the spirit of personal release, liberation, and abandon, does not represent freedom; she represents chaos, and only an outsider would do it. Only an outsider could be so irresponsible to the music. Insiders know that the music and dance, like all other artistic expression, require a commitment to form. As is the case with all other artistic expression, they achieve freedom not by giving in to the emotions but through self-control and refinement of technique. Swinging the blues and swinging *to* the blues, however free they may seem to the uninitiated listener and onlooker, are never acts of wild abandon; they are triumphs of technical refinement and are among the most sophisticated things a human being can do.

U.S. "black" folks dancing to the blues, in no matter what tempo, would be no more likely to disregard the music and give themselves over to their physical and emotional urges, cravings, drives, and impulses than a Hemingway bullfighter (or any other kind) would start stabbing and hacking away as soon as the bull entered the ring or a huntsman would start banging and thrashing away at anything and everything as soon as he heard a rustle in the brush.

But nothing exposes the confusion of so-called white U.S. social critics and pundits more than the astonishing but well-known fact that these same antisensual intellectuals far more often than not may be numbered among the most dedicated dialecticians of the so-called Sex Revolution, the most esoteric apologists from the cult of psychedelic experience, and the time-honored literary champions of universal freedom of the pornographic press!

It should also be easy for so-called black U.S. writers to spot the intellectual one-sidedness involved in the self-therapeutic concern that most people express about the effect of slavery and oppression. Somehow or other most people seem always to assume that oppression dehumanizes the oppressed more than it does the oppressor. But not only do such people overlook the unmistakable implication of antagonistic cooperation, it is as if they also deliberately ignore the most obvious fact of all: The oppressor who is already so dehumanized at the very outset that he can regard fellow human beings as chattels becomes even more dehumanized in the all-consuming process of maintaining an inhuman system. The violation of the humanity of others becomes for him a full-time occupation, a preoccupation, and a way of life!

The oppressed, on the other hand, are not necessarily dehumanized because their humanity is being violated by others. Indeed, there is evidence that the effect is quite the opposite. At the outbreak of the Civil War, for instance, it was an oppressed "victim" such as Frederick Douglass who upheld what was noblest in the American ideal of civilization, not a full-fledged citizen such as Robert E. Lee. Douglass was not dehumanized by suffering. Lee, however, was all too dehumanized by privilege. So far as Douglass was concerned there was no choice but to be for freedom and the nobility of all mankind, while Lee apparently felt that there was a choice, and for all his fine sentiments about civilization he gave his considerable support to those committed to legalizing human bondage even at the expense of seceding from the Union.

Nor should it be overlooked that even as these words are being written, oppressed Americans who are defining their political and economic aspirations in terms of human rights and values, are being resisted, obstructed, and even violently opposed at every turn by people who, far from having been *humanized* by freedom, seem to have become so *dehumanized* by being a part of a system that oppresses other people that they actually place the value and security of *property* above the welfare and fulfillment of *human beings* without even thinking twice about it. It should surprise no one that such people substitute statistics for wisdom and compassion, confuse human beings with machines, and assume that human behavior, including artistic expression, is mechanical and predictable. Human beings, however, unlike machines, may give high-octane performance on low-octane fuel and often give low-octane performance on the highest-octane fuel in the world. Deprived machines always gasp in desperation and run down; deprived human beings, on the other hand, may become immensely creative. But perhaps the catch in this is the fact that it is not really possible to deprive human beings as one deprives a mechanical device. After all, a human being can always wish and dream, and he can never be reduced to zero. Not as long as he is potentially capable of defining himself in terms of his own aspirations.

As for the blues statement, regardless of what it reflects, what it *expresses* is a sense of life that is affirmative. The blues lyrics reflect that which they confront, of course, which includes the absurd, the unfortunate, and the catastrophic; but they also reflect the person making the confrontation, his self-control, his sense of structure and style; and they express, among other things, his sense of humor as well as his sense of ambiguity and his sense of possibility. Thus the very existence of the blues tradition is irrefutable evidence that those who evolved it respond to the vicissitudes of the human condition not with hysterics and desperation, but through the wisdom of poetry informed by pragmatic insight.   ,

V

Kenneth Tynan, the British journalist, drama critic, and aficionado who was with him at the time, reports that when Ernest Hemingway referred to himself as being an honorary Negro one night in Havana he did so "with a good deal of pride." Hemingway was responding to a performance by a trio of Cuban Negro musicians who had just serenaded him with a special song, repeated a Mau Mau chant he had taught them, and rendered a Spanish lament for which he had written the lyrics. There is reason to assume that his remark and the pride that Tynan noted, however, also included Negroes he had known elsewhere.

On another and far more impressive occasion he had already recalled with what was undoubtedly a very special satisfaction another honor, one that U.S. Negroes had bestowed upon him. The incident in Havana occurred in 1959. In 1954, at one point during all the excitement that went with being awarded the highest of all prizes for literary achievement, he found time to tell Robert Manning, then a feature writer for *Time* magazine, about how a Key West Negro announcing him as referee for a boxing match had introduced him as the world-famous millionaire, sportsman, and playboy. "Playboy," he chuckled, knowing exactly what the so-called black American connotation had to be, "was the greatest title they could give a man. How can the Nobel Prize move a man who has heard plaudits like that?"

In Venice earlier that same year Hemingway, perhaps as a straight-faced gag and perhaps not, told A. E. Hotchner, his sometime traveling companion and self-styled Boswell, about how during the trip to Africa from which he was returning, he had attained an admirable position in a Wakamba tribe during the temporary absence of his American wife by taking unto himself an eighteen-year-old African bride and in keeping with local custom had inherited her seventeen-year-old widowed sister, who became their bedmate. He showed Hotchner pictures of the bride and later in Aix-en-Provence told him she expected a child by him to be born in September. "Before I left I gave a herd of goats to my bride's family," he went on. "Most overgoated family in Africa. Feels good to have an African son."

Hotchner, who was never quite certain which of Hemingway's stories to believe anyway, seems inclined to regard this one as more fabrication than fact. But the implications are the same either way. With a writer like Hemingway, facts must always become fiction anyway; and, as Hotchner would probably be the first to admit, it is the fiction that perhaps best represents Hemingway's sense of significance. It was not with the incidents he reported but with the ones he made up that he expressed his most profound sense of actuality.

Indeed, if there seems to be something faintly familiar about the remark that Hemingway made to Tynan in Havana, it may well be due to the fact that both the statement and the circumstances are somewhat similar to an incident in one of his finest works of fiction. At one point in *The Sun Also Rises* there is a brief but easy exchange between Brett Ashley, dancing with Jake Barnes in a Paris nightclub, and a friendly Negro drummer that is loaded with "honorary Negro" implications and possibilities. Jake looks on and makes no comment, but Brett feels the need to account for the intimacy. "He's a great friend of mine," she says. "Damn good drummer."

Ad Francis, the belligerent prizefighter in "The Battler," is also an honorary Negro of sorts. He travels around the country with Bugs, his realistic and uniquely compassionate Negro friend, who looks after him (and his spending money) as if they were members of the same family. Ad Francis is an honorary

Negro in precisely the sense that Benjy in William Faulkner's *The Sound and the Fury* is not. Luster, as much as Faulkner admires his humanity, takes care of Benjy because it is his assigned task to do so. There is something about Ad Francis, however, even in his punch-drunk state, that qualifies him for acceptance.

One fundamental clue to what is involved in Hemingway's conception of his honorary Negro status (as well as his honorary Spanish, French, and Italian status) is an observation he made during his first visit to Africa. "*They had that attitude that makes brothers,*" he wrote of one beautiful group of Masai warriors in *Green Hills of Africa*, "*that unexpressed but instant and complete acceptance that you must be Masai wherever it is you come from. That attitude you only get from the best of the English, the best of the Hungarians, and the very best Spanairds, the thing that used to be the most clever distinction of nobility when there was nobility. It is an ignorant attitude and the people who have it do not survive, but very few pleasanter things ever happen to you than the encountering of it.*" (Italics added.)

There are other clues in *To Have and Have Not*. Hemingway, like most people almost everywhere, also responded to the Negro idiom of motion, an orientation to African-derived dance rhythms that most Negroes everywhere seem to retain, which makes for an ease and coordination of body movement that is not only efficient and practical but also beautiful to behold. Some people have always confused such emphasis on rhythm with psychopolitical theories of race, while others regard it as unmistakable evidence of primitivism. Actually, it is fundamentally a cultural (or environmental), not a racial phenomenon and not necessarily an evolutionary one. There are non-African primitives who are as awkward as some Europeans.

It should not be at all difficult for anybody who has even a casual knowledge of the history of the slave system in the United States to realize that the traditional U.S. Negro idiom in music and dance, for instance, retains a strong African rhythmic emphasis not simply because the Negroes are born that way, but because the slaves, although forbidden African drums and rituals, were not only permitted but also encouraged to sing and dance. The slave masters rather enjoyed the African rhythmic emphasis (as they did the unusual timbres and harmonics) so long as there were no disturbing overtones of tribal communication and re-volt—and besides, they were probably only too happy to note that the dance rhythms were also work rhythms that increased time and motion efficiency.

Harry Morgan, the rugged but ill-fated hero of *To Have and Have Not*, is hardly the kind of white Southerner who would refer to himself as being an honorary Negro. His response to the prac-tical application of dance-oriented Negro coordination, however, is no less significant for being somewhat tainted. Moreover, in some ways he is less tainted with racism than, say, the average northern white journalist, intellectual, or even philanthropist. He can even see a "black" man killing "white" men in a gun battle in Havana and not only make no sentimental identification with the white men because of race or color but also can admire the "black" man's courage and cool efficiency as frankly as some "white" sportswriters came to admire the boxing skill of a Joe Louis and a Sugar Ray Robinson. When Harry, watching the Negro empty a submachine gun and switch to a shotgun while still under fire, says, "Some nigger," he is expressing his (and no doubt Hemingway's) profound appreciation for any man, who-ever he may be, who can perform under pressure with grace and style. Back on his deep-sea fishing boat later on, when his client questions the extra expense of taking a "black" man to bait the hooks, Harry explains that the man can do it faster than he him-self can under pressure. "When the big fish run you'll see," he tells him. Racial, primitive, or cultural—it is apparently all the same to him. He accepts the fact and shows no concern at all about the whys and wherefores.

He does indulge his curiosity about another very special im-plication of dance-oriented movement, however. He notices that his hook-baiting expert comes on board sleepy every morning and concludes that he has "been on a rhumba every night." Nor is this the extent of his curiosity or his involvement. One night while he and his buxom, passionate, and devoted wife, Marie, are making love and she suddenly expresses curiosity about what it is like with a "black" woman, it turns out that he has already known, presumably from personal experience, that it is "like nurse shark."

Since "black" men could hardly regard making love with a "black" woman as being anything like tangling with any kind of shark, Harry Morgan would seem to be deliberately disqualifying himself as an honorary Negro in that category. Not that there is the slightest evidence that he needs to be one. He and the ever-passionate Marie seem to do better than all right for themselves as things are.

Nevertheless, Harry Morgan provides important clues to at least some of what was no doubt involved when Hemingway referred to himself as being an honorary Negro. Morgan's appreciation for Negroes is fundamentally practical. It is never really exotic in spite of his language, and along with it there is a genuine feeling of human identification that enables him to respond with fraternal compassion when a "black" person behaves in a way that is somewhat less than admirable. Obviously, he hired Wesley for the rum-smuggling trip (which turned out so badly) because he needed someone special with him on a difficult mission; but when Wesley becomes bitter and irascible after being shot in the leg while they were being chased by the revenue agents, Harry, whose own wound is much more serious, not only remains considerate but even responds with humor when Wesley threatens to cut his heart out. "Not with no whetstone," he says, looking at the object in the Negro's hand. "Take it easy, Wesley."

But perhaps no clue to what being an honorary Negro meant to Hemingway, who once described a group of Senegalese soldiers as being too tall to stare, and once advised his brother not to trust anybody with a southern accent unless he was Negro, is the account that Harry Morgan gives of the departure of the hook-baiting expert.

"So Johnson gave the nigger a dollar and two Cuban twenty-cent pieces.

" 'What's this for?' the nigger asks me, showing me the coins.

" 'A tip,' I told him in Spanish. 'You're through. He gives you that.'

" 'Don't come tomorrow?'

" 'No.'

"The nigger gets his ball of twine he used for tying baits and his dark glasses, puts on his straw hat, and goes without saying good-bye. *He was a nigger that never thought much of any of us.*" (Italics added.)

There is much in the fiction of F. Scott Fitzgerald for all contemporary U.S. writers to admire and study. *The Great Gatsby, Tender Is the Night*, perhaps *The Beautiful and the Damned*, and certainly some of his short stories, including "May Day," "The Diamond as Big as the Ritz," and "Rich Boy," represent an indispensable dimension of life in America. No other U.S. writer has made a more compelling literary statement about the dynamics and the implications of the U.S. rat race for material success and social status than Fitzgerald did with the story of Jay Gatsby, for instance; and perhaps even "black" intellectuals will, on close study, concede that confidence man Gatsby, *né* Joey Gatz, is as significant and as fundamental a personification of the eternal U.S. problem of self-identity as is Joe Christmas, the race-confused "mulatto" in William Faulkner's *Light in August*.

These same "black" intellectuals, however, will find very little that has any functional or even suggestive affinity with any distinctive aspect of the blues idiom, either in subject matter, selection, point of view, or aesthetic approach in the fiction of the writer most often mentioned as typifying the so-called Jazz Age. They will look in vain even in *Tales of the Jazz Age* for anything remotely resembling either the spirit of the blues or the jazz sensibility. What they will find in his best work is outstanding twentieth-century fiction written by an ambitious, genuinely talented, but essentially naïve although intelligent American who, very much like so many others among all the sad young white men of his generation, obviously confused the blues and jazz with razzmatazz, hotcha, and hot diggity dog.

Fitzgerald was (among other reasons) always too busy trying to be a 100 percent "white" and naughtily successful darling of high society ever to have even kidded about being an honorary black man, even in a nightmare. Nor is it likely that he would have been able to qualify as one had he wanted to. Nor would any obstacles have been more difficult for him to overcome than the fact that the very aspects of riches and power that seem to have held such great fascination for him would have been regarded by "black" certifiers as being dull and unsophisticated. Indeed, Hemingway was well on his way to honorary blackness when he replied to Fitzgerald's starry-eyed claim that the very rich were different from other people by saying, "Yes, they have more money." Riffed with the inside information of a blues musician! Spoken like one who really knows something about what "black" doormen, headwaiters, bell captains, and chauffeurs are actually thinking behind those stylized masks of stylized smiles and stylized dignity and concern. "Man, they can have the difference. Just give me that checkbook."

It was Hemingway, not Fitzgerald, who saw what one sees when one looks beyond the clichés about the blues. What Fitzgerald saw was essentially what a good conventional musician sees in the great metropolis; and what he wrote might well have been written by a truly gifted but essentially conventional small-town boy who has become "urbane" by way of an Ivy League campus, which he uses for family background as a young nobleman might use his ancestral manor.

Almost any black, brown, or beige chauffeur, doorman, bellboy, waiter, or Pullman porter of any experience at all would be able to spot the eager "young man from the provinces" beneath the Brooks Brothers veneer of Fitzgerald at first sight. Perhaps such a "black" person would also be inclined to smile somewhat complacently at the ofay quality of some of Hemingway's physical involvements. But even so, far from dismissing Hemingway as being unsophisticated, he would probably recognize him at once as a man from beyond the horizon, a very special man from whom he might be able to learn a thing or two and thus extend the dimensions of his own experience.

Hemingway, who evolved his own highly individual style and wrote only in his own personal terms, qualifies as an honorary blues musician precisely because he was always writing blues stories without ever trying to do so. What he was always trying to do, as he says over and over again, was write as accurately as possible about how he really felt about the things he really knew. It was only through the process of trying to write straight honest prose on human beings that he came to represent in fiction that fundamental aspect of the contemporary U.S. sensibility that the blues express in music.

Questions of derivation and adaptation aside, U.S. writers and intellectuals who think in terms of the blues idiom (and tradition) will find that a typical Hemingway situation is not only the archetypal situation of contemporary man but also a blues situation. The Hemingway hero is a blues hero, or a man with blues insights and responses. His conflicts and complications have blues ambiguities, and his resolutions, like those in blues problems, are always based on a confrontation and acknowledgment of the fundamental facts of life without illusion, facts that are sometimes as incomprehensibly absurd as they are ugly.

Blues-oriented readers can come to immediate and personal terms with the central statement in almost any Hemingway story simply by giving the title a blues twist or by playing verbal improvisations on the key characters or circumstances. *In Our Time,* for example, is composed of a series of thematically interrelated stories and vamplike and rifflike sketches, bridges, or interludes, the mood of which suggests *Blues in Our Time, Blues for Our Time,* or even *Blues Panorama*. And of course it is easy enough to read *The Sun Also Rises* as *Jake's Empty Bed Blues, Blues for Lady Brett, The Postwar Blues, Lost Generation Blues,* or even *Rocks in My Bed*. As for *A Farewell to Arms,* the hero gets *The Volunteer Blues* or *Crusader's Blues,* the *Empty Talk Blues* or *Nothing Sacred Blues, The Getaway Blues, Separate Peace Blues,* or *Hors de Combat Blues,* and ends up with the *Cold in Hand Blues*.

Among the short stories in a book that might as well have been called *Blues for Men Without Women* are *Blues in Another Country, The Fifty-Grand Blues, White Elephant Blues,* and *Ten Indians Blues;* and "Now I Lay Me" reads like nothing so much as *Now I Lay Me Blues* or *Blues After Midnight*. Nor should the *Undefeated* or *The No-Comeback Blues* be overlooked; and "The Killers," after all, is not the story of an actual murder. What the two cold-blooded gunmen actually do is give Nick Adams *The Cold-Blooded Blues*. They make him realize not only the fact of death, but also, and perhaps even worse, the cheapness of life. What really horrifies Nick is the fact that the intended victim is as resigned as the gunmen are casual, and in the outchorus, the story riffs on what might be called *The Blues to Be Gone* or *No Hiding Place Blues:*

" 'I'm going to get out of this town,' Nick said.

" 'Yes,' said George. 'That's a good thing to do.'

" 'I can't stand to think about him waiting in the room and knowing he's going to get it. It's too damned awful.'

" 'Well,' said George, 'you better not think about it.' "

But no statement by any contemporary U.S. writer extends the literary and philosophical implications of the blues further or gives them a more profound complexity than the inscription that Hemingway composed for *Winner Take Nothing*. At one juncture in *Death in the Afternoon* he had already written: "All stories, if continued far enough, end in death, and he is no true-story teller who would keep that from you." But as if that were not blues-confrontation disposition enough, and as if to reemphasize the significance of the title inscription to *The Sun Also Rises*, he wrote:

> Unlike all other forms of lutte or combat the conditions are that the Winner shall take Nothing; neither his ease, nor his pleasure, nor any notions of glory; nor if he win far enough, shall there be any reward within himself.

To which he could easily have added a refrain he is reported as using in conversation many years later: "How do you like it now, gentlemen?" Now, that is, that you have found out that the blues go with winning as well as losing. Instead, he wrote and included a story that might have been called *The Clean, Well-Lighted Blues, Blues for Nothing,* or even *Blues About Being and Nothingness,* a story about an old man and a waiter who are in good health and have no apparent social, economic, or political difficulties but who have trouble sleeping nights because they are lonely and because they have become aware of the ultimate void that underlies human existence. "Some lived in it and never felt it," Hemingway had the waiter conclude, and then goes on, "but he knew it all was *nada y pues nada y nada y pues nada.*"

Nothing and then nothing and nothing and then (and perhaps even for) nothing. Or as the epigraph to *The Sun Also Rises* suggests so strongly: All is vanity. What profit hath man of all his labor wherein he laboreth under the sun? Or to put the whole matter of blues statement in still another way: In Jake Barnes, Hemingway has created a hero whose predicament is such that what he must acknowledge every day is the fact that he "woke up this morning blues all around my bed." Maybe he doesn't stomp, jump, or swing the blues. Nonetheless he is blues idiom hero enough to look at the world and say "Good morning, blues. Blues, how do you do?" And make the best of a terrible situation.

It is easy enough to write sincere and urgent propaganda

about the necessity of food, clothing, shelter, freedom, and justice. Being for such things is only a matter of being in favor of adequate political structures. Not that bringing such structures into actual being is by any means simple; but as eternally complex as social, economic, and political problems always are, there are others that are not only far more difficult but also more fundamental and even more urgent. Most essential of all are problems that are directly involved in the affirmation and justification of human life as such. "There is but one truly serious philosophical problem," wrote Albert Camus in the opening paragraph of *The Myth of Sisyphus,* "and that is suicide. Judging whether life is or is not worth living amounts to answering the fundamental question of philosophy. All the rest . . . comes afterward."

Nobody was ever more firmly dedicated to the accurate definition of the eternal condition of man than was Ernest Hemingway. And certainly no twentieth-century U.S. writer ever stated the fundamental issues of human existence more comprehensively. Perhaps the most influential contemporary American statement of these issues is found in *The Waste Land* and *The Hollow Men.* But in these two unsettling poems, T. S. Eliot implies that the problems of nada are somehow peculiar to contemporary life and that it is essentially a problem of the renewal of lost connections and energies. The title of *The Waste Land* and the crucial image of the Fisher King clearly establish the fact that Eliot assumes that "things ain't what they used to be," that evil days have fallen upon a once prosperous kingdom of once blessed people. And one hastens to concede that his observations, which are not at all like the assumptions of revolutionary politicians, are valid as far as they go. Eliot does not, however, confront the allegation that even in the best of times in the most fruitful lands the winner shall take nothing.

Hemingway did not hesitate to make the confrontation nor has anybody ever insisted more firmly than he that the immediate functional value of the evidence for affirmation never be compromised. It was all very well for William Faulkner to declare in a speech on a happy occasion that man would not only endure but would prevail, but what Hemingway always wanted to know was how man would prevail and on what terms.

He did not assume that any of the answers to the riddle of human existence would be comprehensive, or that they could ever be reduced to a code. His fiction indicates that he proceeded on the assumption that wisdom would be found in bits and pieces through trials and error from the arts and in experience itself and that he tried to shape his insights not into codes but into the rich, suggestive ambiguity of literature. Assuming, as he obviously did, that art was nothing if not the most basic equipment for living, Hemingway would probably have said of his collected works what he said of *Death in the Afternoon*—that they were not enough but that they represented at least some of the things that he felt had to be said. "These fragments," he may have added, playing another one of his riffs on T. S. Eliot, "I have shored not only 'against my ruins,' but also against my *ruin.*"

The experience in which, according to Hemingway, writers are forged as a sword is forged involves more than anything else the confrontation of human existence in the raw. Nothing seems to have impressed Hemingway more than the fact that Tolstoy, Dostoevsky, Stendhal, and Flaubert had been firsthand witnesses to human behavior in the very worst circumstances and still found amid all the inhumanity enough evidence to enable them to write about human existence in terms that are not only affirmative and not only viable but that also suggest delight and magnificence.

What all contemporary U.S. writers can never afford to forget (no matter how strong the pressure to become engagé) is the fact that no social or political responsibility is greater than that which comes with the realization that there is more earthly chaos and human confusion than there is form and that he who creates forms and images creates the very basis of human values, defines accurately or not what is good and what is not, and in doing so exercises immeasurable influence on the direction of human aspiration and effort. Not even the commander in chief of a revolutionary army assumes a greater responsibility to mankind. After all, revolutionary commanders, no less than agitprop writers, are essentially errand boys. Seldom are they engaged to help establish a social order based on their own conception of what life is about!

EPILOGUE

O nce the writer accepts the obligation which comes with knowledge of the chaos which underlies all human life, he must also accept another. He must presume to go beyond established categories. As with the self-elected dragon slayer who would save his fellow citizens, he must choose his own weapons and proceed as a one-man expeditionary force into the unsafe territory of the outlying regions.

As with all self-designated Sphinx-confronters he will use all the relevant scholarly advice and tutorial assistance he can get, of course, but in the Ordeal itself he must take his chances with his own improvisations. Not only because established categories (conventional conceptions and clichés) are a part of the problem itself but also because, as Ernest Hemingway presumed, the only admissible answers to the questions asked by the Sphinx are those, however fragmentary, which one really knows, not those one is supposed to know because they are taught in the great Universities.

And yet James Joyce, for example, was not really being presumptuous at all when he wrote about a group of inhabitants of the grimy ghettos of Dublin, Ireland, in Homeric terms (whoever Homer was and however much he did or did not presume when he wrote in epic terms about the Reconstruction Problems of a Selected Number of Greek Veterans of the Trojan War). Joyce was being a very practical literary craftsman. He took such fragments as an Irish writer of his intellectual background and sensibility could scrape together and forge into an urgently needed device with which to encounter the actualities of his existence. What Joyce, like all other writers, presumed, no doubt, was that he could "signify" about the nature of time, place, and personality and by so doing could make life more interesting not only for himself but also for those who read him.

Conventional categories and hand-me-down reverence aside, it is only natural for contemporary U.S. writers to proceed as if Ralph Waldo Emerson, for all his New England stiffness, would have been moved by Louis Armstrong and would have acknowledged him as a Representative American Artist, a poet whose melodies "ascend and leap and pierce into the deeps of infinite time."

Perhaps it is also presumptuous, but it is no less natural for contemporary U.S. writers to assume that Jack Johnson—who in his conception of the potential of U.S. citizens would have conceded nothing to Abe Lincoln and could have had only contempt for sad Woodrow Wilson—was himself an American Work of Art to compare with anything in the major phase of Henry James; that Jelly Roll Morton and Fats Waller would have done better than hold their own with Mark Twain, jive artist become fine artist. Nor is it at all outrageous to assume that Walt Whitman would have been bewitched by the infinite flexibility of the Kansas City 4/4 beat of Count Basie or should have been. Or that Herman Melville having made what he made of the crew of the Pequod may have gained new dimensions and resonances from a world tour with the Duke Ellington Orchestra.